THIS IS A CIRCLE
(Mary and Joseph)

What if Jesus was Born as a Native American?

A Story about the Rebirth of Love by

Steven WinterHawk

iUniverse, Inc.
Bloomington

This is a Circle (Mary and Joseph)
What if Jesus was Born as a Native American?

iUniverse books may be ordered through booksellers or by contacting:

iUniverse
1663 Liberty Drive
Bloomington, IN 47403
www.iuniverse.com
1-800-Authors (1-800-288-4677)

ISBN: 978-1-4620-7321-4 (sc)
ISBN: 978-1-4620-7322-1 (ebk)

Printed in the United States of America

iUniverse rev. date: 12/12/2011

THIS IS A CIRCLE

(Mary and Joseph)

These Words (Do Not Belong to Me)
By
Steven WinterHawk

These Words do not belong to me . . .
Do with them as you see fit.
These words were given to me by Crazy Horse . . .
If you believe them, you might be tricked—they are Coyote words.
These words were given to me by Chief Seattle . . .
Do not seek to own them—It would be like thinking you can buy a tree.
These words were given to me by Geronimo . . .
He did not die protecting words.
These words were given to me by The White Buffalo Calf Woman . . .
They were whispered in my ear as I awoke from a Dream . . .

Acknowledgments

I would like to say Miiguetch (Ojibway for thank you) first and foremost to my Mother and Father for providing the perfect way to learn to walk the Traditional Native American Spiritual path—just by being themselves. I was born of a white Christian Mother and an Ojibway Father. Both my Mother and Father encouraged me to follow my Dreams. I will also say Miiguetch to my Soulmate who called me into the Dreams and Visions, and then appeared in my waking Dream as my partner Cidalia to share her Heart with me—like White Buffalo Calf Maiden in the story you are about to read!

I also thank my good friend Heather (Isabela) Embree for the hours of copy editing. And I thank my close friend Tony (Youngfox) Kitchen who is an intuitive photographer, for the cover art in the form of a picture of my original Medicine Wheel that I created and gifted to my friends and family at Christmas in 1992. The poem was the beginning (although I didn't know that at the time) of this book. Miiguetch for the Mystery that is part of our lives!

Chee Miiguetch

Disclaimer:

This is a work or fiction, based on the authors' Dreams, Native American stories that were passed down orally through generations, and last but not least—my personal view of the Bible (and the prophesies therein). All of the characters in this story, are symbolic, but are not so named by co-incidence.

I stated above that this is a work of fiction. The question this raises for me, is whether our dreams are fiction? However you look at this is up to you as far as I am concerned. One way of interpreting Dreams (that works for me) is to see everything and everyone in our Dreams as a part of ourselves. This leads me to wonder about this connection in our so-called waking world. My Native ancestors tell me that we are all part of a Circle of Life. This Circle is beyond time and space, seeming to change (while repeating), retaining the Integrity and Respect even for those that do not recognize this to be so. This Circle is a Dream of the Creator, and allows for many Dreams (and Dreamers) in the experience of the Sharing of Love. This being said, I am writing about my Dreams and experiences with Spirit, and this is not an attempt to prove anyone else wrong.

In one way, this is part my Dream Journal, and this is part of the reason that time (and space) in this story does not always follow a logical sequence. I hope this is not confusing to the reader, but for me, it makes non-logical sense and supports my belief in the Mystery that my ancestors talk about in the stories that have been passed down since the beginnings of time

As I stated above concerning Dream interpretation, I recall this Dream world, through the eyes of the people I write about, acknowledging the filters of myself as a male. Chapter 7 begins: "He tossed and he turned in the bed that night." At that point in the dream, I did not know who I was—waking up. Until I looked in the mirror, and sensed the man I was, I only knew that I was waking in a world that was to be one of the pivotal experiences of the story. In this dream, I get to know a lot about who I really am—and my reason for writing this book. Smile, if you will but this chapter is one of the first connections of myself in the Dream. Until then, I am happily seeing the world (mostly) as a curious Joseph, who has found his SoulMate.

Most of this story originated in a Personal Vision Quest that took place over the span of about a year and a half. Once I attended a wake for a man who had ended his life due to family problems. I need to tell you with certainty that this is not what my Native Relatives mean when they say: "Today is a Good day to Die." Life is Sacred. It is a Gift from the Creator that is to be cherished. This is something I will share about in this book. At this wake, I talked to a Catholic Priest, and he said something that has stayed in my mind even to this day. He spoke about Religion being a bridge to Spirituality. At that moment, it came to me that many of us (myself included) might be trapped on that bridge, fighting our fears and Demons(s) that people who came before have so conveniently named. And so this story is really about my seeking inspiration in the Bible and then crossing over—going beyond both my personal beliefs and my Religion. I respect other people's viewpoints, but I would choose a canoe to a bridge.

Prelude

Sirius

A Council had been called by the Elders. Chief Seattle—He of the Talking Stick addressed the Council. "This Circle of 7 in which we will be close to Turtle Island, is about to complete. In this time to come, we will move through the Smoke and the Mist, to be dangerously close together. For a short time, we will almost be as One."

"It is the Creators wish that we take gifts. These gifts will help the Son of our Creator to complete his Earth Walk. It is our Way, to tell our children of their Tribe, and of the Path taken by the Ancestors that came before. These gifts will help him to walk the Path of Beauty. A Loving Father will always seek to make the Earth Walk, the Journey, easier and Peaceful as possible."

"Ho?" A man called Geronimo, questioned: "I know of the destiny that this child will face. He has walked this Path in another dream-time, and the end was not pleasant."

"True. But it was what the People of his birth were ready to accept. It is not our Way to judge. His message then, and now, and will forever be the same."

Geronimo shrugged. "I do not know if it would have been in my heart to accept another man's decision. I do not know if I could have spoken the words of Forgiveness."

That is why I am asking you to be the one who will carry the Arrow." Chief Seattle replied. "Crazy Horse has already agreed to accompany us, and there will also be a fourth member of our Council—who is late to this meeting.

They were joined soon by the fourth member of the Council. Crazy Horse, quipped: "I guess that you take 'living on Indian time,' Sirious-ly?"

The fourth person simply smiled serenely: "It was my kind that invented the saying."

"By the way," Geronimo asked, knowing well of Crazy Horse's odd sense of humour: "Does anyone know why there were only three wise men in the white-faces' story."

Crazy Horse replied: "at that time they could not find more than three wise white-faces on the planet!"

After the two had enjoyed their moment of mirth, Chief Seattle shook his head, disapprovingly. "If I did not know my friend Crazy Horse a bit better, I might be tempted to say that this is an example that, passing into Sprit does not necessarily insure gaining of wisdom. However, I believe it is his way of reminding us, that to the men and women we might encounter, we will seem to be from a dream, but to us, this dream will be very real, and the feelings and memories of our previous visits will become physical again."

"This is a Good thing to remember." The person who had joined their group late, suggested. "It is a good to remember to respect the beliefs of our white Relatives—although we might not agree." And . . . ," with a smile, "I also seem to recall that the three wise men of question were not even white faced people."

"When our People met the first White-faces," mused Chief Seattle, "they showed us their sacred book. At first we wondered why someone would need these written directions, when our People have talked daily to the Creator. But then when we learned to read their language, the answer became plain. There in the first pages, was a warning about seeking knowledge that had been written on the pages made from a tree. Our People were able to see that they had not heeded those first words of warning. The words that followed detailed the history that they have been repeating since the beginning of the time that they left the Path of the Heart, in favour of the written word. These words have now been translated by men seeking to hold power by appointing themselves the only source of true knowledge. These so-called "Men-of-God," have denied the true Creator, by pretending to be able to speak for Him."

"There are other warnings, within this book, that might indicate that, despite the attempt of a group of men to control the Spiritual paths of their followers—they could not hide the Truth." The fourth member of the group spoke again.

"Indeed," replied Crazy Horse: "and this might lead to a new interpretation of one of their stories—involving the coming of Four Horse-Men?" He chuckled aloud.

The travelers then grew silent, as the moment of the folding of the blanket of time and space was at hand.

This is a Circle

The East is the Beginning

It Begins with the Gift of Life

It is the Moment that is Now

To Live Now

Is to Live in Forever

This is the Gift of Life

The Gift is to Live the Gift is Now!

.... Steven WinterHawk (1992)

Chapter 1

The First Gift

Mary and Joseph Renauldi found themselves in unfamiliar surroundings. They had been driving since early the previous morning, searching for a place to spend the night. Every motel that they stopped at, or passed on the freeway, only confirmed the blatant, flashing signs outside: "NO VACANCY!" The old jeep was overheating again, had been doing so, most of the afternoon that had become twilight.

"We will have to stop soon, just to check out the water in the rad." Joe shook his head. "I am so sorry to put you through this, in your condition."

Mary's "condition," was late months of pregnancy. She was well into the end of her eighth month, but before the trip, her doctor, had assured her that they would be back before the baby was born. "He is in no hurry." The doctor smiled confidently. "This baby will come into this world in his own time. Perhaps he believes in "Indian time?"

Mary was a full-blooded Ojibway—as full blooded as you can be, born as it were, on the land of her ancestors, on Indian land. Mary's husband was of Spanish—Portuguese descent. Joe's ancestors had come over from Spain with Columbus, in the Santa

1

Maria and when the Spaniards returned home, the first time, Joe's relatives remained behind, lived among the Indians, and some even intermarried. But that was before the Aboriginals were declared "nothing more than animals."

* * *

The Story of The White Buffalo Calf Maiden

At the beginning of remembered time, the People (the two-legged) and the animals—all Life, could talk to each other. All Life had Respect for each other, and All knew that that they were Related, and depended on each other for survival, The Red-skinned People, especially, recognized, and lived by the pact, the Respect, for All other tribes. The Red-skinned, two-legged People hunted the Buffalo for food and clothing, and promised to Sing and Dance the Spirit of the Buffalo that they killed, back to Life.

In the beginning, the People were content to live as One, and Share with the four-legged tribes. At some point, however, the Spirit of the People became restless. They began to stray from their path, and the Elders sent out hunters and warriors, in search for a way to re-connect—a Way that the Elders knew would be shown, a Way that came to the Elders in a Dream. This Dream, as the Great Mystery, the Creator of all Life, showed, would come from their Sharing with the Buffalo.

Three hunters had traveled a great distance from their camp, and one day, they discovered an entrance to a hidden valley. The valley was lush with vegetation, and abundant with animals of all kinds. On a wide rolling plain, in the centre of the valley, the hunters found a great Buffalo herd grazing. The three hunters were tired and very hungry, one of men said: "these Buffalo have been given to us. We are hungry. So let us hide behind the rocks and tall grass, and sneak up until we can get close enough to kill one. I need food now."

"This is not the Way." Another man said. The four-legged are our brothers and sisters. We must Sing and Dance. We must honour the Spirit of the Buffalo, and ask to be allowed to kill one of our Brothers for food."

"Ask—for something that has been already given to us?" The first man complained. "My stomach is empty, and the Creator has provided these Buffalo. I do not see anything else that is needed. I am taking my bow and arrows, and I am going now." He would not be stopped. In fact, he did not wait for the other two men to join him. While the two remaining men sat quietly, and prepared to sing their songs as they had been taught by the Elders, the first man stealthily approached the Buffalo.

When the hungry man was very close to the Buffalo herd, he fitted an arrow, and drew back his bow. Feeling very confident (and hungry), he stood up, among the tall grass, and . . . his bow-string broke before the arrow could be released.

"Aiiiiiiee!" He cried out, and stepped back, and tripped over a rock.

The sound of his voice, startled the Buffalo herd, and they stampeded, in all directions, trampling the man in the tall grass, to death.

The other two men, in the safety of a grove of trees, heard their companions' cries, but could do nothing to help. They then knew that the advice of the Elders had been correct. They knew that the correct way to Share with their four-legged Relations must be followed, or they too would not leave this Sacred valley with a full stomach.

While the Buffalo thundered past the circle of trees, the two remaining men, sang a song, asking for a sharing—asking for a Buffalo to give himself to the fire that they had lit. As the men Sang, the thundering of the Buffalo hooves seemed to go on forever. Finally, the dust, and the rumbling settled, and the sound of the herd dwindled in the distance.

The two men, now having completed their Sharing Song, peered out of the grove of trees, to see a lone Buffalo, a straggler, limping toward them. In the minds, the two men, still echoing with their Song, they heard the voice of the approaching Buffalo: "My time is come." the Buffalo said. "I have heard your Song, and I know that in giving my body to your Fire, you will Dance my Spirit back." This Buffalo collapsed nearly at the two hunters' feet. The men, using their knives, accepted the Buffalo's gift, and were very thankful that night.

In the morning, the two men stepped from the safety of the grove of trees, to find the great herd of buffalo back, grazing quietly on the open plain of swaying tall grass. They were well fed, and rested, and were now prepared to complete the renewal of the pact with the Spirit of the Buffalo. They began to chant and Sing, as they had promised, to sing the buffalo back to Life, to take this gift back to their tribe. They sang and danced to the sound of the Mystery of Life that was in their Heart. A sound came to their ears—the sound of a drum, matching the sound of their heart. Another sound came from the mist, in a place near the centre to the Buffalo herd.

"This is the sound of my daughter singing. She is Dancing there!" An Elder, an aged man stood before them. He pointed to the direction of the herd. The mist cleared, and there, where a moment ago was a White buffalo calf, danced a beautiful maiden. This young maiden was more beautiful than any woman the two hunters had ever seen. They were both struck, like an arrow in their heart—at once with a reverence, and a primitive longing that was near unbearable.

"This is my daughter," the old man repeated. "She is from the Buffalo. She is from our Mother Earth. She is from the Creator of all Life."

"We are the Buffalo," the Elder continued: "My Daughter is dancing for you, so that one of you will be her husband. You will take her home with you, and your tribe and our tribe will be as one."

The two men looked at each other. Both hungered—a new and different hunger than the day before. "This maiden will be my wife." The first exclaimed aloud. "No—she will be mine." the second echoed. The old man simply smiled.

Fighting back his hunger, the first man said. "She is from the Mystery. She will bring great peace and help our people find their

4

way back to the source of all life. We must respect this maiden. We must respect her wishes. She will choose who will be her husband."

The second man was too overcome with the hunger. He wanted this woman so greatly, that his lust to have her blinded his heart to anything else. "No!" He exclaimed. "Did you not hear this man? The old man said that his daughter would be my wife. He gave his daughter to me!" He took a step toward the Buffalo . . . and then he recalled the fate of their companion, the evening before. He grasped a flaming branch from the campfire, and holding it before him; he approached the Buffalo once more. The Buffalo parted before the man who held the fire-brand. This torch in his hand was like the fire in his loins—ablaze with every step close to the dancing buffalo calf maiden, until he could no longer restrain himself—he bolted into a run toward the woman, to claim his prize. Throwing all caution to the wind, he ran through the scattering Buffalo, and a moment before he reached the beautiful woman, he tripped, like the man before him, and fell headlong into the tall grass. He fell directly on his flaming torch, momentarily stunned, and the grass all about him burst into a mystical fire, that consumed him within a few moments.

The young maiden continued to dance—protected, by the Buffalo and the grass, and the Earth, and soon a rain cloud formed overhead. The fire was extinguished, the cloud disappeared, and the Buffalo calf maiden danced on.

The remaining man witnessed all that had transpired. He too longed for the maiden, but his resolve to do what was right prevailed. "I will sing my courting song," He said to the maiden's father. "I know that a man can Give-Away all that he owns—but he does not own his children. Our children are from the Creator, and a daughter must have the right to choose, and be respected for herself. This is the first Gift that your daughter has given me. If there is to be a Gift of Sharing, it must be with Love and Respect. I will sing my courting song, and then I will approach this beautiful maiden, and ask for her to come back with me, to help my tribe. And if I meet my death—if I am trampled by the Buffalo, I will say now:

It is a Good day to Die—for the Love of this woman, and for my People."

This man, held out his arms to the dancing maiden, and sang the song that was in his heart. It was a song about his Love for her, and about the life that he would Share, and about his tribe that waited for his return. When the song was nearing completion, the young woman stopped dancing, and when the song was finished, she held out her arms to him. He then, took a great breath, and walked respectively and reverently among the great buffalo toward the waiting maiden. The young maiden, who had transformed from a white buffalo calf, also began walking, and met this man half-way, with open arms.

The hunter took this young maiden home to his tribe, and she taught him how to build a Drum—she taught him to listen to his Heart. She brought many Gifts to Share with his tribe, to help them find a Good Way to Live. Many of these gifts might be lost or forgotten, but she would always be there, as his Sister, his Mother, and his Companion, to rekindle the gift of his Heart.

*   *   *

Joseph Renauldi first saw Mary MorningStar at a wedding reception (to be more accurate, at the wedding ceremony) for a good friend—a man that he had grown up with. It was all pretty quick. Joseph had been on vacation in Portugal for a month, and when he returned, his best friend Jake asked him to be the best man. "How long have you known this woman?" Joseph enquired in amazement. "How long do you need to know your soul mate—when you find her?" Jake replied. "You—just need to show up for a fitting for the tux, and then the church this Saturday." Joseph's Portuguese friend was marrying a Native woman, and Mary was her bridesmaid. As the ceremony lengthened, Joseph's gaze wandered about the church, and came to rest on . . . the most beautiful young woman he had ever (in his young years) seen. His heart leapt out of his chest. The ceremony going on around him became a blur. Anything that Joseph had ever heard about "Savage wild Indians" was erased at that moment from his mind. This woman was an Angel come to Earth—there was no doubt about this in his mind. When her sparkling brown eyes met his—his heart melted away. He did not even hear the prompting by the priest—and needed an elbow from his friend, to remember why he was standing there today. He produced the ring, and when his eyes returned to the object of his amazement, the young woman had averted her gaze, but Joseph was almost sure that he detected a smile.

"Who is that beautiful woman?" Joseph asked another man, who had joined him at the bar, when the reception formalities and the meal dishes had been taken away. The most he had learned, through her speech about her friendship with the Bride, was that she was very well spoken. Her monologue was short, articulate, open, and Spiritually inspiring. Joseph hardly remembered his meal—his mind was completely occupied.

"Which woman?" The man, another friend of the groom queried. "Oh—that one." He followed Joseph's eyes to where Mary sat at the head table, conversing with the bride. "Take a bit of advice . . ." The man turned away, and shook his head. "Keep away from that one—or you will get burned—or worse."

The man absently stroked his Jaw.

"She doesn't seem the type to . . . ." Joseph began.

"No she is not the type . . . to anything." The man turned away. "And her two brothers never let her out of their sight . . . . if you get my drift?"

Joseph did understand, when he noticed (how had he missed them), two rather muscular Native men sitting at a table near the front of the room. While Joseph sipped his glass of wine, leaning at the bar, he observed that, the two brothers, mingled amicably with the wedding party, but, at a moment's notice, either stood by their sister's chair, presumably seeing that her water glass was filled, and whatever else she might need. She had nursed a single glass of wine, combined with ice-cubes, throughout the whole seven course meal.

"Careful." Joseph warned himself, even though he had not (well . . . maybe a few) . . . "sinful" thoughts. Then he corrected himself and his musing—"I do not have anything but the most respect for her" . . . and what he was feeling was something more than an urge. He was, he admitted to himself, awe-struck. His heart reached out to her . . . until, she seemed to know, and . . . "did he see a smile again? Or was it just wishful thinking?" Either way, brothers or not, he had to find a way to meet her. From his teenage, he recalled a statement by another Native girl he had met in one of his high-school classes: "a Gentleman is just a Wolf . . . with patience." His youthful hormones had read a different meaning in that statement, than he was now beginning to understand.

Joseph returned to one of the tables that had been pulled aside after the meal to encircle the dance floor, and engaged in idle conversation with his friends. All the while, however, his mind was seeking a way to meet with Mary—at the very least, he knew her name. Then the disk jockey announced that the dancing was to start, with the married couple, and the married couple would then bring other dancers onto the floor, when the first dance was over. Lo-and-behold—the first woman that the groom selected was the maid of honour, and the bride selected the best man. At this point, Joseph was on the dance floor—not dancing with "her," but at least beside her. Mary MorningStar danced like a dream—like she was born to dance. Joseph was no slouch himself—after all he had been taught to dance at an early age by his Portuguese mother, and had been taken to many such wedding receptions with his parents, even before he was old enough to dance. He had become proficient in all of the "traditional" and non—traditional dances of his people, and later he was thankful, when he found that it was an excellent way to meet young women.

As the dance floor began to fill, and each dancer coaxed another person onto the floor, the near inevitable meeting took place. Mary was letting go of her present dancing partner, when she heard: "I think that the maid of honour and the best man should have at least one dance?" Joseph's answer was a smile, as she offered her hand.

Joseph had been right in his estimation of her dancing ability. As he guided his partner through the twirling dance steps of what some people might call "ball room dancing," she was at least his equal, anticipating, it seemed his every move. "I have been studying your dance." She confided, as the music change to a waltz, and Joseph realized, that the other couples had changed partners three songs back—but he was not about to confide this to his seemingly willing (dance) partner. "Everyone else has changed partners." Mary echoed his thoughts, her breath tickling his ear.

"I am aware of that." Joseph continued with the waltz. "I was wondering . . . ?

"I am not dating." She answered. "I cannot date—at this time I am on a Sacred Quest for my People." She qualified her first statement, as though (perhaps) saying that this might change in the future? (Joseph hoped). The waltz ended, and the disk jockey put on a fast rock. "This is too much like my People's music—like my traditional dancing," she excused herself, as if to say, that this was not what she needed to be doing, at the moment, and that her brothers would be watching, and might begin to wonder. She retreated from the floor, following Joseph's appreciative "thank you." Joseph found his way back to his table, saying another (silent) thank you to the "forces that be," for his good fortune.

Chapter 2

The Tower Of Babel

The Friendship Tower, they called it, but already, it had acquired other names, pseudonyms, by the local people, the common people of New Rome. One name in particular, considering its projected importance, and scope. When completed, it would be the tallest free-standing structure in the New World—in the known world at large. The Friendship Tower was to house numerous businesses and otherwise private offices and endeavours, all inter-connected to each other and the World, by the most advanced broad-band, telephone and Internet technology available (and growing). The President of the U.S.N.R (United States of New Rome) chuckled to his advisors: "From the capital city of New Rome, when we broadcast God's word, we will be the hub of communication for the whole democratic world." Though, he thought to himself, "it would not be wise to shake the foundations of Rome, quite yet."

Joseph was more than happy to accept the job, to help build this architectural "miracle." He would be part of a group of contractors that would install the finishing touches, the interior design and office building. Joseph was originally a carpenter—learning the trade from his father, and then, after extensive design courses, had made a name for himself, at the very young age, not yet thirty years. His life had been his work—a female interest had not been part (except for the occasional dates his friends arranged), until now.

And now, with the elusive Mary constantly at the edges of his mind, he was hired to be part of "Black Wolf Interior Design." Black Wolf was a well—known, exclusive company that made you part of the team—"the family", as they almost called it. While at the office, he was required to wear a smock with their logo sewed over the heart, and when while working, a stylish denim shirt and jeans, the latter exhibiting the same logo. But; "it pays," he resolved in his mind. And it paid well! Most of the office complexes were a modular design, not the kind of craftsmanship Joseph would have preferred, but it was elegant nonetheless, a space age kind of elegant.

He put in many long hours, as the tower raced skyward—often, it was dark when he started work in the morning, and dark when he finished. Then drive home, collapse on the bed, alone, sometimes waking only to undress, wolf down a quick meal—sitting until the wee hours in front of his computer. That was when he would research the history of Mary's people. He was driven to know all he could about this unobtainable Angel who had captured his heart. In the middle of this, one night, he came upon an internet link entitled "Wounded Knee," and upon accessing the story, he was blown away. He leaned back in his chair. "How could this happen?" He took a great breath of air, to clear his mind, and read on. "How could one group of people do this to another?" And to make it almost unbelievable (and unbearable), many of his not-too-distant relatives would have been involved in the atrocities upon Mary's ancestors. In the beginning, some of Joseph's ancestors, had stayed behind. After the first contact with the "Indians," many more had come over, during the conquest of the New World he now knew as the United States of New Rome. To be sure, Joseph also found, in his searches on the web, numerous incidences of barbaric retaliation by the Natives. Many settlers and their families were brutally tortured and murdered—some trapped in a fiery death within a log cabin or church. The "Indians" reacted like wounded animals (he realized that this was very close to the truth). These people who claimed a brotherhood with the animal kingdom, were quickly labelled by their would-be conquerors as no more, or better, than animals themselves . . . . and in the Roman Christian interpretation of the bible, the animals were given to man to use as they saw fit. This may have been a rather broad painting of all Christians, but Joseph himself was beginning to seriously worry about the way the animals, who were to become food in his world, were treated The animals were no more than meat, right from the beginning, force fed, and injected full of steroids—whatever it took to get it to market. But that was another story . . . . or was it?

In Joseph's mind, now, it all seemed to originate with the birth of the Roman version of Christianity. When the original Christian beliefs were combined with the logical Roman way of looking at the world, a new religion had been born. This new religion said that everything was black or white. There was no in-between. There was no grey area. Imagination and intuition were given no credit in the creation of the electronic age that had blossomed since the turn of the twentieth century—almost overnight.

In Rome, men like Einstein and Edison had to be very careful in the wording of how their ideas came to be, lest they be labelled as "heretics." Many potentially great thinkers, in early Rome, had been burned at the stake for following Pagan ways. Shortly after the Emperor of Rome declared Christianity to be the one and only way, he had put to death the man who was responsible for the prophesy of the eventual downfall of Rome. This man named Nostradamus had been the Emperor's private consort, and after a couple of too close brushes with death, as prophesised, Emperor Constantine decided that the man was genuine. It was rumoured, in whispered circles, that the last incident—now available for Joseph to read on the World Wide Web, that Nostradamus had seen the Emperor meeting his death in a duelling match. An anonymous soldier was sent, dressed as the Emperor, wearing the Emperor's armour, and a closed visor. In a freak accident, the opposing man's lance pierced the view plate, and for a short time everyone believed that the Emperor had been killed. Emperor Constantine went into seclusion, temporarily, and when the Roman world seemed doomed to collapse, he resurfaced, claiming to be the "reborn" head of the new Christian church. Christians and former Roman dignitaries alike accepted Constantine with open arms. All statues and evidence of the Pagan God's were destroyed. Nostradamus and the Pagan Gods disappeared together. A new, logic-based view of Christianity was declared. Anything that could not be seen, nor experienced by the five senses was deemed not to exist. For a great time, after a man named Copernicus was beheaded for his "theories" that the Earth, and hence the Roman empire was not the center of the universe—no other land, or world, existed outside the boundaries of the Great Roman Empire.

Joseph scrolled back up through the text on his computer, drawn to the part which involved Emperor Constantine and the "rewriting" of the bible to fit the Roman way of looking at life. The words flashed by, until he saw something "new." It jumped out at him:

"Truth cannot be Hidden or Changed."

"What?" He shook his head, and returned to the page in question.

"Where had that come from? I don't remember reading that the first time through?"

The page had gone by too fast, so he stopped, and scrolled back.

"Nothing."

The words that he had read were not to be found.

"Did I imagine that?"

It was late, and he was bone tired.

"My mind is playing tricks—I need sleep."

He stared at the computer screen for a long minute, before exiting the browser, and shutting down. Joseph did not consider himself a religious man.

Sure, his parents had taken him to church as a boy, and encouraged him to read the bible, but after he left home, to make his own life in the world, he had left that all behind. It had been forgotten, until now—until Mary appeared . . . . and now, her influence was somehow making him question, searching for something—a Truth?

"Truth?"

""Truth cannot be Hidden or Changed."

" . . . . ummmmm?" Something was at work here. It was something like Déjà Vue? "Or—more like synchronicity? No—something that had never happened, was happening again?" He chuckled aloud at his musings. "None of this makes sense." He decided. "Stop talking to yourself and get to bed before it's time to get up for work again."

*   *   *

With the newly interpreted bible as its' credo, Rome grew in power, extending its' "protective" boundaries—conquering all that stood in the way, freeing all of the pagan countries, saving them from their ignorance. In the course of half a century, Rome was in control of the entire known western world—the countries west of "the Great Ocean." As they conquered, they declared each country as "freed," and "invited" the inventors and thinkers to join a growing elite technological group in within the hub, at the centre of the original city of Rome. For these great minds, virtually no expense was too great—nothing was held back that might halt the march of progress. They were given complete freedom to create, with one criteria—that whatever they invented or worked at, be toward the glory, and furthermost of Rome and the Christian church. Therefore, included with the weapon and technology that would be used in the ongoing Crusade of the Cross, beautiful statues and artistic paintings were created, depicting biblical greatness, and (on the other side) great downfalls of mankind.

The Bible of Rome, the New Testament, as interpreted by Emperor Constantine and a small group of Spiritual advisors, was a compilation of previously written religious manuscripts, by various prophets since the dawn of (known) time. The original text, was re-interpreted, and edited for content that would fit the logical view of the Roman civilization at the time. A number of "books,"—chapters that were in the previous bible, were omitted, if they did not conform to Roman logic. According to the Roman viewpoint of God, while being omnipotent (the only force greater than Rome), had the human characteristics of Jealousy and a need to be worshipped, and was often (as pointed out in the Holy Scriptures) given to fits of Anger and Revenge. After all, it was pointed out, it is written, that mankind was created in the image of God—therefore, God, the Father, must be somewhat like his creations. It made logical sense. It also made sense that as mankind had a "dark side," usually called his natural and therefore sinful side; there was another, dark "God," called Satan that was constantly tempting mankind to commit sinful acts. The religious (and lawful) view of the World was a constant battle for supremacy between God and Satan. It was the Roman Empires' duty, therefore, to make and enforce laws that would protect all Godly humans from themselves (their natural and intuitive selves). A Godly human was interpreted as someone who followed the Roman laws, paid their taxes, and who was forever on guard, and mindful that they were all inherently sinful.

As the Roman Empire expanded, the conquered countries were encouraged to retain their previous structure of government, so each country still had its own "King." At the onset, a King was recognized as someone ruled as he saw fit, beholding only to final Roman authority. With this in mind, no country, including the Isle of Great Britain, could ever be ruled by a Queen. A woman, per the Roman bible, was the helpmate to man, and also, the instigator of Original Sin. Women were to be protected, and loved, but they could not hold higher official positions of government—even in the country states of Rome, where "democracy," and voting for a local government representative became prevalent. Over time, women gained the right to vote, but not to hold higher office.

Every evening, via the internet, Joseph delved further into the history of the Roman Empire. He became more aware of the development of the "Father Country"—how alike were his own countries' laws, and customs—after all they had been (and still were) designed to follow those of Rome. Known on the world stage as the United States of New Rome, with its' capital city of New Rome, had a President as a leader, who might easily be called King. The latest President, named Gerald Forester had been elected, but even then, the final approval had to be granted by an Emperor from across the Great Ocean to the West.

For a great time, there was only the Empire. The Empire, in its' logical way of determining what is right or wrong, did not recognize a world outside its' boundaries. For many years whatever lay beyond the Ocean to the East, did not exist. Gradually, however, black and yellow skinned people made their way to the shores of Rome, and became yet another land to save from its barbaric ways—especially if the countries where these people originated were found to contain riches. Countries with gold and oil were at the top of the list to be rescued. It made it even easier, when those countries had dictators that were abusing their people, to justify it as a Holy Crusade. Africa was one of the first countries to be liberated, due to a tyrannical king, who used his subjects for his own pleasures. When the torture and starvation of Africa was halted by the now technological might of the Roman forces, a problem arose. If you are to liberate a people, is it not logical to consider those who you deemed needing to be saved, as any less than equal to the Godly citizens of Rome. The problem was that the conquering of Africa had taken at least half a century to come to light. Before oil was discovered beneath the desert sands, Rome had shared another type of "trade" with the country of Africa; namely slaves. The former dictator had not thought twice before selling his people to the highest bidders of Rome. Officially, the Roman church did not approve, but it had taken the approach (as per usual), that we are all sinners, and therefore our darker side should sometimes be tolerated, as long as it was not harmful to the well-being of the Empire. So, when Africa was taken over, the slaves were also declared free people—but beneath the surface, the learned custom (of slavery) within Africa and Rome continued. China (for the present), and Japan, both in the throes of civil upheaval—at the sword and scimitar stage, did not appear interesting nor threatening, to the Roman Emperor. The current (papal) head of the Roman church, in a meeting with the Emperor, suggested that both countries be noted as needing saving, "sometime in the near future."

Time marched on, and the Roman technology grew. Unrest, within less fortunate Roman countries also grew. For whatever reason, perhaps it is due to teaching passed on from parent to child;

some races seem more adept at certain skills and tasks than others. Some people are able to find a way to prosper, where others will not. Since the advent of Roman Christianity, the Jewish people had prospered. Their financial prosperity had grown through shrewd and very legal means, and through sharing among their own—even to jealousy among the Roman aristocracy, so when, within the country of Germany, rumblings of dislike for the Jews became louder by the common and impoverished German people, it was not a surprise that Rome turned a deaf ear. There were many Jewish people living in Germany at the time—side by side with Germans. Before being conquered by Rome, the German people had only known a war-like lifestyle, and now that was gone. The poorer Germans were forced now to buy their food and clothing, when they could afford it from the more affluent Jewish. Into this melting pot stepped a small man, with dark hair, a dark moustache, and an even darker disposition. Adolph Hitler, it was rumoured, had been an abused child, shipped from orphanage to orphanage until he ended up first, on the street and then in jail. While in jail he was left to brood about the state of his life, until, he found someone to blame. Adolph blamed the Jewish people—after all, they had everything, and he . . . . he was a victim.

In the next couple of years, following Adolph's release from prison, he wrote a book about his life, and how he was mistreated (like all other members of the Aryan race). In the impoverished state of Germany at this time, it did not occur to anyone that this dark little man might not even have Aryan bloodlines; it was too easy to empathize with his being a victim. A once proud race of Germans was also easy to convince that they were actually the pure noble race that had been used by the Jews. In no time, Adolph was elected to the head of government—a government that began a systematic campaign against their "abusers." In the course of months, all Jewish institutions and shops were confiscated by the German government. In the beginning, the wealth was shared, but, almost overnight, the money began to disappear—never to be found. While this was going on, Rome turned a deaf ear and eye—even when Jewish people were put into prison encampments, tortured, and murdered en mass.

While the extinction of the Jewish people continued, the German army and their "pride" grew, until Adolph convinced them, and himself, that the great War-like Aryan race was destined to be restored. His next step and his mistake was when his army invaded Poland. Whereas many of the smaller countries within the Roman Empire had been protesting in the senate about what was happening in Germany, until then, the Emperor had dismissed it all with "countries need to be allowed to work out their internal differences, on their own."

But now—Poland had long been a property of Rome! Rome was rudely awakened.

The Emperor of Rome sent a hand-delivered message warning Hitler to withdraw. The answer, in return, was the severed hand of the messenger.

"What is this?" The Emperor demanded. His position as such that not even his consorts knew his linage, nor his true name. He was beyond a King—he was head of the one and only Church of the World, he was . . . . THE EMPEROR!

"This is the hand . . . ." The advisor began to explain.

"I know what this is! I am asking—how this came to be?"

The military and religious advisors to the Emperor, were not dumb enough to begin explaining how this had gotten out of hand. "Would you like to order an assault on Germany?" They were all too sure that the superior technological might of the Roman army and the air force would crush Hitler's aspirations within a matter of days.

"Yes . . . . ummmm? No!" The Emperor pondered. "We could stop them in their tracks, this is true, but, I have been following this . . ."

"Oh really?", the military advisor thought to himself.

"Yes . . . this German uprising—these German people come from desperate beginnings.

"And what of the Jews?" wondered the religious advisor.

"We need to send a message that they will clearly understand—for some time to come." He appeared pensive again. "I have been hearing that the People that live on that island—Japan they call it . . . . I have been hearing that they have been making tremendous breakthroughs in electronics?" This met with a nodding of heads from all present.

"It seems that they may have borrowed our ideas and are advancing at leaps and bounds?"

Another nodding of heads.

" . . . . and from what I can understand, they have not yet been Saved from their Pagan ways?"

Both the military and religious advisors could see where this was about to lead. "A Crusade is long overdue." Both advisors were on the verge of suggesting, but they had not yet guessed the scope of the Emperor's plan.

"How is the progress on that new bomb? The "H-bomb," I think you are calling it." The Emperor asked.

"We have conducted small tests, but a full test would be devastating. I truly believe that it would not be safe. It would leave the test area uninhabitable for years due to radiation." His eyes narrowed, and he averted his gaze, as he began to comprehend.

"But you are sure that it will work?

"Yes . . . . but . . . ?"

"But what? Have you not heard of the phrase "To kill two birds with one stone? Better yet, why use only one stone. I would like two of those new aeroplanes that our military have been testing in the air by the end of this week. If I am right about the intelligence of these Japanese People, it will not take them long to steal this technology, and soon have a bomb of their own. We must strike before it is too late."

The very Earth shuddered once, and then again, as the cities of Hiroshima, and Nagasaki disappeared from existence. At that precise moment, another message was delivered.

The German army received their second and last warning. This time the messenger returned to Rome unscathed. Within a matter of days, it was noticed by the German people that this diminutive, dark skinned man called Adolph Hitler, did not even resemble the pure Aryan race that he claimed should rule the world. His own Honour Guard unceremoniously dispatched him, while he ranted and raved insanely from a podium, about how he would deal with the Roman Empire. Afterward, it was noted, in the message of surrender to the Emperor of Rome, that the German people had been deluded by a mad-man, and that they were sorry that everything had gotten so out of hand. There was no apology, however for the near genocide of the Jewish people—nor did Rome ask. What was investigated by Rome was the disappearance of the former wealth of said Jewish people, and this was found to be lost . . . . at least this was the official declaration of the Church of Rome.

Notation: "The near annihilation of the Jewish people brought about (with the consent of Rome) the forming of an alliance of all the collective countries in the Western world. This alliance called by many, in the years to come, a lame duck, was known as "the League of Nations." One of the (possibly) few acts of any consequence by this League of Nations resulted in the passing of what became known as "the One Child Act." With the passing of time, various individuals came forward with books, and personal protests that "it was not possible that one million Jews (as previously recorded) could have been killed by the followers of Hitler." To deal with these hate-mongers, the League of Nations brought into being a law, that stated "the number of people murdered during a war is not to be questioned! So long as One Child is unlawfully put to death the act must be punishable to the extent that One Million had died." It was a noble undertaking, which was to be easily overlooked (when convenience demanded), but it provided a way to quickly deal with the holocaust deniers. These men were quickly dispatched to a prison as dark as their hearts."

"Perhaps giving up some freedom may be worthwhile after all?" Joseph pondered, as he read the notation on the web site about the One Child Act. "But, it should not take the horrors of war nor the loss of freedom, to make us wake up, and realize that we know the difference between the right and wrong way to treat our fellow human beings!" At this, he wondered, again about the reference that he had read concerning "Wounded Knee."

Joseph searched the web again for the site that he had read about Wounded Knee. When he clicked on the link (he was almost sure that it was the same site), however, he found a different, an edited version of the text that he had first read. It was "sanitized," cleaned up. The main point of the entry, was a story about an Indian uprising that had needed to be suppressed. According to this version, the government had decided to release from prison a war-like tribe of Indians as a gesture of good faith. During the end of the Indian wars at the turn of the century, these Indians had been captured, and put in a "holding area," pending negotiations, and relocation to a new reservation. Upon news of their release, however, the Indians began to do a banned war dance, and refused to stop. After many warnings, the troops that were to take them to their new home were forced to defend themselves. Sadly, in the battle that followed, after a great sacrifice on the part of the threatened government troops, all of the Indians were killed.

Joseph was taken aback! This was definitely not what he had read the first time. He wondered if he had clicked on the right link, but when he followed all of the searches that his web browser located, there was only this one "new" version of the story. "What was the truth?"

"Truth cannot be hidden or Changed."

This phrase came back to him, from when he began this quest. At that time, it was, he was sure, in reference to the possible altering of the Bible. He could not be sure if the author was the same that had posted the first version of the Wounded Knee story, as it had not been signed—there had not been anything except the words that flashed up on the screen. "Who, after all can be said to possess the One and only Truth?" In the world that Joseph knew, this was self evident—at least in the mind of Rome. There was only one Truth. Anything else was deemed blasphemy or treason, and either could bring about severe punishment.

"Soma." A name came to him. He recalled hearing that name somewhere? Something he had heard on an evening news program. Of course! That was the name that came up from time to time in reference to terrorists' activity. Just recently, he recalled a suicide bombing in downtown New Rome. The official from President Forester's office had attributed the act as being perpetrated by "one of the followers of Soma." "Who, or what was Soma, and what was the connection with the edited story that I read?" Thinking back, this story had been signed: "Truth is the Way of Soma!." Why, only now, did he remember that? The other message, the one that was not signed, must be from another source? Somehow he felt this to be so? But how could he know? "And this would mean that there was a third person (or persons) involved. Joseph was not sure what was the scariest part—that some person (he guessed government) was overseeing the content of the web, or that this terrorist organization was publishing stories to undermine the free world. "The free world?" Who was he kidding? No—the frightening thing was that an intuitive part of him had believed that original story. The only sane voice seemed to be . . . . ? Something that he had thought at first was his imagination:

"Truth cannot be Hidden or Changed."

Chapter 3

Between Worlds

Work on the Friendship tower preceded with its usual overwhelming haste. Joseph had little time, in the next week, to think of anything but meeting deadlines, and sleeping. In the course of the week, he did note a couple of familiar faces that were part of the high steel construction crew. Both of Mary's brothers were part of the team that worked in the top-most part of the unfinished tower—scaling heights that made Joseph shudder at the very thought. He saw them one morning, waiting for the construction elevator. If either recognized him, there was nary a sign . . . still, a seed of an idea began in his mind. Who better to find out information about Native history, than someone whose ancestors had lived it? He had heard that the Indian way was to pass on your tribe's knowledge through oral means. So Joseph hatched a plan that might allow him to talk to one or both of Mary's brother's.

"I think it would be a goodwill gesture that would unite the workers' efforts, if we were to provide a lunch for the men who are building the frame of this tower," Joseph suggested to his employer, the head of Black Wolf Enterprises. "After all, this is to be named `the Friendship Tower.' "It might even be good publicity, when the Government is considering future contracts?" He had a feeling that the chance of new contracts would help it happen.

And so, Black Wolf hosted a lunch one day, during which members of the crew that would be doing the designing and installation of the office suites, would barbeque and serve the other workers. Joseph, of course, volunteered to be head cook. The barbeque took place on a Friday afternoon during a shift change in the courtyard at the rear of the building. The courtyard was not yet completed, but when it was, it would occupy a circular space with trees and fountains, partially surrounded by the semi-circle foot of the tower. The actual construction of the Friendship Tower was a central spire that would house the electronic communications and be capped off with the highest antenna in the known world. Joined to the spire, on either side, forming a partial circle, were the two individual "wings" that made up the office suites. Gazing upward, Joseph was impressed at the elegance of this structure that, on a day when the sky was overcast, would pierce the clouds above.

Seizing the opportunity for publicity, President Forester's office supplied the steaks from animals butchered at his personal ranch. Before being elected president, Gerald Forester was one of the top cattle ranchers and oil men this side of the Great Ocean. The Presidents Beef was very well known throughout the USNR, and shipped to the Empire of Rome itself. His cattle were known to be "genetically engineered for taste." This was part of the motto and included in all the TV advertisements. Joseph had seen the ad many times. In the TV ad, and the billboards, was the President's wife, declaring: "our beef is created for its taste!" Now, while tending the barbeque, a thought crept into Joseph's mind, about how there was not a mention in any of the ads about where that meat came from. True, there were pictures of very healthy cows, but the word was "beef," not cows, nor animals. Thinking about them as animals, would also have been right, since the edict of the Roman Church, was that MAN, in capitals, had been given dominion over all animals, in the Garden of Eden . . . . "Whoa there!" Joseph returned his mind to the task at hand. "Where did all that come from?"

"What do you know about Soma?" Joseph sat his coffee down at the table beside Mary's brother. Only one had shown up for the free meal, and he was consuming his third steak with great gusto.

Most of the other men had left—either gone home, or went up the elevator to begin their shift.

The man stopped eating just long enough to offer in a low voice: "do you have some sort of a death wish?"

Joseph was taken aback. "I beg your pardon?"

Bart Brown Bear (as Joseph learned later, was his name), shrugged. "Yeah, I guess you would not understand—else you wouldn't have asked? For you it might not be as risky. Still, you might lose your cushy job." He resumed eating.

"Please excuse me." Joseph replied. "I'm finding that there is a lot more to the world than I can learn in the city of New Rome?"

"You got that right Mr. Wolf." This time his eyes twinkled ever so slightly.

"Mr . . . . ?" Joseph smiled, realizing that he was wearing a jean jacket with the Black Wolf logo. Despite Bart's concentration on the rapidly disappearing steak, he had let the other man know that he was not unaware of his surroundings—that he was not "unaware," period. His previous reply to Joseph's initial question was a definite "this is not a subject to be talking about in the present surroundings."

"So you like my sister?" Another straight-forward remark. Bart Brown Bear was not someone to skirt an issue.

"I won't lie, that I found her to be a very interesting lady, to say the least."

Who was he kidding—definitely not the brother, nor himself. There was hardly a day that had gone by that Mary had not been on his mind, in one form or the other.

"Interesting?" Bart picked up the T-bone, to chew the last morsels.

"I mean . . . I only met her once, at the wedding . . . and I was impressed at her complete . . . how can I say . . . openness. Is she always . . . . are all your people so . . . I can't find a word—without guile, is all that comes to mind."

"We have learned who we can trust. It is that simple. But we are here to protect Mary . . . and it does not take a genius to see that this could be dangerous for her."

"Dangerous? I respect your sister—in case I didn't make myself clear."

"Yeah we know that—and that is the dangerous part." Bart rose, indicating that it was time for him to leave.

"How so . . . ?"

"Just think about your first question, when you came over to talk to me. My brother Simon is not so easy thinking about this. Simon says that you spell trouble—and maybe I agree . . ." He broke off, and then added. "We know why you organized this little cook-out."

As Bart rambled on his way, Joseph wondered to himself: "so if you knew this, why did you show up? Maybe the other man just liked to eat (that was true), or had he come to extend a warning to keep away from their sister?"

Joseph lingered long enough in the courtyard to aid in clearing up after the barbeque then he took one of the main elevators to complete the finishing touches on the office suite he was presently installing. He was just getting started, when one of the supervisors from the high steel construction showed up at his door.

"I need you to come with me." The man explained. "One of my workers has taken ill, and he is asking for you."

"But I am not a doctor . . ." Joseph began.

"I know that, but this man says he knows you—Bart, one of the Indian brothers from Kansa."

"Yes, I know him, but how can I help? Should he be taken to the hospital?"

The other man sighed. "That's the policy, but with these men from the Rez . . . well we treat them a bit different." Then, at the raising of Joseph's eyebrow, the man went on: "I mean that, I personally, respect their beliefs, and after all, they are here in New Rome as part of a cultural goodwill exchange. One of the big time priests from the New Roman Cathedral is down in Kansa, attempting to "save the heathens." Between you and I, they do not need saving. Bart and his brother are two of the hardest workers I know—and honest and trustworthy as the day is long." The man waited at the door for Joseph to follow him.

In the elevator, on the way up, the supervisor started talking again. "In the not so distant past, some people might call me an "Indian lover," but you know, those people have been given a raw deal, I do not believe in the least, that they are connected to any of the terrorist activity. It's just too bad that the real bad apples hide out somewhere in the badlands deep in the Rez. If it wasn't for the shaky treaty, I am sure President Forester would be sending bombing runs over Kansa, to flush them out."

"You could be right," Joseph agreed absentmindedly. "And with the increasing number of suicide bombers lately, I would not rule that out."

"You brought your cell phone?" The other man inquired, as they stepped out of the elevator on the uncompleted fortieth floor. "I will hope you can convince Bart that he should get checked out—you might need to call an ambulance."

The two men found Bart, bent over double, sitting on a bench by a beat up picnic table. "All the conveniences of home." Joseph remarked to himself, and then was glad that he had not said it aloud. "What seems to be the problem?" He bent over the large Native man.

"I guess I ate too much." Bart managed a smile that was more of a grimace.

"Maybe we should get you to a doctor?"

"No—no doctors. I asked for you, because I need to get in touch with my father. He will tell you what to do. After all you and your meat, are partly to blame for this."

"How am I to blame for you overeating?" Joseph wondered.

"It's not you." The man winced again. "It's those doctored up cattle. My father warned me to go easy on the meat here, but I guess my craving got the better of me?" He gasped. "You will find a phone number in my shirt pocket. I need you to call my father—he will tell you what to do."

Joseph extracted a piece of folded paper from Bart's left shirt pocket, and began to dial the number on his cell phone.

"I will leave you in capable hands." The construction supervisor said to Bart. And to Joseph: "We are working one floor up. Just give a yell, if you need help."

Joseph nodded, waiting for an answer on his cell phone.

A man answered, who Joseph learned, was Bart's father. When Joseph explained the emergency, Bart's father asked him: "Can you bring my son down in the elevator? I will be right over."

"Can you walk?" Joseph asked Bart. The other man was sweating and breathing hard now. "Your father asked for us to meet him in the court yard at ground level. I am thinking you need an ambulance?"

"Don't think too hard about that, Mr. Wolf." Bart steadied himself on the edge of the table, to stand—not without a great deal of effort, and Joseph's assistance. "That is not going to happen. I am not about to go to one of your hospitals, unless . . . . well, it just isn't going to happen!"

The sun had set on the city and the courtyard when Joseph and Bart exited the rear doors of the Friendship tower. In the encroaching darkness, the circle at the base of the tower, deserted now, was illuminated by a nearby street light, and the raising full moon.

"Wolf's moon." Bart commented, as Joseph helped him over to one of the temporary wooden benches at the perimeter of the courtyard. There were future plans for a majestic fountain, and encircling concrete seating, but at the present, there was only bare earth. Joseph acknowledged his ailing companion's remark with a shrug of his shoulders. It reminded him of how he had been driven, since meeting Mary, to find out more about her, and Kansa (or the Rez, as most people called the land southwest of the Red River).

In a few minutes, a Yellow cab stopped under the lone streetlight, and an aged Native man got out. The man paused for a minute gazing up at the ripe moon, pushing his wispy grey hair back from his face. "There is something out of balance here." He exclaimed as he made his way over to where Joseph and Bart waited. "That has the feeling of a Wolf's Moon, but how can that be? A Wolf's moon is a Winter moon . . . ." Then he looked directly at Joseph. "This night belongs to you." The Elder said, as if that explained everything. "I came to look after my son, but the Spirit has called me for you."

"My name is Edward Wind-in-his-ears." The old man extended his hand and forearm in a traditional greeting. "I was named this because I can hear the Spirits that are in the Wind."

Before Joseph could form a question in his mind, Edward turned to greet his son: "Bart, the mad cows have you again?"

"Yeah. Once I get started, I can't stop." Bart agreed.

"Come to the centre of the circle." The Elder instructed. He opened the nap-sack that he had brought with him, and took out, among other things that Joseph didn't recognize, a folded Navaho blanket. Edward spread the blanket out, and motioned Bart to lie down.

"What about . . . ?" Joseph began.

"No one will see us. The Spirits have told me that this Moon time belongs to you," the old man assured him.

Joseph shrugged—he found himself doing this a lot lately. There were too many things happening that completely defied his logical understanding. "Ok, what's the worst that could happen?" He didn't want to think about security finding them—an unauthorized person, in the form of a Native Elder, present on the grounds of the President's tower, after hours, no less . . . ? He breathed a deep sigh, and asked a silent prayer—for his job, and who knows, perhaps his future?

Meanwhile Edward Wind-in-His-Ears was giving his son a drink—a brownish liquid, in a bottle. Then Bart stretched out on the blanket, and the Elder began shaking a rattle over his prone body, while chanting in low voice. After a few minutes, he stopped, with one final shake of the rattle in the direction of the full moon. He stood up, and made his way over to the picnic table at the perimeter of the circle. "You might want to sit over here with me." He said to Joseph. "You look kind of conspicuous out there in the moon light. You don't want to call attention to yourself, if anyone looks out the window of the tower."

By now, Joseph was at odds, what to believe—until he saw the faint beginning of a grin on the old man's face. "But you told me . . . ?"

"You are getting yourself involved in things that will require learning to trust in the Mystery." He was now putting the bottle of medicine that he had given Bart and his rattle back in his nap-sack. "This is a lot like the Medicine that was given to a man called Soma, when he freed our people from the prison camps that they called Reservations." He remarked.

"Soma?" Joseph was at once called to attention. "I asked Bart about him earlier, and he said that it was not safe to talk about this subject?"

"That was true at that time—in fact this is a dangerous thing about which to talk about, at any time. There is, however, a time and a place that Spirit will pick—and this Moon time was given to you."

"This story about mad cows and Medicine began when a man called Columbus first came to our shores. He is famous now, for discovering "the new world." There is even a day named after him. You would almost think that our people did not exist, until our land was "discovered." But we have been here since the Great Mystery, the Creator put us on this world we call Turtle Island. There are stories, lies, to hide the fact that we belong here. These lies say we came over a land bridge from the other side of the Great Ocean. But we know that we were here to greet the first people who came that way, and we welcomed those people, and called them brothers and sisters."

Joseph listened intently to the story as told by Edward Wind-In-His-Ears. This story had been handed down from generation to generation in the oral tradition of these people. Although the story was about many nations, that had been incorrectly, collectively named Indians (by the aforementioned Columbus), Edward narrated this story from the viewpoint of his ancestors, his tribe, called the Anishinabe—a word which the Elder translated as 'Man Put on this Earth, The People, or Original People.'" The Story as told by Edward, came to life in Joseph's mind, as he leaned back, and gazed up at the darkened night sky—captured in the moment by the magic of the Wolf Moon.

Chapter 4

The Other Side of the Ocean

The People learned many moons later, that Columbus had come to the land he called "the new world," without the consent of Rome—without the Emperor even having any prior knowledge. The King of Spain had heard that there was a new world called India, that was full of riches beyond compare, and so, he agreed that Columbus could take three ships and search for this new world. It was not within their plan, as to how this might be (or not be) shared with Rome. The King actually believed that Columbus would sail off the edge of the world (Rome kept all other countries in the dark about life and lands outside the known boundaries). If the truth be out, it was Queen Isabella who persuaded the King to let Columbus make the voyage. Some countries were ruled (almost jointly) by a King and Queen—except in official dealings with Rome.

Columbus did not find the land of riches that he sought. Instead, he found an inhospitable climate that would have been the undoing of the Spanish, who were trapped, and forced to spend the winter. If it were not for the help of the people who Columbus called Indians, the captain and crews of the Nina, Pinta, and the Santa Maria would not have survived that winter. Come the Spring, Columbus and most of his crew high-tailed (actually, with tails between their legs according to the stories passed down by the People) back to Spain. When Columbus returned to his homeland, the story he had to tell was about a vast unconquered land—and a proud, sharing red-skinned people that he had discovered. This was the story that eventually made its way to the ears of Rome.

The King of Spain and his explorer were called before the Emperor, to account for their indiscretions against Rome. "And when were you to tell me about this world beyond the Great Ocean? Before or after you had gathered the Gold and Silver for yourself?"

"Great Emperor . . ." the King began: "it was in the name of Rome that this undertaking was begun . . . . and I am sorry to say that this India is not the land that had been rumoured."

The Emperor had heard the rumours. " . . . and what did you find?" He addressed Columbus directly.

"A land of great forests, wild beasts, and equally untamed people, who live with the animals like brother and sisters."

"Another Pagan land—like Africa, and China? Perhaps there are natural resources that would make it worth our while to save these people from their Sins? If this land is so uninhabitable, why then did I hear that some of your men stayed behind?"

Columbus and his King did not have an answer, at least not one that they cared to discuss with the Emperor of Rome. The men who remained behind had told Columbus, that these people had something that was not to be found back home. They had used words like trust, and sharing, and freedom—but this was not what the Emperor needed to hear, if one valued his life. Over the months to come, those who had returned from the land across the ocean, shared their experiences with their countrymen, and eventually the word spread, about this land of great forests and fertile plains, unsettled, there for the taking, and a groundswell of eager farmers petitioned Rome to be allowed to make this their new home.

The exodus began quietly enough, first a few ships from Spain and Portugal, followed by eager settlers from every country within the Roman rule. One stipulation for the claiming of this land (in the name of Rome) was that, no one would be allowed to take modern technology, except for weapons to protect themselves and devices to communicate with the Father land. It was speculated that the Emperor was either sceptical about their motives, or he wished to punish them for disobeying his laws concerning the absence of "land beyond the boundaries of Rome." Either way, the homesteaders, as they became known, took the first horses, which the natives marvelled at, and having no name for this beast, called them big dog. The horses multiplied quickly, and soon many being "freed" by the Indians, grew wild, and roamed the plains.

At first, the homesteaders and the Natives lived peacefully, sharing the land and its bountiful resources. Then, as boatloads more Europeans arrived, and towns grew into cities, the Indians retreated, pushed further into the wilds, until one day, gold was discovered . . . "but, I am getting far ahead of my story." The old man, Edward Wind-in-his-ears halted, almost as though he could remember, almost as though he had been present . . . and then, Joseph recalled reading that the Native tradition of passing on the history of their tribes was through oral means, and he realized that Edward's father and mother, and Grandparents must have been responsible for the story that he was now hearing.

"In the beginning, when the White faces began to settle on our lands, we shared, and helped them to survive. Then, as more and more of them arrived, the Red man was pushed further west, toward the plains, off the rich, fertile land in the centre and Eastern part of Turtle Island. One thing I want to clear up, at this point in my story—our land was not always the island as we know it to be now. We agree with the white face that there was once a land bridge, connecting the land of the white face people, with the land that we call home. My People also believe that the land bridge was removed by the Creator, to protect us from the greed of the white skins."

"I find that version of the story acceptable." Joseph said. "But, why, then, did the Creator not protect you from my ancestors? Why did the Creator not hide you from their greedy eyes?"

"Our People have a Way," the old man sighed " . . . and the Heart of this Way is Responsibility."

With that, he continued his telling of the story . . . .

Chapter 5

The Aztec
(the Fall from Grace)

Following Columbus' first journey to the "new world," the collective beliefs of the Red Man were shaken. The prophesies of the Hopi tribes became reborn in the minds of the People. There would be a great payment extracted, if the Red races did not regain the balance that they (at one time) shared with the Earth and all of its creatures. In many gatherings, this was discussed to great lengths. The truth was apparent, that although many of the Tribes still honoured the four-legged and the winged brothers and sisters, there had been rifts created. The Land was divided, due to different beliefs among the Red men and Women.

In some instances, where there had been Respect, this was eroded by powerful leaders, who began to claim that "their Way" was the only way. The Spirit Path was slowly being replaced by Religion. A powerful tribe on the south-west part of Turtle Island, called the Aztec, worshipped more than one hundred "Gods." For these people, the One Creator was forgotten—replaced by a Sun God who demanded constant human sacrifice.

For many moons, numerous seasons, the Aztec carried out horrendous acts of carnage, all the while, mindful of a misplaced (?) belief that a god-man called Quetzalcoatl, the feathered serpent, would one day "return" to change their lives, and make them rulers of the entire known universe. As the sacrifices continued, however, a man arose to power, called Abraxus, a caring man, in the middle of all of the mayhem. Still, although, in his heart, he knew that there was a better Way, it was difficult for him to disregard the teaching of those that preceded him, so the ritual sacrifices continued.

One day, a man with white skin was captured by the Aztec, and brought to Abraxus to become the next in a series of seasonal sacrifices to the Sun God. As this man was led up to the great alter at the top of the pyramid of the Sun, Abraxus noted that he was unafraid—he was dispassionate about his fate. Something, about this man's willing acceptance of his death, touched Abraxus. As this man waited his hands bound behind him, on the altar, to be beheaded and disembowelled, Abraxus motioned away the other priests. He bent toward this man, and questioned him.

"You do not seem to fear death?" It was more of a statement than a question.

This man, who had been living among the Red People for most of his life, had learned to speak a common language of the People. This, in itself, amazed Abraxus, and he believed this man to be a sign from the Gods.

"Why should I fear?" The man gasped, from his knees. "I will go to be with my God. My God is the One God, the God of Love and Mercy."

"If this God is so great why has he not protected you from being here today?" Abraxus demanded.

"My God has sent me to you." The man winced in pain. "I will willingly sacrifice myself—as his Son has done for me, so that his Truth will be known."

At this, all of the teaching of Abraxus' people welled up in his mind, and did battle with his heart. At once, a keen "Knowing" began to take hold of him, and before it could change his mind, he quickly raised his sacrificial sword, and beheaded the man who kneeled before him.

Nightmares haunted the man called Abraxus. Dreams that he could not dismiss. He soon feared the night. Each night meant another meeting with his ancestors. In his dreams, the ancestors showed him the future of the Red skinned People. In his dreams, the white race conquered all of Turtle Island. The Red man, and his women and children was tortured and murdered to extinction. Abraxus could take no more. Ragged and weak from lack of sleep, he surrendered to the dreams. "What can I do to change this?" He asked. That night, he had a different dream. In this new dream a man appeared to him. This man led a group of dark skinned people, but this man's race could not be known.

For a time, this man was accepted by the white skinned people—the same people who appeared in the previous nightmares. Some revered him, and bowed down to him, while others feared him. His message was one of peace. "We are all the same. We are all Brothers and Sisters." He proclaimed. "My Father has sent me to tell you this." It was a simple message that bothered those who feared him greatly, until they spread lies about him. He was tortured by the white skinned people, and put to death.

Abraxus awoke from this dream with his head full of wonder. "Is this what has happened, or is this what is to come? Perhaps, we are not the first people to make these mistakes." Having only his previous experiences, and the teaching of the former Aztec priest, however, he was at a loss to understand the dream. His mind only understood sacrifice, as a way of pleasing the Gods. "I will sacrifice that which is most precious to me." He resolved. "Perhaps this will cause the God of these people to take pity on us. Perhaps this will bring forgiveness." It was a result of his mind and heart engaged in war.

In the presence of a gathering of his people, Abraxus gathered up his first-born son, to carry the boy to the altar at the pinnacle of the pyramid. With each step, his heart became heavy, with the knowledge of what he was about to do. He laid the small child on the altar. The astounded crowd at the base of the pyramid were silent. The boy cringed in terror, as his father raised the sacrificial sword above his head. "Oh God of these white skinned people." He exclaimed to the sky. "Please hear my cry. Please tell me that you will accept my sacrifice, and show our people forgiveness."

Abraxus paused. He listened, expecting . . . he did not know what to expect

But the battle between his heart and mind was raging beyond control. All that he heard was silence. Even the birds had ceased their cries. The world held its breath. Abraxus breathed a deep breath, from his stomach. He looked down at his quivering son. He looked up at his hand, and the upraised sword. He released the sword . . . and it clattered to the rocks below. He gathered his son into his arms, sobbing quietly. And in the continuing silence that followed, he heard a gentle voice:

"I am the Creator of all things. I would not ask you to do harm in my name."

"But, I have heard that you sent your Son to these white skins, knowing that they would put him to death?" Abraxus raised his teary eyes, but saw no one. He and his child were alone at the top of the pyramid.

"Did I ask you to sacrifice your son? Did I stop you from doing what you knew was wrong?" The Voice was like a gentle breeze.

"You did not." Abraxus replied. "I am responsible for the Good or the Evil. But . . . why did you give your son to those people to do as they pleased?"

"I have sent my Son, to be the Way—to Show the Way. I sent my Son, to show them, that they have a Choice. Would you wish harm for the child in your arms?"

"I was insane—my people were worshiping the God of Fear—who knows what I might have done . . . . ?" Abraxus clutched his son to his breast.

"This is MY Way. It is the Way that I have given to all People—to the Black man, the White man, to the Yellow man, and the Red man, and to all creatures. It is the Way that will teach you to listen to your Heart. Do this, and when you have learned to walk the Path of Beauty, I will be true to the Promise that I gave to your Ancestors—I will send a Messenger, to take you home."

A sound arose, from below. The people began to chant: "Hail to Abraxus . . . . he has shown us the Way."

The People followed Abraxus, out of the city, away from the pyramids. They removed all of their gold ornaments and statues, and returned the gold to the Earth. They became planters of grain, and learned to live in harmony, and waited (still) for Quetzalcoatl . . .

. . . much time passed, and when a man called Cortez, who had heard rumours about a land of gold, came to the shores of the land that had previously been ruled over by the Aztecs, he found the cities and pyramids . . . and the humble dwellings of a People who had made their home in the valleys . . . . deserted.

This is a Circle

The South is a Dance of Sharing

It is about One

It is about Two

It is not about a Number

Sharing is not about One-way

Sharing is a Two-way

The One that Gives Is equal to the One That Receives

They are the Same

One

. . . . Steven WinterHawk (1992)

Chapter 6

The Little Big Horn—Prelude

As the homesteaders arrived by the boatloads from across the great water, the red-skinned people shared with them—they shared food, and anything else that their new friends needed—including their land. It was not the belief that the People owned that land. The People believed that the land (Mother Earth) owned them. They were the children of the Earth, and her protector. The new people, the white-faced, however, claimed everything, including the land, as their own. With the passing of many winters, the white-faced people kept coming, and even though they were not allowed to bring technology (by decree of the Emperor of Rome), the weapons that they carried were far superior to the bows and arrows of the Natives, so little by little, the red skinned People were pushed off their lands.

Eventually, the People gathered in an area at the South-West tip of the place they called Turtle Island (they did not differentiate the name between one continent and the whole of Mother Earth). In the beginning, they offered little more resistance, to a greater force. The skirmishes were small, and some even learned to live among the White-faces. "It is the Creator's wish that we share."

Life became one great Potlatch—a Give-Away. But even the Wolves, will fight, when they are cornered, however, and a sense of impending conflict (anger) was building. As the confrontation grew near, a man called Maco (who had led many skirmishes against the Mexicans) called a war council: "we will dance, and when the Creator has shown us the path (to War)," he raised the talking stick high, "it will be a sign that these people must be driven from our lands."

The War dance proceeded into the night, and into the days that followed—into the years that followed. The People attempted to drive the white faced from the lands that had been given to them by the Creator—until the People found themselves driven back to the river that became the border that separated their new home, the lands that had been taken from them by the Europeans. It was here that the People made their stand, on the banks of what was, by no co-incidence, named the Red River. It was here that they planned to make a final Dance of War.

The People Danced that night with a greater fever in a last desperate cry to the Creator. And in that night, the Creator truly sent a sign. The Earth began to tremble, with such a force that the dancers could no longer remain on their feet. In the morning that followed, Turtle Island had changed. The part that the red man had claimed as a refuge, the whole South Western tip, had partially separated. A wide, powerful river now existed—a much greater version of the gentle Red River, now separated the People, from the lands that had been taken from them by the White-faces. The Creator had spoken—and reluctantly, Maco agreed: "this Red River will also be a sign to our White Relatives that this is to be our home."

Time heals many wounds. The White skinned race flourished, choosing to forget the People on the other side of the Great Red River. Chief Maco grew old, and went to the place of his ancestors, and a new chief, a young man called Geronimo took his place. The many different tribes were united under Geronimo, respecting their differences, and finding a common purpose: to regain the sense of Oneness with Mother Earth. There was another common truth, a weary knowledge that they had not seen the last of those who had all pushed them to the edge of Turtle Island. The Elders, in whom Geronimo sought council, cautioned him that the Creator had saved the red man and surely had a destiny, a plan for them. This plan however was as much of a Mystery as the Creator himself. "We are not finished. Not one of the Creator's children will be complete, until Peace, and Respect for all living things (including the White-faces), comes to be."

The words of the Elders echoed in Geronimo's dreams.

Some of the People kept ties—despite the anger and hatred between the White and Red man, some of the People still had friends among the white-faces, and as the war smouldered, and the smoke abated, they traded again with their white friends. On one of these trading "missions of peace," a ship docked at a small Native village on far southern-most end of the Great Red River, just north of where the River rejoined the Ocean. On this ship were Black Robed men who came to "spread the word" among the pagans. Marvelling at the richness of the land, and the forests, one of the black robes wandered among the trees, and stopped to rest by a small stream. This man bent to drink from the clear water, and his eyes caught a reflection of sunlight on a stone. He picked up the stone, and a look of wonder filled his eyes.

Shortly thereafter, the black robe who had wandered into the forest was seen in an excited discussion with the captain of the ship.

The captain visited the tepee of the chief of the tribe, and declared that the white men would be leaving the next morning, as they had important business to attend to back home. "We will return to trade with you." The captain promised, in parting. The chief simply smiled. He was used to the ways of these strange people, who rushed here and there. It seemed to the chief, that the white-faces were forever looking for something—something to satisfy a craving that they did not understand. He could not have been more correct. In less than the passing of a moon, the white men returned, heavily armed, and slaughtered everyone in the village. The news back home, on the other side of the Red River, spread like wild-fire. Gold had been found on the land that was presently inhabited by the "Indians."

This began what was to be called in the history books of the white race—the Indian Wars. It very quickly escalated into a concentrated attempt to exterminate the "Red animals" who were a threat to the whites that attempted to stake claim to land south west of the Red River . . . . after all . . . it was argued (by the many of black robes): "these are not God-fearing human people like us. They call the animals brothers and sisters! They are no more than animals themselves . . . . and is it not written that God gave us dominion over all animals—to use as we see fit?"

In the time of the Indian wars, a number of men were declared "folk-heroes," determined mainly on the amount of red savages that they were able to kill. In addition these coon-skinned wearing woodsmen, another breed of man made his appearance, in the guise of pony-soldiers. In the beginning the pony-soldiers were given the job of protecting the God-fearing settlers (and pan-handlers) from the Indians, but as the Gold rush reached its frenzy, the aim of the troops led by a man called Custer, became the extinction of the Red skinned animals.

It has been acknowledged since, that many instances of dishonour, and horrific acts, including torture and slaughter of innocents were committed by both the white and red people during the Indian wars, however, the path of the man called Custer, and his followers, was considered (by the red man) as being that of an evil spirit! Not only did Custer and his men wipe out entire villages of Red People, to the last man, women, and children, but Custer's troops were seen in town, after these massacres, wearing the wombs of the butchered women, on their heads. It was rumoured in times to come, that the flags carried by Custer's troops had been altered—that over the simple circle of stars, had been sown two reverse lightning symbols. Perhaps these flags represented the man called Custer's "hero," who had also believed in extinction of impure, lesser races, or was it in fact the true evil spirit who came across the ocean with the white man? Whatever the reason for the actions, the Red men gathered, and asked the Great Spirit to end this man's rein of darkness.

The prayers of the Red People were answered, in part—by true followers of the White man's God. Ancestors of the men who had lived with the "Indians" that first winter in the New World, began to petition their King. Eventually, the King of Spain made the journey to an audience with the Emperor of Rome.

"When I agreed to let people go to this new world, I stipulated that they would get no assistance from Rome. I promised not to interfere in the way they lived, as long as they honoured their heritage."

The king of Spain knew the truth behind the words of the Emperor, and those who settled in the "New World" were well aware that the watchful eyes of Rome were upon them, and ultimately the bulk of their taxes went directly there.

The King wisely held his tongue about these matters.

"I am aware that you have graciously interceded in the past, when acts of gross injustice were being committed." The King of Spain began: "When the genocide of the Jews was taking place, you stepped in, halted the perpetrators, and restored peace to the state of Germany." He spoke, addressing the Emperor as though it was he, and not his predecessor who had orchestrated the end of the Nazi regime. If the truth be known, the King of Spain, and the rest of the world, had no way of knowing which Emperor was on the throne at the time of the war. The succession of Emperors was so seamless, an unrevealed secret, it was as though the original man, who reauthored the Bible was the one that now listened to the plea for assistance for New Rome.

"I have been known to champion the under privileged." The Emperor acknowledged. "But I do not see the need in this circumstance. The people, as you have called them, are no more than animals."

The Spanish King chose his words carefully: "the men of Spain have had good luck in bartering with the "savages." We have been treated fairly, and I am told, that this is more than we have been granted by the men who are staking claims on the Indian land—claims for gold mines and for a new "ore" called Uranium which they have been selling to the representatives of Rome at an inflated price. If Rome were to help these savages, and make them trading partners, surely, the role of these pillagers would be circumvented?"

"What do you suggest that I do?" The Emperor's interest seemed to be aroused.

"All that we ask is for a boon—for Rome to halt the slaughter that is being perpetrated by this man Custer. Anything beyond that would be an act of Grace."

"Indeed?" The Emperor smiled wryly. He appeared thoughtful for a long moment. "I will grant this one favour, with the following information, that I wish you to take back to New Rome."

"Your Excellency . . . ?"

"I would have you let it be known to this man Custer, in whatever means you see fit, that there is to be a great meeting of the Indian tribes, in a place called "Little Big Horn." I have heard about this man's ego from my sources. This will be all that is required. This audience is ended."

On the journey back to Spain, the King shook his head in wonder, but just the same, he made plans to pass on the information as the Emperor had directed.

Chapter 7

The Winds of Change
(The Little Big Horn Revisited)

He tossed and he turned in the bed that night. Sleep did not come easy. The events of the evening played over and over in his mind. It all seemed . . . wrong somehow? Well, maybe "wrong" was not the real sense of the whole muddled conundrum. In that boardroom he had experienced an uneasiness; that something more was going on than a simple attempt by a group of people to prevent the takeover of their company by a large conglomerate. Something else was at stake? Something else was happening in the "background" that he could not put his finger on.

"Shane?" Sarah's voice broke the silence of the bedroom. He remembered. They had spent a more than pleasant evening together, and she stayed the night.

"I am having a bit of problem getting to sleep," he answered. That was not something she would find surprising . . . but when he did try to sleep . . . there were dreams . . . ? He sat up and swung his legs to the floor. "I think a glass of water might help."

In the bathroom he raised the glass of water to his lips, and stared thoughtfully into the eyes in the mirror. "Who the hell do you think you are? Whatever put these peoples' lives in your hands?"

The strong brown eyes in the mirror returned a look of clarity.

"I know who I am . . . do you?"

"I am Shane Little-Wolf, big time, hot shot lawyer. All this . . ." He surveyed the bathroom that was bigger than most peoples' bedroom. "All this is mine. I earned this fair and square. This is what life is all about." A young native face in the mirror smiled back . . . a knowing smile. As he swept the long black hair back into his trademark pony-tail, he recalled how the first thing he did after passing his bar exam was to change his name—his last name. He had been christened Shane Little, but one day during a summer holiday spent with his grandfather, he learned part of another truth. "Little-Wolf has flair to it." He explained to his father. "And by God, I am going to make a name for myself." In his mind, he completed the sentence: " . . . and I am not going to spend my life in some two-bit shoe factory, living paycheque to paycheque."

He settled back into bed. The shoe factory that his father had lived and died in, had come back to haunt him. That was what it was about. That was the gnawing feeling that kept him from sleeping. He sighed. "OK . . . OK . . . I hear you. It's up to me to fight for them. Omega and their corporate lawyers will wish they hadn't come up against me." Shortly after, sleep found a contented smile on the face of one Shane Little-Wolf.

"Little-Wolf. You are in another place."

It was a statement and a question in one.

A log in the fire cracked, and the young brave was jolted into the present.

"Yes." He gazed across the campfire at the aged face of the Elder. "Why am I here?

"Spirit picked you for this. The Spirit of the Wind blew you to our campfire last night."

"I had lost my way." Little-Wolf shrugged.

"A warrior of the People never loses his way." The old man's eyes burned like the coals of the campfire. "He becomes the wind, and the wind blows him places he needs to be."

The young man took a deep breath. He did not wish to disagree with this old man, but his heart was full of other thoughts. "I need to be tracking Yellow Hair." He retorted. The anger flared. "Two moons ago, he and his men slaughtered my family. He burned our

47

camp to the ground, while I was away on a hunt. A camp filled with helpless women and children. My Grandfather, who had known more seasons that any of the People I know, was clubbed to death. More than a part of me died there. More than a small part of our People, the old ways died there!" Little-Wolf shook with anger. He made a move to stand. "I have another place to be. That place is on this man's trail."

"You have it half right." The old man did not move. "Sit. Hear me out. And then you can ride. There is more at stake than one man's anger."

The younger man settled uneasily back onto the ground.

"Here is the arrow." The Elder held out the shaft, feathers first, over the fire.

Little-Wolf reached out and accepted the arrow. The flame leapt stinging his forearm. He did not flinch. This small act would have dishonoured the warrior that he was. He slowly brought the arrow over the fire, and balanced it in his hand. He knew a struggle between his heart and his head. He would not dishonour the old way, and yet . . . there was a different kind of knowing that was slowly creeping into his life. This new way of thinking was fuelled by an anger that smouldered into a flame. It seared his heart like the campfire had burned at his arm. "Tell me what you want?"

"It is not just my want." The old man spoke slowly, choosing each word as though a wrong thought might unbalance the arrow in the brave's hand. "It is the Way. The Wind brought you here."

A moment passed between the two. A long moment, as a man turns over in his sleep, and wonders where he is, before finding a more comfortable way to lay, and once again, regaining his dream.

"This arrow is for the one with the Yellow Hair." The old man explained: "It is our way of speaking to his kind. It is our way of saying to Spirit that the People will honour the Winds of change. With this arrow, we are saying "it is a good day to die.""

Little-Wolf held the arrow up before the fire, seeking a balance that was not within his heart. "It is a good day to die?" He echoed the Elders words. They were a question in his mind. "My heart

48

and my mind burn as one at these words!" He spat into the flames. "There are questions that burn like this fire!"

"And what are these questions?" The old man was serene. He was unmoved at the display of anger.

The younger man's voice rose with his emotions: "Are you so ready to give up? Are you so ready to give in to what this man with yellow hair represents? Are you so ready to let the ways of our ancestors die?" Now he grasped the arrow in a powerful fist.

"Look at the power of your hold on this arrow." The old man's voice was a near whisper. "Would you hold it so angrily that you will break it in two? This is our teaching. That which is held with the heart cannot be broken. When the mind and the heart are at war, the old ways will be broken. "He paused to let his words sink in. "Change is the way of the Creator. To honour the wind of change, and to honour the messenger of this change, is our way. This is why we can say 'it is a good day to die'."

The anger flared in the young man's eyes. "Honour the man who butchers our people? No!"

He stood. And spat again into the fire. "Pthaw! You do not know what you ask! This is what the man with yellow hair deserves!" He reached down into a bundle that he carried, and pulled out a rifle. Holding the weapon above his head he shouted hoarsely into the wind that had sprung up to fan the campfire:

"This is how I will speak to Yellow Hair. A bullet from the weapon that slaughters our people! It is more than he deserves!"

Shane was up early. He laid out the papers from his briefcase on the kitchen table. Within those documents were two choices that his clients and he had seen during the meeting the night before. As far as his clients were concerned, there was only one choice. The small shoe company that his father had worked all his life in was in danger of being taken over. For a while it seemed like a done deal . . . until these documents were found. The documents belonged to old man Watkins, the man who had started the shoe company over 50 years ago. There had been a clause added to these documents, when the company grew into more than a family business. This clause stated that in the event the company was ever to be sold, the employees would have first chance to purchase the rights to the name. It was old man's Watkins way of promising his employees some kind of security. At the time it was all he could offer. It was hard times then, but he took the chance of expanding, without sacrificing his original concept that any shoes they sold would be hand-made. As the older employees remember him saying, with his winning toothless grin: "made with heart and soul."

"Problems?" A sleepy eyed Sarah joined Shane at the kitchen table. "What's all this about?" She bent over his shoulder to survey the papers.

He kissed the hand on his shoulder. "Maybe there is trouble ahead for us."

"How so?" She sat her coffee cup down and picked up the document Shane had been pondering over.

"You know about as much as I do about this by now." He had shared his thoughts the night before. She nodded. He continued: "well there is more. To begin with, if I stand up against Omega, they will pressure the other companies in the area. Omega owns this state—almost."

"And you might lose a lot of big corporate clients?"

"Yes . . . but God Sarah . . . do you know what really scares me?" He took a deep breath. She sipped her coffee; her eyes were clear . . . waiting. "Something in me wants to beat Omega and all that they stand for. I want to say to them . . ." his voice rose, and fell.

"What? What do you want to say?" She asked.

"I . . . I don't know? It's not even my fight. I have no right except to represent my clients in the best way I know how. And that is part of the problem. They asked for my input you know. I've helped a good many companies put it back together—financially. I have a strong analytical mind . . . you know?" He paused, and smiled at a shared memory.

She returned the smile, her lips curling into a broad one-sided grin. "Yes . . . I do know."

She reached over and massaged his neck. "There's more, you said?"

Shane shrugged. "There's this dream I've been having."

"Tell me." She rose to stand behind him, to put more effort into her massage.

"We are not giving up." The old man motioned for the brave called Little-Wolf to sat down. "You have not listened with your heart. You do not understand. When the fire of revenge becomes so powerful, it destroys the balance."

"Then tell me more. Help me understand?" Little-Wolf sat back down quite reluctantly.

"We cannot hold the past." The old man began again: "Change is part of the Creators way, but there are some things that we will not give up. These are the things we know with our heart. These truths will never change. We can forget them, but they will catch fire again within us one day. They will return us to our Way. They will seem to die, but they will not die, as long as the fire of life is with our people.

The young man waited. "But you are saying . . . ?"

"That it is time to honour the Winds of Change. That is what this arrow is about. That is what you were brought to this campfire about. I have seen you. You are above all this. You are on a ridge. There is a battle that you have not been part of. Now I see that you will be part of this battle . . . but first . . . you will listen to the wind. You will ask. You will hold up the hand that touches your heart to the wind. This is how you will know. If the wind blows from that west at that moment, this wind will speak of changes. Great changes are to come. The old ways are about to die before this wind of change. If any other wind blows, the battle will turn another way. But if the wind from the west is blowing, you must ride into this battle with this arrow. It is for the man with Yellow hair. It is to Honour that he is a voice for the Winds of Change—even though he does not know of our ways."

"I am angry!" Little-Wolf shook the rifle again. "I do not have the strength to honour this man's ways—except to give him back what he brings to our people." He drew a ragged breath. "Perhaps I am not the one to do this? If I ride into this battle, I will kill in revenge, I will end his life with this weapon. It is the only way to quiet this pain. My pain is my Father and Mother, and my Grandfather. It is not mine alone."

"I have said what I must." The Elder was firm. "There will be no judgment of your actions. You will act from your heart. There is a truth that you have now spoken. All of the People act as One. What one will do is done by all, and for all of the People. You are free. I will leave with the sunrise to a gathering in the valley of the Great Horned ones. There will be a great celebration. Many tribes will come. Will you ride with us?"

"I would." Little-Wolf managed a smile. "It will be a great gathering. But I must ride to meet that sun. I have thoughts that must be faced. I will look for him. You are right about one thing. He and my path will cross." Little-Wolf's fingers were colorless in the grip of his rifle.

Even while Shane narrated his dream of the night before to Sarah, more images filled his head. The dream continued, like it had a life of its own.

"Your heritage is coming back." She bent to place a kiss on the temple that she massaged. "I want you to be sure of one thing. Just in case you are wondering? I am not with you this morning because of your money." She sat on his lap, and became enfolded in his arms. "And I was not attracted to your brains."

"What then?" He grinned. "It must have been the fire?" His breath deepened.

She answered in another way . . . without words.

Shoe companies, and corporate conglomerates were suddenly part of some distant reality. Even the dreams in his mind receded . . . swept away . . . like a breeze, like a memory of a distant wind.

Later, when Shane pulled out of the driveway, to keep his appointment with some nagging kind of destiny in the board room of the shoe company, the dreams began again:

He urged his spotted pony southward along the sloping mountain path. He was still following the man whose life he had sworn to end. A couple of days back, and many rocky ravines, the trail had turned. He followed a large group of men on horseback, as they circled toward the valley called the "Little Big Horn." The heart within his chest throbbed with his knowing. The old man's words echoed in his ears along with the ever present wind. The wind met him head on, sweeping down the ravine from the south, bringing memories of the old ways. He could smell the sweet grass burning. He could hear the voices of laughing children. Most of all, he could hear the drum that was his heart building to a crescendo. The old memories welled up inside him . . . became thunder . . . rolling . . . rumbling, became . . . the sound of gunfire!

He topped the ridge and it all exploded into his senses. The outcome of this battle seemed evident from his vantage point. There were still many horse soldiers alive, and the death thunder of their rifles was taking a heavy toll on the encircling red skinned people. But the People died, and charged again. They would not be denied. Their numbers and their unyielding purpose would not be stopped this day. This battle spoke the truth of the old man he had met at the campfire. But his heart was heavy. He could see more of this truth . . . more than he cared to see. He did not wish to see at this moment, he did not wish to know. . . . and yet he asked . . . . The wind was strangely quite as he asked; until he brought one hand to his heart and raised it to test the wind. And the wind answered.

He was silent for a moment, gazing into that wind, and then clutching his rifle, turned his pony in the direction of the sloping grassy carpet that led to his appointment with destiny. There was anger building inside his chest—a searing sense of loss that will not be released except in one way.

The crunch of the car tires on the gravel as he turned off the highway into the parking lot brought Shane back to the reality at hand. He turned off the motor, and sat for a minute, partly to clear his head, and partly to let it all fall into place. There was no stopping the dream, his only choice was to let it be. Where this was leading was not within his logical grasp. All he could do was to devote as much of his attention to the matter at hand, and let the rest take its course. "I think I am badly in need of a holiday after this is put to bed," he muttered to himself as he walked to the front entrance of the factory. He paused. It was Saturday, there would be no one working in the plant. He decided to try the entrance door on the side of the building.

The side entrance was unlocked. He pulled the heavy door open and stepped inside. The pleasant smell of leather brought back memories of his father. It was, he realized, a good number of years since Shane Little had accompanied his father though this same door. When teen age came, the attraction for his father's work gave way to other things, one of those "distractions," he smiled, being Sarah. 'No, Sarah my love, you are definitely more than a passing distraction'." Sarah had been there at the beginning, when other dreams, a young man's vision of becoming a lawyer were not more than a passing fancy. Even then, she was one half of a strong friendship, and a mutual attraction, that burst into flames at a moment's notice. He listened in the empty factory for the sounds that his memory expected. From far in a back corner, a sewing machine buzzed into life. "Who??? There should nobody working today??"

A familiar face greeted him. The gray hair was different, there were so many added wrinkles, but the eyes held that same twinkle. A huge hand engulfed his in the way he remembered, as a boy. The hand that threatened to pump Shane's arm from its socket had the constituency of the leather that the old man worked.

"Mr. Bonitas? What are you doing here?"

"Shane? It is you? I wanted to talk to you at the meeting last week, but you came and went like the wind. I guess I had a lot on my mind that wasn't clear then, that is now. Shouldn't you be in the board room? The meeting must have started already?"

"I am trying to understand it all?" As Shane spoke, his eyes were drawn to the work bench. "One way or the other, things are going to change around here." He stated the obvious. "Will that be OK with you?"

"Oh you mean . . ." The elder man chuckled. "I am remembering when we did it all by hand. Not so long ago for me. Shane . . . we do have a few modern machines at use here. Nothing that will take from the quality of the workmanship. That is what it's all about . . . you know?"

"I'm not sure I do know?" Shane was blatantly honest. "You must be putting all that you own at stake—you and the other men—to pull this off? It's a big risk."

"It is." Jose shook his head. "But what is a man's life if it ends at the loss of his heart?"

Shane shook his head. Not in agreement—necessarily, but more to clear the echo. "Jose? What is happening?"

"That is at risk. It is what we are . . . don't you think? I . . . we have a chance . . . to make a difference. Is that not what my life is about?" He pointed to a washed out cardboard sign that hung above his work bench:

"Arrow Shoes: made with Sole and Heart"

"Hand crafted in the Southwest since 1933"

The sounds of gun fire, and screaming horses blotted out everything else. The war cries of the men around him drew Little-Wolf into a web of concerned effort—that had no other purpose, save one. Red men on ponies circled, and surged forward, the rifles answered. A man and horse collapsed together at Little-Wolf's immediate right. He knew that his purpose was to ride on, but the face of the man stopped him. He leapt to the ground oblivious to the gunfire . . . the smoke, and the blood.

The face of the old man who had given Little-Wolf the arrow did not show surprise. Pain ridden eyes gazed up at him from beneath the fallen horse. The animal rolled in its death throes, foam and blood issuing from its mouth. The old man was freed. Little-Wolf bent to help.

"No—go on." The Elder coughed hoarsely.

"What are you doing here Grandfather?" Little-Wolf momentarily ignored the old man's words.

"This is a place for the young braves?"

"We were waking up when the horse soldiers attacked. Everyone who could fight joined in. These horse soldiers made a mistake. They thought we would break and run. We will not run again. They made another mistake. In their pride they did not send scouts, or they would have known how many of the People had gathered here—how many tribes. Spirit has given me a chance. This is a good day to die!"

The old man's words halted abruptly. His eyes went far away. He whispered a question: "The Wind? How did the Wind speak to you?" And he was gone the way of his eyes before the younger man could reply.

Little-Wolf gently eased the Elder back onto the blood soaked Earth. He raised his eyes from the face of the Elder, to see a man with yellow hair: one foot on his fallen horse, a pistol in both hands, firing without letup, into a sea of encircling, nameless red faces. Little-Wolf searched about the battle field. His own pony stood waiting a few feet away—a black and white ghost horse that should have run . . . might have been hit by the erratic rifle fire, but. . simply waited for him. The rifle lay at his feet. He picked it up, and flung it in the direction of the man who would never know of the Ways or the reason for Life, of the old man he and his troops had killed. "Take this back. It is not for me!" The young warrior screamed in a tongue that they would not have understood even if they could have heard him above the din of the battle. "Yellow hair! I have something else for you! This is the answer of my People!" He drew the arrow from his pouch, notched it to his bow, and leapt to the back of his spotted pony in one move.

Somehow, Shane was in the main lobby of Arrow Shoes. How he got there he did not recall. He paused and drew a sheath of papers from his briefcase. He was searching for a logical answer—something to ground him. The familiar words, detailed written manuscripts, usually did that for him. He had a sense of the answer—almost. He opened the main lobby door, and stepped outside. The sky was turquoise blue . . . , and the wind was still. He brought one hand to his heart, and then held it up to a cloudless, silent sky . . . .

After making his way to the boardroom, Shane paused with one hand on the door. He listened to the voice that he knew to be the corporate lawyer:

"You were about ready to claim bankruptcy before Omega came along." The man's words were sharp, like the retort of a rifle. "The way I see it you have no other option but to accept the buyout gracefully. "A moment of silence followed. "I don't believe there is any more to be said on this matter!"

Shane swung open the huge oak door. All heads turned in his direction. He strode purposely over to the end of the table opposite the man who had spoken.

"I have something more to say on this matter." He grasped a copy of the offer by Omega in front of him, and slid it up the table in one movement. "Take this back." He said evenly. "This means nothing to these people! You have no idea what you are talking about here. You have no idea what Arrow means to these men and women. You will never own Arrow, if we have anything to say about it—and I happen to know that we do."

Shane Little-Wolf took a deep breath. "Change is a part of Life to be Respected, and Honoured, but some things never change, and will not be compromised. It is time for you and others like you, to listen. There are some things that cannot be taken by force, nor bought or sold—at any price."

*   *   *

In the quiet that followed the Battle of the Little Big Horn, a group of women paid a purposeful visit. They thrust knitting needles in the ears of the Yellow haired leader, saying: "since you did not listen to us in this world, perhaps you may hear what we have to say, in the next." One of the mysteries that would be recorded in the white man's accounts of the "Custer massacre," was that body of Custer was neither scalped nor mutilated. This was not a mystery to the People who ended his life.

In the solemn walk back to their camp, a young woman broke the silence: "I saw my Grandfather—I am sure he was there."

"Who? Oh yes the Spirit of Geronimo would have been there—that is for sure!" Another woman agreed.

" . . . . But he did a strange thing." The young woman continued after a while. "I saw my Grandfather take away an arrow. This arrow had been in Yellow hair's heart."

Chapter 8

The Gift of Spirit
(Prelude)

Prior to the relocation of the People to Reservations, a particular young man of destiny had experienced his coming of age Vision Quest. When he returned, he was at a loss to explain the vision that he received during this time. He returned to his tribe, to consult with the Shaman on that fateful morning that Custer led his men on the attack that was to spark the battle of the Little Big Horn. He did not get a chance to find out what the tribal Shaman might think of his vision. All he remembered in the intense times to follow was a name, and a voice from a fire. He had seen a small bush burst into flames. The vision was so real that it shocked his mind. "This was not a dream," he said to himself. "Your name is to be Soma, from this moment on." A gentle voice spoke from the fire. "You will free them from the imprisonment of their body and minds. You will lead your people to a place of safety and Peace that I have prepared."

Those words ran through this young man's mind in the days and years to come, during which, his People were interred on Reservations not of their choosing, and those words were all he had to cling to when he was taken from his parents, and forced to learn the white man's ways. The first thing his vision accomplished, was to gradually free himself from the darkness of the mind that drove many children to suicide or death through simply giving up, when a person is told over and over, that they have been living a life of "sin". Before the residential schools, and the oppression of the white race, these children, and the People they represented, did not know of a word called sin. In times gone by, the children had been taught to recognize right from wrong. They were taught to listen to their Hearts. They were taught that when you learn to sense what your heart is saying, you will be walking the Path of Beauty—you will walk the Spirit Path. Suddenly, now, all of this was wrong. Their soul was taken from them—denied as being worthy. They were brainwashed into believing that all that had gone before was sin. They learned a word that condemned to death in a fiery hell if they did not give over their souls to the church of the white man—if they were not saved by the white man's god. It was too much for many of these young minds to grasp. Those that did survive came to believe that they were indeed sinners—it was the only way they could process the dichotomy of someone who spoke of love, and beat you at the same time.

Soma's memory of his vision quest was his true saving Grace, as he learned later. He learned to keep quiet as a way to survive. He learned that by not challenging the oppressor's viewpoint, he could assimilate the knowledge—these people were light years ahead of the Red race, in technology and logical thinking. He reasoned that they had accomplished this, by denying their Spirit, but if this was what he needed to help his own kind, then this is what he would do (on the surface). Inside he smouldered, but outside, he became a grade-A student—driven by the Spirit, not only to simply survive, but to excel.

Time passed, and the Fire within Soma kindled into a Flame. By the time he graduated from all of white man's schools, his Spirit connection was strong. He began to see smaller miracles grow larger until he had conquered the logic of this white man's world, in his mind. Shortly after graduation, he was offered a job at the United Nations, in Rome, as an interpreter. No one could grasp how this young man had, almost overnight, learned to speak ten of the major languages in the modern world.

Ten years past, and as Soma approached his thirtieth birthday, the Spirit spoke to him again, reminding him of his purpose. Now, a well known and respected member of the United Nations, he sought, and gained a personal interview with the Emperor.

"I will come directly to the reason for my request to speak to you." Soma stood proudly and addressed the Emperor eye to eye.

The Emperor smiled at the man's seeming bravado. "I understand that you have your reasons for requesting an audience with me. But know this, before you speak further: if I did not have a reason for you to be here today, you would not be here."

Soma thoughtfully pondered the Emperor's warning, and calling up his learned diplomatic knowledge, he asked: "how may I be of service to you?"

The Emperor's smile broadened. "Now you are displaying the abilities that got you in my door. I have a need to hire a person who is fluent in difficult languages, and who can be a mediator on my behalf. If you can respect me, I will respect you and when you have come to show your worth, I promise to hear your requests—not before."

That was that. The interview was over, and Soma was given a day to think about the Emperor's words. This struck him as significant. The Emperor must have definite need for his services, or the command would have been: "do it—now." This also meant that the services were of a nature that involved willingness on his (Soma's) part. It was apparent that the Emperor was somewhat aware of the other man's history of assimilating knowledge through intense study, followed by (meditative) retreats from the public eye. "How much do you really know about me?" Soma pondered. "Perhaps you might be surprised at what you think you know?"

The next day, Soma called the Emperor's aid—using the number given to him by this same man. He agreed to the position as "offered" by the Emperor, although the details were more than sketchy. He was told to wrap up his current affairs, and report to the office of the aid—and to bring his clothing, since he was to be staying on-site until what was required of him was accomplished. Two days later, he stood suitcase in hand, at the door to the Palace. The man he had talked to showed Soma to what would be his sleeping quarters, and bid him to make himself comfortable. The Emperor's aid, also said that he would be starting his assignment that very afternoon.

Later that day, Soma received a visit from the man who had instructed him to prepare for the first part of his job. The man brought with him a sealed box. Upon breaking the seal (the Emperor's personal Seal), the man left. "I am not allowed to see the contents. What is inside is between you and the Emperor—at penalty of death." He promptly left the room, and Soma heard a "click" of a key at the man's departure. The room contained all of the necessities of life, and the same man who had locked him in would return at the appropriate meal times. That was all that passed between them until, four days later, Soma reported that: "I have translated the page that you gave to me. This must be a test—as it is very vague, and it hints of more?"

Immediately that afternoon, Soma stood before a beaming Emperor. "I had a feeling that you might be the one to do this." The emperor's smile was sly. You are only the sixth man to try. Sadly, I could not allow those before you to leave this palace, just in case they understood even a bit of what this is about." His eyes became like that of a predator and his meaning was clear. "Not a man came close to cracking this code."

In Soma's thoughts, was a clue to one of weaknesses of this powerful man. "He chose only men to test this. If he had been open enough to choose a woman—particularly a woman with Native ancestry he might have been successful." All this aside, Soma kept a straight face, and a closed mouth, not revealing this life (his life) preserving information. If the truth be known, he (Soma) was the perfect candidate (as the other man had somehow guessed) for the job. The symbols that he was asked to translate were similar phonetically to numerous Native languages. It was as though the language of his people had been accelerated beyond the spoken word, and the symbols brought to life! Wherever this language came from . . . . Soma could only guess? His heart leapt in his chest at the prospect of learning more, but he artfully hid that from his "employer." Soma realized that, this man, and his linguists and scientist could not proceed given their logical approach to the problem. It would take an open mind, balanced in Sprit and the true physical world. And this bit—this snippet of information was light years ahead of the world that Soma and this man who called himself Emperor, knew.

"So . . . tell me what you learned—and keep in mind that I do know somewhat about what this is about."

Soma guessed that the other man must have something more; the "words"—the symbols, implied this. "This is one part of a message—from beyond."

"Beyond where?" The emperor's eyes were steely—at once unreadable.

Soma drew a breath. "It says, not in a literal sense, but in an implied one . . . (Can't give too much away, Soma paused) . . . that this . . . container . . . . or perhaps it is a vehicle? The word is so close that it essentiality means the same. It says that what is contained and carried is from beyond the Void."

The emperor cut short a gasp, and then quickly regained his composure. "And does it explain what this Void is?"

"The word also means Darkness—nothingness . . . . also a place of habitat . . . like the other side of the great ocean? That is all that there is." Even as Soma spoke the words, he sensed a reaching out . . . . to that place beyond the . . . Void.

The Emperor seemed pleased. "I can only say that you are correct. Please return to your quarters. I will ponder on this, and perhaps I will ask you to translate more."

Soma smiled to himself, as he returned to his room. "He is most likely wondering how to get me to translate the rest of whatever he has, without me actually gaining the knowledge in the process? Well fat chance that it will or even can, happen that way."

That night, Soma tossed and turned in restless sleep. A voice, from the Void echoed in his mind: "remember your destiny. You will be the one—you will free your People."

The next day, the Emperor's aid brought another sealed box. "You know what you are to do with this." He instructed.

This began a daily ritual of sorts. Soma translated the symbols, and reported his translation back to the Emperor—with one exception: there was a greater meaning that spoke to Soma, that he did not pass on to his "employer," The literal translation was enough, it appeared, for the other man who noted the information, and congratulated Soma, before sending him back to his room.

After a time, and a when a suitable amount, in Soma's view, had been translated, Soma stood quietly in front of the Emperor, with the fruit of his daily work in his head. He wrote nothing down, but had, in the past days, delivered his translation orally.

"I am waiting." The Emperor demanded.

"As I am," Soma replied.

"Is there some reason that you are not talking today?"

"There is a reason. The reason I requested an audience with you on the first day."

The Emperor frowned, and appeared to choose his words carefully. "I will listen to your request."

"When I first stood before you, I came with a request. I would like you to free my People."

"Free your people? I am not involved in the differences between the Red man, and the colonists of New Rome. If you think your people are somehow imprisoned, why did you not approach the courts in the new world? From what I hear, your people are free to come and go as they please."

"Begging you pardon, Emperor—the men are free to work in the mines and road building, but their wives are not allowed to leave the Reservations. They are given a meagre bit of food for their work when they go back to the Reservations at night and the children have been taken from them."

"Oh yes. Their children have been taken—and provided with the same education that was given to you. If they do not use this education to better themselves, as you have, is that my doing?"

Soma held his head. The Emperor's logic was inescapable, but one-sided. He felt the fire building inside him, but he knew that this man would respond to nothing but his own way of thinking. "Begging your leave—my people want to go back to their home lands." He stated. "And only you have the power to make this happen. The true power for all major decisions in our known world resides in Rome. That is why I came to you for help."

The Emperor sighed. "It appears that you and I will need to come to an agreement." You will do the translations that I require, and with every ten pages of translations, I will send a decree to New Rome, that one of the Reservations will be, as you unjustly call it: set free. They will be allowed to return to the lands south of the Red River."

Soma could (almost) see the reason for the wording of the agreement. To date, the pages given him contained small bits of what might be a larger work. The reason being apparent. If Soma was not allowed writing material, he would logically have a greater difficulty putting it all together. The fallacy in this, which Soma was not about to divulge, lie on the logical viewpoint. The material that he was translating was symbolic, and not logical writing. Each bit hinted of the whole, in a manner that Soma had read about holograms. In a Hologram, each part contains the whole. That is, if the person viewing it can, in this case, stretch his mind to reveal the greater message. This was the second meaning behind the logical translation that was given to the Emperor. "Today is the tenth day of my work. This will be my tenth page of translation."

"Yes—but this is only the first day of our agreement." the Emperor replied.

The fire in Soma's heart smouldered. He would have liked to say more, but he simply nodded, and holding up the numbered page, with the Emperor's seal, proceeded with his daily translation.

Nine days later, following Soma's translation, and the other man writing in his personal notebook, the Emperor announced that he would keep his part of the bargain. "I will send a personal message to the President of New Rome to the effect that the Red Man" (he paused to emphasize those last two words), " . . . that the Red skinned people who are now on a temporary reservation in a place called Wounded Knee, are to be released—unconditionally."

Chapter 9

The Gift of Spirit
(Wounded Knee)

Big Foot's People were working overtime—literally. When the men returned from their daily work, they joined their wives in the day's worth of food that they had been given. Then they joined their wives in the creation that was the result a vision of a Medicine Man called Wovoka. The women were busy sewing vests, from Buffalo hides. These hides and a small bit of Buffalo flesh were smuggled into the encampment at Wounded Knee, by a few white men, a small handful who were sympathetic to the Red People's cause. Wovoka had a vision that with the Ghost Shirts that the women were making, and the Spirit Rattles that the men were constructing, his tribe would be able to dance themselves to freedom—all the while, impervious to the white man's bullets. This last part would definitely be required, since all dancing had been banned, under penalty of death. "When we are dancing the Ghost Dance . . ." Wovoka once explained: " . . . we will be in Spirit. We will call the Spirits of our ancestors with our Dance, and our Rattles, to take us to safety."

One cloudy day, as if in answer to Wovoka's prophetic vision, a pony express rider arrived with a message from the President. The men of the Wounded Knee encampment were allowed to leave their labour, and join their wives. The pony express rider, a friend of the ailing Chief Big Foot, told the people that they were to be allowed to go home—that they would soon be free. The men and women donned their Spirit Clothes, and with their babies in arms, prepared for the journey home. "It looks like this will be a good Dance." One woman smiled to Big Foot."

Big Foot smiled broadly in return. "It looks that way," and proceeded to lead his people toward the old stone archway that was the gate to the reservation.

There was a regiment of soldiers at the gate to meet the band of refuges. The Captain stepped forward and addressed the people: "well . . . . it looks like you are decked out for a celebration?" He remarked. "Just what kind of celebration do you imagine you are going to attend? He smiled broadly.

"We will be dancing when we are on the lands of our ancestors."

Big Foot explained.

"Well . . . I would not start dancing right yet." The man raised his arm to signal the men behind him, and they fanned out, in a semi-circle around the gate to the reservation. "I have not received any legal notification that any Indians were to go on any trips."

"But the message from the President . . . . ?" Big foot began . . .

"What would you Injuns know about any letter?" The man replied. "I heard that you might be relocated, but as I stated before—there has not been any legal notification delivered into my hands."

The men and women grouped behind their leader could read the implied meaning quite easily . . . . this was another lie. They had been lied to so many times, and this appeared to be just a stalling tactic by the white soldiers, until they could get the release papers countermanded.

As One, the men and women of Wounded Knee began to Dance. They circled to the west and danced the Ghost Dance—for their freedom and their lives.

The captain who had confronted them shouted: "Stop the dancing. All dancing is illegal . . . if you continue to dance; I will be forced to make you stop . . . ."

*   *   *

Many miles away, Soma had just begun his evening prayer and meditation. He was shaken from his reverie by a sound that could only be thunder. In that moment, he stood amidst a downpour. In the rain and thunder, another noise was equally deafening—the sound of gunfire. All around him people were falling—his people. Men and women (with children clutched in their arms), falling to the bloodied, drenched earth in a place that Soma knew instinctively was the temporary reservation at Wounded Knee. He reached out, in vain, to catch the falling people, only to find that he was like a ghost. He was present in spirit only! He collapsed in tears . . .

. . . . and then there was silence.

He raised his head from the earth, and his eyes beheld only bodies—quiet and unmoving—except for the soldiers. In this place of carnage one Red Man stood . . . or was this a man? Yes, the great Shaman Crazy Horse stood, where all the people had died. No one else saw this Spirit called Crazy Horse. The soldiers who checked out the dead, searching for any that had so much as a breath remaining, were also unaware of the presence of Soma. The two "men" exchanged looks, then Crazy Horse retrieved a rattle, from Chief Big Foot's unmoving hand in the rain that was quickly turning to snow, and the Shaman's Spirit faded away.

The next day, Soma refused to accept the box containing the symbols to be translated. Immediately, he was called before the Emperor.

"I kept my part of the bargain!" The Emperor fumed.

"How can you say this?" Soma returned: "My People were slaughtered the moment they tried to claim their freedom!"

The Emperor was momentarily stunned into silence . . . . and then: "I kept my part of our bargain. I sent a message to release the tribe at Wounded Knee. Is it my fault if the soldiers of New Rome would disobey my command—although I doubt that they would do so, if they were not provoked? I received a communication that your people began a forbidden war dance, and the soldiers that would have delivered them to their new home were forced to stop this pagan ritual. If you know what happened at Wounded Knee, you must also be aware of the cause? I am wondering also, how you could know about something that happened last night, hundreds of miles away? I will have your quarters searched for some kind of communication device."

Soma was momentarily quiet. "How did I know this?" He wondered to himself. It had not occurred to him to question what must have been a dream. Something was happening—it had begun the moment he had completed the first translation. The symbols that he translated for the Emperor had another meaning—for someone who followed the Spirit Path of his People. The logical translation was true, but only in a logical world sense. Without the Spirit, it was still a great knowledge—but lacking a connection to the True Source.

. . . and knowledge, Soma had come to realize, can be dangerous without Spirit.

*   *   *

"That is all that can be talked about at this time."

The elder called "Wind-in-his-Ears," rose unceremoniously from the bench, and motioned to his son. "Bart, it is time for us to leave this place. The sun will rise soon, and it would not be a good thing for members of the People to be discovered unattended, this close to the white man's place of worship."

"Whoa?" Joseph shook himself out of the dream\story that the old man had been recounting. The eastern sky was indeed beginning to lighten ever so faintly. "What about the rest of the story?" He queried.

"The magic of the Wolf's moon has ended for tonight. This is all that I can say." With Bart in tow, the elder headed for the bus stop at the far end of the plaza.

"That's it?" Joseph was not to be put off this easily.

"For now—perhaps forever. Who can say what the Spirit might decide in the days to come. For now, that is all."

Chapter 10

The Gift of Relationship
(Gaia)

"Last night was like one long dream!"

Joseph lay back on his bed, with the story still running through his mind. "It seems like it was real—like a memory." He mused. After making his way groggily home on the bus, he crashed. "It is no surprise to me, how the Native People were able to pass down their history through storytelling . . . but I still have to learn how the Sons of Soma came about. And who are they anyway?"

In the days and weeks to come, the Friendship tower project went into full gear, and Joseph did nothing but go to work, eat, and sleep—with a bit of Internet and book reading thrown in. Even his meals were rushed. He grabbed quick snacks off the lunch wagon, and picked up a pizza or French fries on his way home at the end of a long day. If only the work had involved more hands on, he would have had less trouble keeping in shape, but with the rush to get the tower completed, he was pretty much forced to take a supervisory role, in the finishing off of the offices. Pretty soon he found himself feeling sluggish and heavy, due to his poor diet, and lack of exercise.

"Is that a spare tire I see?" Jenene gave him a playful poke as she delivered the latest armful of plans—drawings for the layout of the offices. Each office, although modular, was laid out to the specifications of highly-priced clientele. Jenene was the secretary, and the head cook and bottle-washer of the project. If you wanted something done—she was your "man," and if she didn't have the answer at her finger tips, she knew who did.

"I don't know how you do it?" Joseph exclaimed. "You have the busiest job here, yet you are full of energy and . . . . if I might be so bold to notice . . . the best-looking shape of any woman I've had the fortune to know."

"Get outside." Jenene answered. "You spend too much time up here in the clouds. You need to be more down to earth. Get back to nature. And I think I know just the inspiration. Jake and I are going to a conference this weekend. It's about becoming healthier, by getting back in touch with nature. The conference is called Gaia. Gaia is another name for the Earth."

"And why—what would I find to inspire me if I did go along to this with my two best friends?" Joseph had been the best man for Jake and Jenene's wedding.

"Not what—who,." Jenene answered. The guest speaker at the Gaia conference for Global and Personal Health is someone you might remember called Mary Morningstar."

* * *

That week end, Joseph accepted a ride to the conference with Jake and Jenene. His car was in the repair shop, and he was on the verge of letting it go, because the quote for the repairs was just about what the ten-year old car was worth.

"What do you think about a jeep?" Jake suggested. They had just passed a large billboard with a picture of the animal in question.

"Actually—it is on my list to check out," Joseph responded. Jenene's suggestion about this "back to nature" conference could not have been timelier. When the tower is completed, I am thinking about moving out of the city. Or maybe buying a cottage up North. This rat race is driving me crazy, and a jeep would be just the thing.

I can just imagine—motoring down the country roads with the wind in my hair . . . ."

" . . . . and Mary Morningstar in the passenger seat?" Jenene chirped up.

"Yeah—sure. There's a fantasy that has about as much of a possibility of coming true as me surviving a re-enactment of Custers last stand. 'Cause with the way those brothers hover around her . . . . well . . ." He shrugged, and then laughed out loud at the picture in his mind.

"You just never know," Jake offered. "If you are ready to face the kind of commitment that is required? Well, who knows? Just look at me. I got me an Indian Princess, and I didn't even have to learn the Pow-Wow dances. What do you think, Jen?"

"This Indian Princess agrees." Jenene responded with a friendly poke to her husband's ribs. "And Joseph? Mary was a bit impressed with how much of a gentleman you were at our wedding reception." She winked. "And to tell you the truth—I would not be telling you this, if I didn't know you as well as I do. You are both my best friends and if the Spirit is willing—I would like to see you get together."

A musical sound interrupted Joseph's train of thought. He retrieved his cell phone from the pocket of his jean jacket.

"Hello? Yeah that's me. So what did you find out?" A moment of silence. "Ok. That's that, I guess. Just put it back together, and I will drop by on Monday to settle up with you."

"Good or bad?" Jack inquired.

"Nothing I didn't expect, I guess. That was the garage. The mechanic found something when he put my car on the scope. There is a leak somewhere. Head gasket he said. Just one more thing. The car is not worth fixing."

"How about if we get together tomorrow, and check out a car lot? A friend of my mother's owns a Jeep dealership. No co-incidence there. Are you interested?

"Sure. Sounds like a plan. Joseph agreed.

The rest of the drive found Joseph deep in thought. His mind drifted back to Mary. "Holy mackerel!" he mused. "What am I getting myself into? The Natives have a saying about today being a "good day to die." Well if I do not mind my manners like my grandmother taught me, today might be the day. And is any woman worth this kind of risk?"

When Joseph saw Mary again, however—all his concerns about personal safety were somehow forgotten (for the moment at least). She was preparing for her presentation when the three located her, beside the main stage. The minute her sparkling brown eyes recognized him, Joseph was the recipient of a warm and friendly smile. She extended her hand for him, and his heart gave a leap in his chest. For a moment, he was at a loss, until Jenene whispered: "Shake her hand." And then: "But don't hug her. We don't want to deal with a heart attack here."

Joseph managed to return the hand shake, with a reddened face. Mary greeted Jenene and Jack with the aforementioned hug, and as she mounted the steps to take her place beside the podium, she had another kind of smile on her face. She had obviously overheard.

"You son of a gun, you." Joseph chided Jenene. "What was that about?

"I was just being helpful." Jenene chuckled. "Stand up straight—and remember. You are a wolf—not a love struck puppy."

"And now, I want to introduce our very special guest." The announcer's voice boomed over the loud speaker. "I don't know anyone who could better represent the spirit of our conference for Global and Personal Health—Gaia, than Mary Morningstar!"

Then, when a round of appreciative applause had subsided, he continued: "Mary is here today to talk about her People's commitment to Gaia. In case you do not know, Gaia is another name for Mother Earth. Mary is our guest from south of the Red River. She is a real live Indian Princess. What tribe do you represent?" he asked, and turned to shake her hand.

"I am Ojibway." she smiled that disarming smile. "But today, and for the whole of my visit to your beautiful country, I represent all of the People of Kansa." Another wave of applause greeted her. " . . . And I am here today to convey a heart-felt message that is the focus of this conference. Our Earth is in trouble. Whether or not you

call her your Mother, as my People do, the Earth is becoming ill."
She paused to let her words sink in. "It is my duty as a representative
of the Red People to inform you that everyone on this planet needs
to join together in this."

"At this time, in the history of our world, we are hearing about
something called the greenhouse effect. This involves another
controversial idea—that of global warming. Notice that word:
global. If this is true, my People join many who are concerned and
sympathetic to the plight of our mother Earth. This is becoming
an issue of world-wide responsibility. This is something that all of
us need to come together in addressing. This is not just for the
Red People, or our white relatives. The fate of our planet needs
to be a coming together of those of all colours. In our Medicine
Wheel, we recognize that there are four colours, and four directions.
The teaching of the Medicine Wheel is a Circle—this circle is the
Earth."

There was a resounding applause that showed that the crowd
gathered there today was in agreement with the message of this
"Indian Princess."

"What is the meaning of this Medicine Wheel?" Joseph asked
Jenene, as the applause died down.

"'Tell you later." Jenene drew a deep breath. "Mary is really going
out on a limb here. In case you aren't aware of this also—it is pretty
well frowned on by our government to talk about what is considered
Native religious practices this side of the Red River—even though
we do not have a religion as such."

"You got to be kidding!" Joseph exclaimed. "In this day and
age?"

"There are a lot of laws that were never taken off the books . . ."
Jenene halted her explanation, as Mary began to speak again.

"Whether or not you believe in Global Warming, the
Greenhouse effect is a well known truth by the scientists of New
Rome. It works like the greenhouse that it gets its named from. I
don't think I need to get too technical about this? My People do not
need the long drawn out explanation for the way Nature works. We
see the truth in simple terms. For this to work, the heat of the Sun

74

warms up the inside of the greenhouse, but although the Sun's rays are allowed to penetrate, the glass of the enclosure keeps the heat from escaping, and creates an artificial environment for plants to grow. This, as I have said, is a simplified example, because in the world wide greenhouse, there are other things that produce the heat, and contribute to the enclosure that stops this heat from escaping. The enclosure, the great greenhouse, is mostly—about 50 to 75 percent made up of water vapour. The rest is other gases, and this becomes too technical for me. In the grand scheme of things, there is a balance. We need this great natural roof—to shelter us, and keep in just the right amount of heat and atmosphere so that we can live and thrive—like the plants. What is important to know, however, is that we humans, the two-legged, as my People call us, have begun to upset that delicate balance—mostly through the burning of toxic fuels that are gradually increasing what makes up the roof of our world?" Mary paused, to let this sink in.

"Before I continue, are there any questions so far?"

A number of hands went up. Mary pointed to a man in an expensive looking business suit, and one of the attendants gave him a remote microphone. "Let's just say, for the sake of argument, that I believe that this is happening," he began. "I came to this conference looking for ways to improve personal health. I want to know—what does any of this mean to the average Joe."

A murmur went through the crowd that was difficult to interpret if it was in agreement with the man's' line of questioning, or not.

"A good question." Mary nodded in his direction. "And it is quite relevant from both sides of the topic. The best way I can answer is: it means a great deal to all of us, as individuals and collectively as a species. Starting with the last—it is my Peoples viewpoint, and this is shared by a growing collection of concerned scientists world-wide, that, if Global warming continues, the future effects may be catastrophic! Our world could become uninhabitable—or at the very least an unwelcome place for humankind to call home."

This time, the murmur grew into a tumultuous venting of disapproval that took a while to die down. Mary waited patiently.

"I get the impression that most of you do not like what you are hearing?" She said with a firm voice. "Well I am here today to tell you that neither do I. I do not like where this is going. I do not like having to say what I am saying, but it needs to be said. If the truth is an unwelcome pill to swallow, then I for one will be the first to say: do the investigation yourself. Become involved, and prove me wrong. This is all that I ask, because my answer to the first part of this gentleman's question, is that it is something that will affect all of us—individually, and the best way to approach the problem is to start small. We need to start by caring enough about a future, if there is to be one for our children and grandchildren—to do something now."

This time, there was a smattering of applause—tentative, but nonetheless encouraging. Mary pointed to a woman standing near the stage, who had kept her hand up throughout. The woman grasped the mic.

"I believe you." She said nervously. "But what can I do? What can any of us do?"

"It really begins with you." Mary smiled encouragingly. "The first thing you and I can do is to respect Nature. Whether you believe that the Earth is alive (like I do), or not, you can do your part in re-establishing the balance of Nature. I am not saying that you should give up your cars—for example. The fast pace of life that we lead today almost makes our automobiles a necessity. We need to get to work, when our work is sometimes too far away, and the local form of mass transportation is unavailable, or not yet up to the task. And yes—we enjoy a drive in the country with our families, on our day off. I am ready to admit that our life back in Kansa has become almost as technicaly dependent today, as yours in New Rome."

"I have to admit," the woman who still clutched the mic smiled, "that what you just said, is a surprise to me. I pictured the Red People of Kansa as living in tee-pees, and riding horses." She chuckled aloud, and many of the crowd either laughed with, or at her admittance of ignorance.

"Some things change—and some remain the same." Mary smiled approvingly. "I do prefer the slower pace myself, and I like to ride horses, and camp out like my ancestors, but (her face became serious again), too many of our People have become addicted to gas guzzling, polluting cars, either as a status symbol, or because they just want to travel fast. I believe, that the answer to a good many of our problems today is to slow down. We need to be more moderate in our approach to life, or the world, and its inhabitants will be pushed to extinction—including the two-legged, four-wheeled ones.

Now, unless I have not given you enough to think about for now, I will say the rest of what I am here to say, and you can get on with enjoying your day."

Mary addressed a few more questions, and then continued. "I am not here to tell you how to live your lives. I am here to open your minds to questions. And if you have questions, then perhaps you will bring your concerns to your local government officials. But it begins with you. This is my goal. If I only accomplish that, then I will have done all I can for today. We have cities like yours, and our cities contain factories that are polluting the atmosphere. Our farmers have begun to use chemicals that are harmful to the Earth and the creatures that we once thought of as our relatives. There are those of my People, who still believe in the old ways. We are returning to the Traditional Way of living in Balance. The fate of our planet, however, is no longer in the hands of the People you have named Indians. We believed once, and we still do to a lesser extent, that the Red People are the caretakers of the Earth. What I mean by this, is we have come to realize that it is time to walk our walk, and accept that this world is too big for one coloured people to save. At one time, the balance was less complex. If you recall, I spoke before about how a good part of the ceiling—the roof of our greenhouse, is made up of water vapour? At one time there was a simple balance that was maintained by the trees and flowers and the sky. There was air for us to breathe, and when the time was right, it would rain, and everything would be restored. Our People would welcome a Rainbow, to see that all was well with our Mother Earth and all of her children. Now, it will require the cooperation of the

People of all four colours. It is not too late. If we work together, we will once again, see a Rainbow."

Mary stepped back, to show that her speech was finished, and when the applause died down for a last time, she stepped up to the microphone again. "I have an announcement: My Brothers and my Father and I are willing to show that we do not speak into the wind. We have a booth set up, where you can visit with us, and we will talk to as many as are interested, about ways to help the environment. Also we will have a paper that those that wish to join us, can sign up to spend the next four Saturdays visiting your local parks and enjoying Nature—and picking up trash. It is our belief that what you have called Earth Day should be celebrated year round. And if enough people are interested, we will be asking a group to join us at one of the large parks North of New Rome for a full week-end campout."

Joseph and Jenene, and Jake were the first to put their names on the list for the camping trip, and committing to the effort to help clean up. Joseph had a lot to think about as he listened to the other speakers and visited other boots to talk to other concerned people who shared their ideas about reclaiming world-wide and personal health. At one such booth he purchased a small tent, and other camping accessories. His mind was also on his decision to purchase a gas-sucking, off-road vehicle.

*   *   *

"Do you have anything that would be better on gas, and less polluting?" The next day, Joseph had this question for the Jeep salesman, after he had been shown some beautiful and powerful SUVs. "I do admire these cars, and it would be great to own a Jeep. I am thinking of doing a bit of camping, and traveling out of the city, but I am concerned about the effects of these on the environment?"

The sales man shrugged. "Sorry, I don't think I can help you . . . unless . . . ? Would you be interested in a used car? I have one that is about three years old that was traded in for one of these newer models."

"How would that make a difference?" Jake asked. "An older or newer gas-guzzler? What's the difference?"

"Your friend voiced an interest in something less powerful. Or at least that is what I heard. Everyone else is trading up. The older Jeep I mentioned is a four-cylinder. There is not much call for those anymore. Jake—I have to admit, because you are my friend, that the person who owned it complained that it was under-powered. How about it?" He asked Joseph. "If you do not need to get somewhere in a big hurry, this might be the right vehicle for you? The previous owner kept it well maintained, and the mileage is low."

Joseph could not help remember the part of Mary's speech about taking life a bit slower, and enjoying the ride (his imagination added the last part), as he put his signature to the papers to purchase the used Jeep.

True to Mary's words, she and her brothers organized and participated in the cleanup of four major parks in and around the city of New Rome. Joseph had only seen Mary in a long flowing, ankle length skirt. Now he was simply stunned by a form-fitting pair of blue jeans. The four weeks went by faster than Joseph would have liked. Mary was very amiable and talkative, and shared a great deal of knowledge about the local plant life. "We could eat most of these plants that you might think of as weeds." She explained. "And many others are medicinal, but remember that I used the word 'could.' Under different circumstances, the first of which requires the absence of pesticides, and herbicides, the plants that grow wild in your back yard are part of the gift of life from Mother Nature." She also told the group about the value of hugging trees. "This is more than a gesture—it is a way that you can directly re-establish a relationship with the Earth." She demonstrated, and encouraged everyone to follow her lead. While hugging his chosen tree, Joseph found himself watching her out of the corner of his eye. If he had his wish, he would be the recipient of that sincere hug. And then, (did he detect a smile?). He was sure that Mary had caught him watching.

The next weekend, the Friday evening, found a caravan of eight vehicles made up of six couples, Joseph in his newly acquired jeep (packed with camping equipment), and Mary and her brothers and father in the lead, in a rented van. Jake and Jenene were noticeably absent. The night before, Joseph had received a call from Jenene, saying that Jake's Mother, back in Portugal had fallen and injured her hip. They had already booked a flight, and were very sorry that they could not join in the camping trip as planned. It was a six hour drive to the nearest true wilderness park, and the roads out of the city were clogged with SUVs and campers—all attempting to escape for the first long camping weekend of the season. It was dark when they arrived at their destination, and the tents were pitched by flashlight. Joseph gave silent thanks that he had practiced putting up his new tent, in Jake and Jenene's back yard. Mary's brothers quickly had a campfire burning, and everyone was happy to share a quiet moment and a tea—unwinding from the long stressful trek out of the city.

"Everyone get a good sleep," Mary advised. "We plan to be up and on the trail as soon as the Sun comes up—if that is agreeable with the rest of you?"

Every one nodded, and one man (that Joseph recalled from the conference as asking what is in this for me?), remarked. "That is more than agreeable—that is what Erica and I came for. Right Erica?" His companion, a tall stately blond haired woman saluted with the last of her tea.

"If you are not aware of this," Mary had informed the group of potential campers on the Saturday before, "this park is a wilderness park. There will be wild animals, but it will be safe. There are no guns allowed. My brothers will bring bows and arrows, because it is open season only on certain wild-fowl, and should the Spirit be willing, we might eat turkey or pheasant. But an arrow would not be much protection from a bear. Do not be alarmed though. Wild animals will not bother you, unless you go out of your way to bother them. Anyone want to cancel out?" No one did.

*   *   *

"Are we ready to go?" Mary asked. They woke at the break of dawn to a clear cloudless sky, and enjoyed a light breakfast. "I would recommend that you bring a few apples or oranges for lunch, since we will be out most of the day. I brought along a good supply of each for everyone. This land is free of poisons so there will be plenty of edible plants and flowers. I can show you how I was raised to live off the land. My People could travel great distances when there was no game available, eating whatever Mother Earth supplies."

"Are you talking in a symbolic way?" Erica, the tall blonde companion of Sam (Joseph had learned his name, and ceased to think of him as the "what's in it for me man). "I hear you say Mother, like the Earth was your real Mother."

"My flesh and blood Mother has passed to Spirit. Her body is returned to the Earth. But before that—it is our belief that our bodies are created from that which makes up the Earth, and the Stars, and all things. This is the basis of our belief that all things are Sacred—that they are all ONE."

"Dust to dust." Sam quoted. "I would like to think that there is more to us than that. But I have yet to be shown that there is anything else. I am a purely logical thinker. If I can't touch it, how can I know that Spirit exists?"

"Spirit moves in Mysterious Ways," Mary suggested, while shouldering a light back pack. "We are here to enjoy this day. If we are open to that—who knows what we will find on our Path."

Early morning found the group of hikers on a trail that wound its way up a small mountain, sometimes through dense forest and undergrowth, only to break out into clearings giving everyone a panoramic view of the valley below. The pine and oak trees that made up this wilderness "park" stretched as far as the eye could see. Mary, and one of her brothers (Simon) led the way, with Joseph and the other campers close behind, and Mary's Father and her other brother (Bart) bringing up the rear. They made short stops, to rest, and sample the abundant plant life, as Mary had promised. During these halts in the otherwise brisk walk, Joseph realized that any rest

81

needed were for the city people. Wind-in-His-Ears (Mary's father) was in good health for his senior years. He did not seem winded (no pun intended), at any time, and joined in sharing laughter and otherwise contributed to an enjoyable hike. During one short stop, Wind-in-His-Ears sat on a rock beside a young couple who had walked directly in front of him.

"I noticed that new camera of yours seems to have an unlimited amount of film," the Elder remarked good naturedly.

"Yup!" the young man replied. "That's funny! Not so long ago that would be a problem, but Janice and I have two gigs of storage, and we both brought along an extra memory chip—just in case." He held up the camera for the older man to see. "Oh? I just had a thought? Is it against the rules to take pictures—we were not told about it?"

"No—no rules today—except don't do something that might get you or someone else hurt," Wind-in his-Ears chuckled. "But I might suggest that you take a different picture once in a while—that will help you remember, in a Good Way."

"How so?" Janice asked.

"You might remember that the Red People were against having their picture taken at one time? We were afraid of having the camera steal our souls—or that was the story."

"And do you still believe that?" her husband asked.

"Well, I have a slightly different view," he rocked back, clutching his knee like a child would. "That flower that you admired back a ways on the trail? It will look the same for many years in the picture that you took. But if you walked back later when the sun is no longer in the sky, that flower would be asleep. And if you came back this way, when the snow is on the ground, that flower would no longer be seen. But the seeds of that flower would be sleeping (in another way) under the frozen ground. This is about me also," he pointed to his heart. "I am an old man—that is what my son's sometimes say when they are making fun with me. If you took my picture today, and then looked at it in one year's time—It might not be who I am. I may not be in the same Dream—I may be Dreaming in another way, and I would like you to think of me as I really am."

After a moment of respectful silence, Janice inquired in a quiet voice. "Are you saying that it is wrong to take pictures? What should we do?"

"Yes," her husband (Kim) asked. "We want to do the right thing, but we would like pictures to help us remember."

"It is not for me to change another person's beliefs—only to suggest ways to make things better (and that is only my judgement)." The Elder rocked again, clutching the other knee to his chest. "I would suggest that, in addition to the pictures that go into your camera—take pictures with your Heart. Your Heart will see a bigger picture—it will see the Wolf that was watching you from the forest, while you took your pictures of the flowers and the squirrels. And in that picture in your Heart, that Wolf will have young, and grow old—and it might be the children (or Grandchildren) of that Wolf that you will encounter the next time you come this way."

When the hike resumed, another young couple dropped back to talk to the Elder Native. "We couldn't help but overhear your conversation back there. My name is John, and this is my wife Josephine. We are newlyweds—I guess it shows?"

"It does show. I can see the way you look at each other, and hold hands. When you are walking this way—we call this the Path of Beauty. This is the Way of the Creator."

"I agree," John smiled lovingly at his companion, who urged: "Ask him. We are really interested in how you think—if is not an intrusion?"

"Ask me anything." Wind-in-His-Ears replied. "And I will answer to the best of my knowledge. But please remember that this will be my way of seeing, and it will not necessarily be your Truth. Finding your Way of walking the Path of Beauty is always the right thing."

"About what you said back there . . . ? John began rather hesitantly. "Did you . . ." When you talked about the Wolf? Were you talking about yourself? Symbolically—I mean. This Native idea of the Mystery fascinates me—and Josephine."

Wind-in-His-Ears chuckled aloud as they walked together. "It is about simplicity. This Mystery is not about hidden things.

When things are hidden from us, this is usually due to our Heart being closed. You heard me talk about seeing with the Heart? This includes open ears as well. The Wolf could be me. I am the Wolf, and I am the Deer that will become the food for the Wolf. And I am at once myself—dancing on the Mother Earth." He demonstrated a few steps—causing dust to swirl around his feet. "Oops—You did not see that." He smiled broadly.

"What are you talking about?" Josephine looked puzzled. "I mean—what didn't we see?"

"Dancing," his face was momentarily sombre, "it is still against the law of your country for a Native to dance that way."

"Are you pulling my leg?" John wondered. "I read about that—but that was a long time ago."

"Many laws were not removed from your books—as they call it. Crazy as this sounds," the Elder brightened up, "we are simple People" (he continued his previous explanation). "And I do not speak the way I do to attempt to confuse anyone. There was a Wolf in the woods—back there. The Wolf followed us for some times. The Wolf has gone now. I guess it decided that we were not a threat?"

"A real Wolf!" John was amazed. "I didn't see it either. Can you teach me to see the way you do?"

"This is not a Mystery. But if you open your Heart and mind to include the Mystery, then the Wolf will be there—and many other small Mysteries as well. There is a small Mystery that your wife is not hiding too well."

"How could you know?" Josephine gasped. "It is less than three months. I don't—we have not told anyone yet. I don't think I am showing?" She brought a hand to her stomach.

"Your face is showing," Wind-in-His-Ears smiled encouragingly, "and the One-with-the—Mask has been watching you." He pointed to where the two shutter-bugs had strayed from the path to snap a picture of a mother Racoon and her baby.

"Wolves—and Racoons?" Josephine shook her head. Are all of the animals in the forest watching us? And for what reason?"

"For the reason my People have learned to watch our four-legged and winged relatives. We are connected through Spirit—and the animals have not lost the Spirit senses that we have neglected to trust. If you want to know something about the world—just ask our relatives. Then listen and watch."

Mary walked back to join the hikers who watched the mother Racoon and her baby scurry away into the undergrowth. "Please stay on the path." She advised. "And stay together. This is what our Relatives are telling us. They are watching out for us . . . and Dad?"

"Yes, my daughter?"

"Be careful," she kissed him on the forehead, and walked to the front of the line. "Alright people, we need to pick up the pace a bit."

"Is there a problem?" John whispered as he walked a bit faster.

"Not for me," the Elder answered, "there is nothing to fear that lives in this forest. The most dangerous creatures here today walk on two legs."

An hour later, Wind-in-His-Ears' words were to appear prophetic. The group, headed once more by Mary and Simon, had been making their way through a dense bit of forest, where the trail seemed hard to see, except to the experienced guides. They crossed a clearing, and on approaching the other side, there was a great commotion—a whirling of wings, and a flock of wild pheasants exploding skyward. At once Bart and Simon drew their bows. It took less time than Joseph could count,—and Simon had brought down two birds. The rest of the birds flew off in different directions.

When quiet had settled on the clearing again, Sam exclaimed excitedly, "you could have gotten more!" To which Simon replied in a reserved tone: "we only take as much as we need. Two birds will be enough for our evening meal." Then, as he was settling his bow about his shoulder, a lone pheasant took to the air and passed over the heads of everyone watching. "Bart!" he called out. "coming your way, Brother!"

The lone bird flew directly into Bart's arrow. The group of hikers, turned and Simon muttered rather loudly. "Well—what was that about then?"

Bart retrieved the pheasant, and stood quietly sniffing—testing the air in a manner that was oddly familiar to Joseph. "This is about my Brother—or should I say, my Sister?"

"But your Brother already killed two birds," Someone remarked, "and why do you say . . . ." At this point, a large brown bear ambled out into the clearing and stood upright, appearing to imitate the sniffing action that Bart had displayed a few moments earlier.

"Everyone. Be quiet. Do not make any sudden moves," Mary instructed, in a low voice, "Bart?"

Bart nodded. He removed his arrow from the pheasant. With his eyes on the Bear, he gently deposited the dead bird on the ground, and proceeded to slowly back away to the opposite side of the clearing, where the others were gathered. The Bear waited (an agonizing few moments, it seemed to Joseph) and dropped to all fours. Still sniffing, the large animal gingerly approached and seized the gift in its' massive jaws. With one last quizzical, almost human, look in the direction of its' two-legged relatives, the Bear disappeared back into the forest.

Everyone breathed a sigh of relief. "Whoa! That was close!" Kim broke the silence, hugging his wife, all the while trembling in relief.

"You do not know how close," Simon retorted. He confronted Sam, who stood ashen faced beside his blond companion. "You can let go of that gun now," his voice was not loud—but commanding. "Now—you have endangered everyone. A wounded Bear would not be something to take lightly."

Sam withdrew his hand from his jacket pocket. "I didn't mean to . . . . I was afraid!" he stammered.

"We all had our reasons to feel fear," Simon replied, "I am asking you to remove the bullets from that gun in your pocket. I am not asking you to give it up."

"Your damn right I won't give it to you," Sam still trembled, "in this country I have the right to carry a gun . . . and in case you don't remember—an Indian is not allowed to have a gun this side of the Red River."

"Oh Sam!" Erica pleaded. "Please take the bullets out. We could have been killed."

Sam grudgingly complied. "Ok but I still don't feel safe. You must have known about the Bear? And if you did—why did YOU lead us somewhere that was not safe?"

He confronted Simon, with words, but did not look the other man in the eye.

"We were completely safe," Wind-in-His-Ears stepped forward. "And we had plenty of warning. I have heard this Bear since the Wolf first appeared. How do you think I got my name? This Bear was not hunting two-legged prey. It was curious, and looking for a hand-out. This trail may be overgrown in places, but we are not the first to follow it. I imagine that the last group that passed this way have fed the animals—or at the very least, left bits of food behind. I found this:" He retrieved a candy wrapper form his pouch, "and this:" he showed the rest of the group a collection of fast-food wrappers that he had collected along the way. "We will be safe to go on now. I am sure the Bear is back in its' den sharing a meal with her cubs—which I also heard a ways back.

"The question now," Mary spoke up, "is, do we go back to camp, or continue on? I believe that a vote of hands is in order? Those that want to call it a day—put up your hands." No one raised their hand, although Sam gazed at the faces around him, and it was not difficult to see that he didn't want to be the first (or only) dissenter. "Are you sure?" Mary asked a second time. If only one of you do not feel safe—we will turn around here, and I would not blame you—my Heart is still pounding." She glanced directly at Sam.

Sam took a deep breath. "Ok—I am still shaken. But that is really part of the adventure. This is not the first time I have hunted wild game—but I admit a hand gun is a bit out of place."

Simon shrugged and looked to his Father. It was a "you got that right," kind of look. No one voiced it, but Joseph was sure that the silent consensus would have been something to the effect that "this is a wilderness hike—not a hunting party."

"Ok," May said brightly, "we will aim for that tall pine you see way up there." She pointed. "I have a hunch that there is a stream nearby—can every one smell the water?

Right! See this is what it is about. Sometimes a good scare will get all of our senses awake. We will camp up there before heading back."

It was a long hike—longer than it looked at first, to the tall pine tree at the top of the ridge. As the destination drew closer, the smell of water was indeed in the air. Everyone walked briskly, but no one spoke. The ground levelled out as they approached the pine, and the dusty path was replaced with small gravel that became a riverbed. They came to a quiet stream and discovered the source in the form of a waterfall just beyond the grove of pines. From the waterfall, a number of small streams ran out like spokes from a wheel, giving life to the valley and the forest below.

"This was worth the climb. Don't you think?" Mary addressed the party of mentally and physically tired hikers. They collapsed on the ground and agreed.

"We all need a rest," she suggested, "and then, if a couple of you will help Bart and Simon gather some dry branches, we can start a campfire. I will clean the birds—with a little help, and we will enjoy a meal of pheasant and oranges and greens that I have gathered along the way. How does that sound?"

Everyone brightened at the picture that Mary painted. It would be the first time for most of them to experience what it might really be like to live off the fruits of the Earth—given freely (including the wild-fowl).

"You can find a bit of grass where you are, but I might suggest that we sit, or lie, in a circle so that we can support each other in letting go of the stress. There was a lot to learn on our journey here, and we experienced it as a family—we have become a tribe—I hope you will not forget this day?"

When they were settled. Josephine asked. "Is it Ok to talk?"

"This is your time." Mary lay back on one of the patches of grass that dotted an otherwise sandy riverbed. Nature had provided the perfect gathering place—smaller resting places for those who wished to be alone, and larger blankets of soft grass for those who chose companionship.

"I was just thinking," Josephine lay with her head on Kim's' lap, "actually I was wondering about how your People are about forgiving? If that is not too personal? You spoke about letting go?"

After a brief silence, Wind-in-His-Ears spoke. He had chosen a place to sit between Sam and Erica—who selected to sit apart. "Letting go, if I may, is a personal thing—how you let go, I mean." He smiled in the direction of his Daughter, and she smiled back a thank-you. "When you come to know our People, you will find that most of us agree to follow a personal path. That is to say we respect that everyone does not think the same. The best way I can say this is by telling you how I have learned the meaning of forgiveness. I have a car back home that I enjoy to drive." This brought a curious bit of laughter. "Do not be surprised." He leaned back on his hands. "It is not a polluter of the air. It is a Volkswagen. This automobile was designed by this beautiful young ladie's ancestors (he addressed Erica, who reclined at his right), at a time when their country was at war with the world. Think of this—does this young lady look like she could be at war with anyone? I am sure you all know better. And I love my Volkswagen dearly. It has never let me down," he gave his words time to sink in.

"And this gentleman," Wind-in-His-Ears turned his head in Sam's direction at his left, "this man's People and my People were at war—a terrible war in a not-so-distant past. Our People—yours and mine, "(he spoke directly to Sam) "did things to each other that some might think are unforgivable. There are scars that exist to this day. But I need to tell you that you have not done anything knowingly to harm me. Back there on the trail you acted in a way that I do not understand. But if something had happened as a result—I know that it would not have been because you meant it to be so. This is how forgiveness works for me. We need to learn from our ancestors, and respect that they lived in different times and thought in different ways. It is as simple as this for me. The past is past. I have not hurt you and you have not hurt me. There is nothing to forgive, and if there is to be in the future—that is not now." That said, the Elder reached out a hand of friendship, which Sam accepted with a sheepish smile on his face.

No one else spoke, or needed to, until it was time to start the fire, and clean the birds to be cooked. The men helped to gather dry wood and fallen branches from the forest, and the women joined Mary at the rivers' edge. She used a knife from her backpack, and showed them how to remove the feathers with the aid of cold water. First, though, she carefully saved a number of the larger feathers, and bundled them away.

Soon a fire was blazing. Mary waited for the flames to die down, and then Bart put the two pheasants that were now cleaned and gutted, on a branch, over the fire. "I have kept all that we will not be eating to be burned in the fire before we go." She informed the non-Native hikers, "we will accept the Gifts of Mother Earth and our winged relatives, and we will leave this spot the way we found it—to be enjoyed by whoever comes this way—be they two-legged or four."

While the pheasants were being set to cook, Joseph wandered over to the tall pine tree that had been the focus of the last part of their trek. All the while, it had seemed to be calling him. Now he stood apart from the group looking up at a nest in its' further most branches. "Is that an Eagle's nest?" He asked aloud, not expecting an answer.

"Yes it is. You have good eyes—for a Wolf." Mary stood beside him craning her neck to gaze skyward.

He was about to reply with a joke about his working for Black wolf construction, and that the Wolf stuff was Bart's idea, but Mary spoke again.

"Do you think I did the right thing? I mean bringing these city dwellers out here and exposing them to danger—not to mention filling their heads with the beliefs of my People?"

"Of course. And it was our choice, after all." He turned to look at her concerned (beautiful) face. "It might not surprise you to know that many city dwellers have a need to escape the rat race, as much as you would not choose to be part of it. Besides—there is a time to speak out about what we know to be right. This is a good thing for me right now, because I have been feeling stuck. You—and your family have been an inspiration for me in this way."

He felt Mary's gentle touch—a silent "thank you" on his forearm, and a gust of wind, high in the pine tree caused them both to look up once more. The wind moved the top of the tree, and was gone, but something was dislodged, and came drifting down, to settle at their feet.

"An Eagle Feather," Simon spoke. He stood beside his sister. Mary's hand was gone from Joseph's arm. "This must be a Gift for you. It is the Great Spirit telling you that your visit to this country was a good thing."

"No," Her reply was soft, but firm, "this Feather is for Joseph. This is a strange thing. But it has been a strange day. And this is for our eyes only. See how everyone else is busy with their own thoughts?" And she reaffirmed this to Joseph. "Please pick up the Feather, and hide it away. The government of this land has a law about anyone except a person of Native birth possessing an Eagle feather. This is one of the good laws that they have created, but this like many other laws, are not concerned in matters of the Heart and the Great Spirit. I do not understand what this means, but it is right."

Joseph glanced from Mary to her Brother. Simon's face was unreadable. Then, he did as she suggested, hiding the Feather away in his shirt—to be transferred to his back pack at the earliest possible moment.

"The birds are cooked." Someone called from the fire. "We just need the rest of the fixings, and we can eat."

The hike back to camp was less eventful, and quicker than the trip up the mountain—it was downhill, in more ways than one. The group made fewer stops, and they were mindful of being watched. For some it was a pleasant feeling—one of belonging—that someone (the animal relatives) looking out for their well-being. For others the encroaching evening shadows held fears—of what might be lurking around the next bend in the trail. The sun was dipping low behind the grove of trees, when they reached their camp on the small hill on the other side of the valley. Bart and Simon had a fire blazing before the darkness descended on the circle of tents. Prior to the trek back, Mary had invited anyone who could brave the cold mountain water, to bathe, or clean up in whatever way was suitable to their sense of privacy. "I have been raised in a culture that embraces the respectability of a sweat lodge," she announced, "and we are roughing it," she reminded everyone. "There will not be hot water available tonight. I suggest that we do this in groups—first the men will go to the waterfall beyond the pine, and then we women will take our turn. Joseph found the cool water invigorating—and stimulating to his senses. The effect remained even as he was tidying up his small tent.

When he rejoined the group around the fire, the atmosphere was light. Someone had brought marshmallows to share. "How about a sing-a-long?" Josephine suggested. Joseph retrieved his battered guitar from the boot of the Jeep, and Erika handed out spoons—while someone else overturned a water bucket to serve as a drum. "Now it is our turn to surprise the wild-life." Kim joked. Soon the band geared up, and strains of "Kum-by-ya" and many other time tested campfire songs drifted out into the night. And as the night wore on, even the Beach Boys, "Help me Rhonda," was offered up to the star filled night sky. Joseph grew somewhat nostalgic, recalling many evenings shared with his friend Jake, when the two young men first came to the New World from Portugal. Joseph had gone on to pursue his craft as a carpenter, and Jake formed a band that claimed a degree of recognition. Sitting there "howling at the Moon," as Bart called it, Joseph missed the company of Jake and Jenene, but "there must be some good reason that they were not able to come?" He had begun to believe that a Greater Force or Destiny was at work in his life.

One by one, and in couples, the campers yawned, and departed to their tents for a well deserved rest. Mary smiled her good night, went to the big tent that she shared with her Father, leaving Joseph, the two brothers, and Wind-in-His-Ears to watch the fire die down. As the last of the singers took their leave, a singing of another kind had begun. Perhaps the wolves had joined in early, but now, in the still of the night, they seemed nearer.

"Your Brothers are asking you to join them in song again?" Bart suggested.

"Coyotes—maybe?" Joseph ignored the remark.

"No—they are Wolves." Simon agreed with Bart. "What do you think Father? Are they looking for kin?"

"Most likely." The Elder stretched and yawned. "They do seem closer than before. What do you think we should do?" He turned his head questioningly to each of his sons, and then to Joseph. "We should do something." He stretched again, and stood up.

"What are you going to do?" Joseph wondered.

Just then, Sam, who had left the fire just before Mary, called out from his tent. "Is everything ok out there? Those animals seem a bit restless."

"Everything is under control," Wind-in-His-Ears answered, "or at least it will be soon. I think you should do something, or your Brothers will be paying us a visit," he addressed Joseph.

"I don't understand," Joseph looked for help in the faces of his three companions. The Native men wore serious faces.

"You have called your Brothers. They heard you singing to the Moon. Pretty soon they will be in our camp. I think it would be good, if you were to mark your territory?" Bart suggested. Simon and his father shook their head in agreement. "Haven't you seen any of those wild life documentaries, where the hunters wake up in the middle of the night and go out to mark the boundaries of their camp to keep the Wolves at bay?" He asked Joseph.

"You mean . . . ? That I should . . . ?" Joseph recalled seeing the movie that the other men described.

"Yes. And the sooner the better," Wind-in-His Ears walked to the edge of the circle of the campfire. "We will help, but the Wolves are your Brothers, and they will recognize your scent. Ho! You out there!" He called to the darkness. "This is the camp of Black Wolfe, and he will be letting you know this is so." He motioned to Joseph.

Joseph was rather unsure if he was being "put on" but the call of the Wolves did seem closer, so he joined the two brothers and their Father at the perimeter of their camp.

"Make sure that you save enough to encircle the camp," Simon instructed, as the men walked the circle in a clockwise direction, pausing to urinate—marking the boundary of their territory.

"Well—I will sleep a lot better now," Simon announced. "I have not enjoyed a good pee like that since my last two-four. Too bad we weren't able to bring a case of Bud. I think I will turn in now—I am getting too thirsty for water."

"I will stay up until the fire is out." Bart announced. "Good job there Black Wolf—I knew you had it in you." He exchanged a smile with his Brother. Their Father was already unzipping his tent, without so much as a good-night. The way the Elder hid his face pretty well convinced Joseph that he had been had. "Still," he shrugged and played along. "I can take a joke as well as the next person." He thought to himself.

"The Wolves have quieted down, so I think I will call it a day too." Joseph beat a hasty retreat to his tent. Once inside, he lay on top of the sleeping bag thinking in the darkness. "What a family!" He drifted off, to dream about a large black Wolfe. It spoke to him in the dream, but he could not understand a word it said.

He woke with a bit of a start. The tent was illuminated by an unearthly glow—he guessed that it must be moonlight. Was that what woke him? No—something else—and it was not the sound of a tent zipper. That was barely audible. It was a voice—which he had grown to love. She was whispering something about the moon . . . ? He couldn't make it all out, but the reply was clear.

"Be careful to look out for wolves," the old man's tone was not as much a warning—it was more like a private joke. Joseph's face reddened in the moonlit tent.

"Don't worry about me." She whispered back. "I get along with all animals—even the two-legged kind."

Joseph pulled the tent zipper down carefully—just enough to see an angel, with a long flowing shawl clutched about her shoulders and head, disappear into the forest. He considered the folly of following her. "I might be intruding?" he mused. But the dream and the wolf were lingering in his memory. "Ok—so I was the butt of a joke. But it still doesn't seem right to let her go into a dark woods at night all alone. I should follow little Red Riding Hood, just to make sure she is safe from any other wolves." He chuckled at his musing, and remembered her parting words—and realized that he was already dressed.

As quietly as possible, he slipped out of the tent. The moon was full above his head, and the clearing where they had made camp was near bright as day. He set off in the same direction as Mary had taken. In attempting to orient himself, he came to the conclusion that this would lead him to the top of the small hill that the camp was located on. It was a short walk through a dense growth of trees and shrub. He calculated in his mind that he had walked about fifteen minutes—more or less, when the trees thinned out, and the ground levelled off. He halted at the edge of the tree-line, and watched—caught up in enwrapped attention at a scene that could only be called mystical.

Before him Mary was dancing. She held the shawl out like wings, as she swayed and circled, her ankle length skirt flowing with her fluid movements. She appeared to hear music where none existed. Joseph held his breath, and was reconsidering his previous thoughts about intruding, but he was caught up in the moment—the moonlight, and the dancer who had captured his heart . . . . and then . . . a sound—a barely audible click. He looked around—wondering about a camera that could take pictures at night, with only moonlight. There was no one to be seen, at far as he could see. But he was sure of the sound. Mary was still dancing—if she had heard anything, she did not seem concerned. The dance was the most important thing right now. Oddly enough, it was something he had said to her that afternoon that surfaced in his mind: "there is a time to speak out about what we know to be right." "And there is a time when actions speak clearer than words." He added to himself.

Her dance completed, and she raised her hands from her heart to the full moon above. Her back was to Joseph. "Did you meet any wolves on your way?" She asked, and then she turned to face him. "Please forgive my family. They would not have joked with you, unless they respected you, and knew that you would take it as it was meant to be. It is about recognizing you as one of our People—even for Simon. The Wolf is your animal self—it is your totem."

"I guess I was a bit miffed at first. But that was because some part of me really believed . . . . but it's my turn to apologize. I should not have intruded. That was a beautiful dance. I just couldn't help my self—strike that. I made a choice to follow my instinct."

"It was a good choice. Following your heart is always a good thing. I danced the Eagle Dance," she explained, "the drum that I was dancing—the music was the beat of my heart. The Eagle Dance is about asking the Creator of all things to help restore the balance. Sometimes this is called the Rain Dance—for the same reason. The rain will come when the clouds have become full. It will bring a cleansing. It is also a gift that we can request. Some of our dances are what your people call a prayer. Other dances are just for fun—about the enjoyment of life." She became silent—as a thought occurred. "Come—sit awhile and we will talk about this." She went over to a fallen tree that made a perfect bench.

Joseph sat beside her on the log. There did not seem to be anything that needed talking about. A thought about the phrase "bad blood," popped into his mind.

"There has been much misunderstanding." She seemed to read his mind. "I wonder how one kind of dance can be wrong—when another is right? Perhaps it is about the memories that are present? The past is difficult to heal when we do not learn to recall it in a better way?"

"I wish I knew something to say that would help." He reached out to cover her hand that rested on the log between them with his. She did not attempt to draw away. After a few moments—a twig snapped in the forest behind them.

"On the morning that I was born, a White Buffalo Calf was also born on our farm. My family took this as a sign, that I would be the one to restore the balance for our People—to restore our Relationship with the Earth. I came to your country seeking to reclaim the souls of my People. But I see that we are alike. This is the quest. This is the purpose of my being here."

"I agree with that." He replied. They were still faced apart—gazing out on the moon-lit valley. "It's definitely a good thing. . . . but . . . ?" Some part of him (the wolf?) grew brave. "I think it might be a good thing to consider that healing can be about the sharing of Love?"

She did not reply, but from the corner of his eye, he noticed that certain smile. Finally, she sighed. "It's time for me to get some sleep." He reluctantly let go of her hand. "I think it will rain in the morning, so make sure that your tent is secure." Before she went her way, she appeared to remember something. "The singing and music was good. And you play guitar quite well. My People like to drum, but the flute is one of our favourite things too. You might like to try it?" With that, she disappeared in the direction of the camp.

Joseph remained a few minutes, so that should anyone be awake (her Brothers), they would not be seen together. When he returned to camp, his suspicions had been correct. Simon and Sam sat facing each other across the ashes of the fire. Sam was poking at the ashes, as Simon spoke.

"Yes we knew." Simon was saying to Sam, as Joseph crossed the clearing toward his tent. Simon scarcely paid him notice. Joseph heard Sam's partial reply while unzipping his tent flap.

"Then why . . . ?

"My sister and my Father believe that this was a good chance to improve our People's relationships." Then when Joseph closed the zipper, the voices dropped to a muffled, barely audible exchange. After a few minutes, Joseph heard the zipper in the direction of Sam's tent, and the night was silent.

As the morning approached, and the moon disappeared, Joseph overheard an animated exchange—a woman's and man' voice—none of the words were discernable. Shortly after, there was hustle and bustle, and occasional flashlight use, intermixed with mild cursing. Eventually all noise ceased, and he heard a car start up, and drive away. Joseph did not look out, since it was pitch black, but it wasn't a hard guess that Sam and Erica had departed.

In the morning, the sky opened up, as Mary had promised. It rained steadily until almost noon, and Joseph gave thanks that he was in the company of experienced campers. Anyone who chose to pitch their tent in the small valley would have been forced to pack up. Joseph only peered out from the warm and dry sleeping bag and tent to confirm his suspicions about the early morning departure. He returned to his thoughts, to wait until the grass was dry enough to venture out. Around noon time, Bart and Simon started a fire, with wood that they had covered the night before, and everyone enjoyed a cup of tea and light breakfast-lunch of eggs and toast. After clean up, a short hike preceded breaking camp and the lengthy drive back to the city.

Chapter 11

One Story Ends
Another Story Continues

And just like that, a chapter of Joseph's life ended. He returned to work, at the summit of the tower the next day with a weary heart. Some part of his life was missing—he felt emptiness, and this emptiness had a name! He proceeded to immerse himself in his work, but his mind did not have the drive that had been present at the offset. He brooded for over two weeks, and could scarcely sleep. Finally he came to the only decision that might give him peace. He phoned Mary's home. She had given the number where her family was staying while in New Rome, to all of the people at the beginning of the hiking weekends. The phone rang a number of times, until a sleepy voice said: "Who is this?" The voice on the other end of the line belonged to one of Mary's brothers.

When Joseph apologized for waking the brother (it was eleven o'clock in the morning), he asked if he could speak to Mary.

"Mary's gone back home." The brother then unceremoniously hung up, without as much as a simple good-bye. The meaning though, was quite plain: "Don't bother to phone here again."

*   *   *

That night, Joseph worked later than usual. He decided that since he would not be able to sleep with his mind in a state that it was, he might as well do something useful with his time. The evening shift of workers came and went, and he receives a visit from the security guard.

"Just checking in to see that you are OK? How much longer are you going to be here?"

"I am just finishing up." Joseph answered. He looked at his watch. "Holey cow! It's 11:30! I will be right down." The guard said good-night, and Joseph heard the elevator begin its descent. Everything was deathly quiet, and as Joseph gathered his belongings together to leave, he heard the elevator again.

It was coming back up. He wondered if the guard had forgotten something . . . or what?

The elevator stopped on the floor, outside the room where Joseph had been working. The door opened, and Mary's brother—the one Joseph was sure had answered the phone that morning, walked in. Actually, he staggered in. He was obviously sloshed.

"Simon?" Joseph blurted out. "What are you doing here? Didn't your shift finish a while ago?"

"Yeah—it sure did. And do you know what? It was my last shift for this Unfriendly tower." He chuckled as though he believed he had made a major joke. He abruptly blinked, and tried to refocus his eyes. "And do you know what I have been doing? I have been celebrating. I brought a bottle and found a safe place to hide until everyone was gone. And do you know why?"

"You told me that you were celebrating your last day here?" Joseph ventured. The man stepped closer, and pointed a finger of the hand that still held the bottle, at Joseph's chest. His breath reeked of alcohol. "Yeah—that, and there is something more. I came to warn you. Stay away from my Sister! Understand?" And he prodded Joseph's chest with the finger.

"Your sister is gone back to the reservation—isn't she?"

"Yeah. She's gone back home, but I know your kind. You don't give up. We get lots of you white boys on the rez. You come down there thinking that you can have your way with our women. You don't know the meaning of respect."

"Whoa!" Joseph kept his hands down, so as not to further antagonize the man, but kept a close eye on the bottle. "Not all white men are the same. Just like Red men have different personalities. I would like you to know that I do respect your sister—very much. And I am not saying that I do not like her. All I would like is a chance to be friends—with respect. What is the wrong in that?"

"I saw the way you looked at her when you were dancing." The man staggered, almost falling, and then regained his balance. "That was not about respect!"

"That was a long time ago." Joseph answered: "I smiled at her. That's all. I danced with your sister at Jenene's wedding because it is our custom for the best man to dance with the maid of honour."

"The Sacred Dance." The man corrected. "I saw you watching her dancing the Sacred Dance. Our Dances and our women are Sacred!" He teetered, hesitating, perhaps not sure what to say next. His mood seemed to be changing—perhaps he had said his piece, and would . . . . ? "OK. I need to go now." He took a step back, and leaned against the nearest wall for support. "Just you remember—stay away from my sister . . . you should learn to respect her."

"OK." Joseph agreed. "I am ready to go too. Just let me get the rest of my things together, and we can leave together."

"I need to leave now." Simon stated emphatically, and while Joseph was turned away to pickup his briefcase, the brother stumbled to the door—the wrong door. The door he opened, lead to a part of the building that was in a lesser degree of completion than the office Joseph was working in. Joseph heard the door open, and by the time he turned around, the other man was outside.

"Good Lord!" Joseph exclaimed, and bolted for the open door. "Simon, wait. That way is dangerous." "That way," led to a temporary platform, that was enclosed by a short, railing—and beyond that open sky!

"I am not afraid!" Simon muttered his reply, and by the time Joseph made it through the door, he had one leg over the railing, and a foot on a single beam that extended ten feet to nowhere! "This is why they pick a Red man for this job,"

He swung the other leg over and stood unsteadily on the steel beam. "We are not afraid of death. Today is a good day to die." He shuffled away from the railing, his arms extended, like a tight rope walker. "What do you think, Mr. Wolfe? Are you afraid of death?" Despite his drunken state, he seemed almost clear minded.

"I am respectful of Death." Joseph answered, with a sigh.

"Oh sure! Like you say that you will be respectable with my sister?" It seemed between a dare and a taunt.

"More so. What can I say to convince you of my respect?"

"Talk is cheap." Simon shuffled further along the beam. "White man's words are always cheap—he is always looking for a way to break his promises.

It is action that speaks clearer than words." He now appeared completely aware of his surroundings. Perhaps (Joseph wondered) the drunken Indian act was just that?

"I believe you. And I agree," Joseph wondered where this conversation was heading.

"If you agree with me, then join me here." Their eyes met, and Joseph gazed into a pair of strong brown eyes that were full of purpose.

"So this is a test of some kind?"

"You might say that? And if you pass the test, you might get to talk with my sister again. It is the duty of my brother and me to protect our sister. If you do not pass this test, you will not talk to her again."

"How do I know that if I go out on that beam with you—that you will not just push me off?"

"You do not—except for respecting my word that I will not do that. That is the test. If you can trust me—then I know that you will keep your word about respecting my sister."

Joseph drew another long breath, and considered the possibilities. Beyond his heart-felt desire to see Mary again, there was more at stake. He was not completely sure about Simon's statement "today is a good day to die." Did the other man mean??? Simon's eyes told him that the man was committed to his action, but what was the consequence? Would he really take his own life to protect his sister from disrespect? Yes—most likely, but can that kind of man be trusted? Joseph decided "yes, again" and carefully stepped over the railing.

"Take my hand." Simon offered. Meanwhile he backed up another step. "I cannot ensure that you will marry my sister, but you will be a friend for life—of our People and my family."

"Sure. Sure," Joseph replied, "it's just how long that life-time friendship will last, if we both take a dive off this beam, that has me worried." Still he inched toward the outstretched hand.

*   *   *

"Sometimes, when you want something bad enough, you need to be ready to lay your life on the line to make it happen—at least to make it possible." Joseph mused to himself on the way down in the elevator with Simon. "Maybe this is the meaning of the Native saying: 'today is a good day to die?'" To take that chance, to go out on a limb (or a steel guider, one hundred floors up), might not always involve a literal brush with death. Essentially, it means being willing to risk changing life as you know it—to sacrifice it all for your true destiny. Something spoke to Joseph that very first night that he danced with Mary Morningstar. That something told him that she was part of his destiny. . . . and when he came to that moment of decision, he had a choice. He could have refused to follow Simon out on that beam, he could have . . . ? No. Even though, as Simon told him up front, that there could be no certain outcome in a future relationship with Simon's sister, this was his chance that would not come again. When he took that first step, he did willingly die—to his past.

Back in the safety of the penthouse of the almost completed Friendship tower, Simon had congratulated him with a hearty slap on the back. "Welcome to our family brother Wolfe. Now how about helping me find that elevator? I seem to be a bit tipsy." Simon's drunken condition miraculously returned, as quickly as it had disappeared. He leaned on his new "brother" for support, and they boarded the elevator together.

When the elevator doors opened on the ground floor, Simon disengaged his arm from Joseph's shoulder, and as he staggered in the direction of the nearest bus shelter, he muttered something to the effect that "that fire-water is gonna be the death of me yet." He waved off any further assistance. "I can find my way home from here . . . my father is waiting for you on that bench—over there"

Joseph shrugged. He watched until his new-found "brother" was safely supported with his back against the side of the bus shelter, and the latter pulled out and lit a cigarette, while he waited for the next bus to arrive. "OK?" Joseph turned toward the park bench at the far end of the semi-circle that was yet to be paved (or covered with cobble-stones). This would eventually have a fountain (so he had been told), and become an elaborate welcoming at the main entrance to the Friendship Tower. At the present, it was bare earth, with a light dusting of the first snow of the late fall season. It seemed, (Joseph marvelled, as he made his way gingerly over to where the Elder man sat waiting), it seemed like only yesterday! "How long ago was it?" He asked.

"Was what?"

"How long ago was it that we sat on the picnic bench in the centre—over there?" Joseph motioned with his hand in the general direction, as he seated himself beside Mary's father, whom he also knew as Edward Wind-in-His-Ears.

"This has happened for you to understand what we call '"Indian Time"' The old man answered.

"What has happed?" Joseph leaned back. A full moon broke through a clouded night sky, illuminating the area that was directly in front of them—the centre of a circle that was bounded on the one side by the tower itself. "What IS happening?"

"The Creator is showing you the Mystery that is part of your totem. It is so clear to me—I know what needs to be done at this moment. If we had any doubts, it is clear now."

"The moon? You are talking about this moon?" Joseph attempted to understand.

"Yes. We began the story with this same moon. Now it has come full circle—and it is the true season. It is the time of the Wolf's Moon. This is the time of the Relationship of the Earth and the Moon—this moon is Sacred to your totem."

"So, does this mean that you will be telling me the rest of the story?"

"It does. We have one night to share. I will be leaving in the morning for Kansa, the home land of my people."

"But—will we have enough time?" Joseph wondered.

"This is your Moon." The Elder replied. "Indian time has another side that most people do not know—Indian time is about now. When you are living in Indian time there is no reason to hurry—everything that is destined to happen will happen, and that which is not—will have its' own time."

"It sounds like you are talking in circles to me." Joseph chuckled.

"Yes. It is all about a Circle." The old man agreed with a broad smile. "Now let us continue. This is a story that has happened before, but a new story is always beginning . . . ."

*   *   *

"You have the Ark." Soma confronted the Emperor. He had little to lose, at this point, and both men needed what the other could provide. Either way, his very being had been changed—somehow, giving him a knowledge that eclipsed death itself.

The throne room was pregnant with silence.

"The Ark? Ah yes. I have often wondered why it was called that. Is it because it is like the ship that was supposed to have been built by Noah? . . . not sure I even believe that fable. This is too small to hold more than one man—I doubt it could have been built to carry away anyone to safety at the end of the world. But who cares anyway. I have it. And I have discovered other uses for it. Yes. I took control of the thing when I conquered the Holy city. It was in the temple. It was no longer working."

"It was broken?"

"Not exactly. It quit working when the man they called Jesus was put to death. At first I didn't see the connection. All that appeared to have happened was that the thick curtains that the Israelites use to enclose the Ark were torn when Jesus died . . . and it shut down. My first clue came from examining the curtains. They were lead lined. They were meant to contain the energy that the device emits. And here is something I am betting about the construction details that are outlined in the Bible—the only thing I think the priests actually had a hand in building, was the curtains. I am beginning to think it came from a space craft that crashed a long time ago, and the Israelites found it. When they realized some of what it could do, they immediately believed that it was a gift from their God—to help them overcome their enemies?" The emperor laughed aloud.

Considering that Soma had learned about the Emperor's utter belief in the religious teaching that he represented the supreme commander, he was only mildly surprised at the other man's words. He was more interested in why he was now being brought into the Emperor's confidence, and he was very curious about the so called Ark of the Covenant. "What you are describing does not seem to be the Ark that is talked about in the Bible?"

"But it is. All that about how they built the Ark, and the cubit by cubit dimensions are meant to throw off the reader as to its' true origin and identity."

" . . . Which is . . . what?"

"Isn't it more than obvious? This could not have been constructed by people who used it. They did not have the technological knowledge. It had to have come from another world—or time."

" . . . Or dimension—as in parallel world—another dream, as my People might describe it?"

"Do you really think that is possible?" The emperor took a step back. "I am beginning to believe that anything might be possible—after all, I am the living proof."

And then it struck Soma—what the other man had blurted out about having taken the Ark, after defeating the Israelites. The man, who stood before him, was the same man who had been the Emperor of Rome all those centuries before. Here was the man who, had taken the advice of a seer called Nostradamus, and averted the Fall of Rome. Not only had he changed the fate of the world at that time, but was alive today to tell of it. "What else did Nostradamus tell you? It must have been something—for you to have put him to death? By the way—you do not look a year over . . . . how old are you, anyway?"

"That is for you and I to know. Unless you want a message sent to New Rome about how your people have become expendable. Here is another thing that is between you and I. The only thing that halted the extinction of the native race was a decree from me that I had need of them. If the President of New Rome had his way, there would not be reservations along the banks for the Red River. The man, who is in charge of New Rome, does not think that the riches have all been found. He is sending geological expeditions across the river, and a new bridge is under construction. It will be called 'the Golden Gate Bridge.'"

For the first time—since he had gained the wisdom, and found peace within himself—Soma was shaken. Not for himself, but for the fate of his people. He took a deep breath and contemplated what to say next.

"You need us?" He managed.

"Of course. Why do you think I have allowed you to talk to me in this way? Do you think we could ever be considered at the same level? I AM THE EMPEROR! I am the ONE who has cheated death. I am the ONE TRUE representative of GOD on this forsaken world! This device that we have spoken of was delivered into my hands for a purpose—a purpose known only to myself, and GOD! And you—and your people were sent to me, to help me fulfill that purpose."

As Soma listened to the ranting of the other man, he regained his state of quietude. He had a purpose too. And his purpose also depended on the survival of his People, but not in the way this

107

self-appointed "man of God" viewed life. Everything the Emperor believed and lived for was for and about himself. Soma's destiny was not even limited to the Red race that had fathered him—he knew that now. This conversation, this day, had been taught, had been shown him by this man he saw as the Enemy. At that moment, he experienced serious questions regarding any further translation of the message from the Ark—and now, he knew where the symbols originated, that he had been given so far. He was not about to reveal, however, how much the knowledge had transformed the person who did the translation. Perhaps, he mused, whatever the Emperor had done to shield the energy of the Ark (lead lined curtains—or a room thus protected) did not truly halt Spirit, or whatever comprised the energy the device emitted.

"Are you ready to resume the translation?" The Emperor had regained his composure too—noting the silence of the other man. "Now that you are more aware of the consequence of your inaction. If you are not . . . think of this: I will make sure that the end is not quick for your people. They have been treated gently as of late—even allowed some freedom to work for their keep. As of this moment, I have decided to cut off the food supply, and not allow anyone to leave the reservations . . . until they die of hunger, or you begin the translation again. What is your answer?"

Soma had received a Dream—a Vision of the future. Perhaps this was the future that Nostradamus met his untimely end in disclosing. Be that as it may, if he did not resume his task, his people would have no future whatsoever. As for himself, Soma did not fear—he was able to look beyond the "Void," and to see even beyond the "end of the world."

"It is a Circle." Soma sighed in resignation.

"What kind of answer is that?"

"My People—the Elders have taught that life is a Circle. I have believed, until this moment, that this was a Symbolic teaching. And all of my logical knowledge, gained in the white man's school has reinforced this belief. But now, all of that has dissipated, and that logical knowledge has been replaced by a feeling—a knowing. The device that gives you answers is not responsible for this change, any more than it can give you this true meaning of life. "Soma was, to some extent (and even he did not know how much) telling a lie, in some desperate attempt to help the other man see. "There is a Great Danger in what we are about to do here."

"I will be the judge of that." The other man declared. This is my destiny. It is my purpose to find the meaning of life—discover the blueprint and to conquer death—once and for all"

"Do you not already have the Gift—the Gift of Eternal life?"

"I have learned that I might live forever . . . . as long as I remain close to the Ark. This is a truth that I should have you put to death for knowing (but would not do—right now, at least). This is the curse that comes with being the keeper of this great source of knowledge. I want more! I want my freedom—and the knowledge too. And I will have this, no matter the cost! The Israelite priests who gave up the Ark, begged me to keep it safe. They said that all of the knowledge—past, present and future, is available to the one who has the Ark. They told me that the original manuscript of the Bible originated from the Ark. The Bible, in its' simpler form, contains a manual for the use of the Device that helped produce it."

"I agree." Soma spoke, slowly and carefully, weighing each word. "This Bible does appear to have been inspired—to come from a Source of great truth. But . . . . if we both agree on this, then we might also agree that this manual has included a warning—in the very first chapter. This warning is about 'eating from the tree of knowledge of Good and Evil.' Is this not so?"

"Clever—very clever interpretation. But this is a warning about proceeding with caution. This is also about the Tree of Life. There may have been two trees, or does it symbolize the two halves of our brains? I have had a lot of time to think on this. Exposure to the Ark seems to harmonize both parts of our brain. I am a living example that Life (and death) can be conquered—all I need now, is to learn how. I believe that the Ark—and the tree (or trees) would not have been given by God, if He did not expect us to make use of them."

Soma was silent. He had learned in the white man's schools that men will go to any attempt to see what they want to see, and to prove their rightness. He had (just as silently) read many accounts of the greatness of men like Custer—heroes who had bravely fought the savage Indians. History books are full of the truth—as told by the side that won the war. His was a simple reply. He bowed at the waist, with his hands clasped to his heart. This was something he also learned while attending school—from a schoolmate who was a true Indian man, from a far off land that Columbus thought he had discovered. The act, called Namaste, means "I recognize and respect your divinity—my heart to your heart." And he could only hope that this was true.

"I am ready to resume the translations."

Chapter 12

Blood and Sacrifice
(. . . continues)

In the days and months that followed, the translation of the "alien" glyphs continued as before, except Soma was now more aware of the process that he was part of. He learned that as the symbols were translated, a new group appeared—apparently in the air above the Ark. The device seem to "know" when the last translation was complete. It seemed to be part of a Spiritual test, programmed into the device by whoever had created it. He was also given additional information through random conversation with the Emperor, at the time he delivered his translation.

"It was almost by accident that I discovered how to wake up the device." The Emperor spoke. They were nearing a point that would give them some key information about what the latter called the human genome—the DNA. "I had been reading about how the former owners of the Ark had conducted sacrificial ceremonies, in which they placed their "sins" upon a bull, and following a ritual killing the animal, they sprinkled the animal's blood upon the alter of the Ark. I tried this with some animals—but with no results. I believe that (for some reason), the Ark would accept animal blood no longer."

"Perhaps you will recall that the sacrifice of the man called Jesus changed all this?" Soma suggested.

"How perceptive. Perhaps that is true? Whatever the reason, I decided to go to the next logical step. The President of New Rome had contacted me, to say that he was interrogating a savage—one who he believed to be only a step above an animal. This man, who the Natives called a Shaman, was considered to be a holy man. The President asked my advice (for once) if it was prudent to make an example of this pagan. He was afraid that the savages might go into a killing frenzy, but he also wanted to get a point across about your people's sinful ways. That man (the president) is quite a coward—you did not hear that from me."

Soma shrugged and nodded, wanting to learn more.

"I had this man called Wovoka, sent to me, and instructed the president to tell his tribe that it was a diplomatic mission. Under armed guard, I brought him into the room that I keep the Ark, and explained to him (much as I explained to you) what I had in mind. Essentially this was the easy way—or my way. He spoke good English, and actually found the idea agreeable.

"I will be pleased to sacrifice my blood—for the good of my People." He said, and asked for a knife. He seemed to be quite aware of what was involved. I stood behind one of the armed guards, and observed while he drew the knife across the palm of his hand, while holding it over the altar. The minute the blood touched the altar, the device was alive—and the first symbols appeared in the air.

"I know the meaning of this." The red man exclaimed to me. That is how the first translation began. And that was how I learned that there was some connection between your people and the symbols."

"So why didn't you continue with the Shaman called Wovoka?" Soma wanted to know.

"I believe now, that being that close to the Ark for any length of time does strange things to a person's unprepared mind. I have spent lifetimes a bit every day, in close proximity to the Ark, and bit by bit it has changed me—I admit to that, but I have become in sync with the energy it emits. Both of my guards went mad, and the man called Wovoka . . . . well he became crazy in another way. He began to believe that he was the reincarnation of Jesus, and that he was reliving the crucifixion."

"He was mostly correct." Soma said, in a calm voice.

"What? You cannot believe what you are saying?"

"I do believe this. This is the true meaning of Sacrifice, as shown by example—by the man you call Jesus. Sacrifice, in the true sense of the word, is the offering of your life (or your blood) for another person, or as Wovoka saw it—for his People. My People are in agreement with the acts of this Jesus—this was one of the things he was born on this Earth to change."

"Nonsense! Not that I do not believe in Jesus, but I find it absolutely astounding that a man of your upbringing—a savage, could try to tell me about Jesus. As I explained before, the Israelites had been conducting ceremonial sacrifices since the beginning of time."

"In this part of the world, the concept of sacrifice was wrong." Soma replied. "That is all I can say . . . . except, it is not a sacrifice for one person to kill another, including animals, without this man or animals' desire to sacrifice themselves. No Sacrifice is real, unless it is genuinely given. That is why your Ark no longer worked after Jesus' death. He changed this for all time. And that is why Wovoka was able to re-activate the Ark."

The Emperor appeared thoughtful, for a few minutes. "And my story about Wovoka is the reason I will never let you nearer to the Ark than you have been to date. I had to send Wovoka back to his people . . . and you know the ending to that story? It would be best if you kept your mind on finishing the translations, if you know what is good for you, and your people."

At a later date, Soma learned that after Wovoka left, the Emperor attempted to enlist the aid of other Natives, from the various reservations along the Red River, but with little positive results. Not surprising (thought Soma). These people were physically and spiritually tired—they had nothing left to give.

So, in an effort to keep the Ark alive, now that it had been re-activated by Wovoka, the Emperor began trying other types of fuel, as he had in the past. Then, one day he tried water, from a nearby spring, and the energy, and thus the fading symbols, returned. Again, Soma was not surprised, since the pure water, from the spring, was indeed, the blood of the Mother Earth. Soma experienced a silent, inner smile, when the Emperor had told him that he had previously tried water—that was blessed by priests (under his supervision).

*   *   *

"There is so much more to learn." Soma bit his tongue, and discretely, did not say that it would be pure ignorance to imagine that the Mystery could ever be explained. Instead, he pronounced that: "We are at a critical step of understanding. When I give you the translation of this current group of symbols, you will have the information that you were seeking."

"How could you know the goal of my quest—beyond being free?" The Emperor became adamant. "I have been seeking to conquer Death. That much you have been told, but I hope to complete this for the good of all mankind. When my work is done, I will have a cure for illness and suffering that I will share. This is the reason that no one—nothing can be allowed to stand in my way. Any one person (or race) must be sacrificed if it is for the Greater Good—including your People—do you understand what I am saying?"

Soma did understand, and he spoke no more of the Emperors' idea of sacrifice. One of the symbols he was about to translate was a spiral and the others . . . he wondered why the other man did not see . . . ? Yet he knew also, that the Emperor wanted a logical translation of something that the accumulation of glyphs had done to the translators mind. This, he reasoned, was the necessity of having a translator in the first place. It would take someone who can think in Spanish, be able to tell an English speaking person the real meaning of a manuscript that was written in the language of question. And now, the Emperor waited for him to . . . .

"Before I tell you, I have one request?"

"No! Tell me first, and then I will consider your request." The Emperors' eyes flashed dangerously, and he stepped closer, menacing.

Soma was unmoved. "I have agreed to give you the information you requested. But my request is a simple one, that will help my People survive, until you have put to the test that knowledge that I am about to share."

"So you do understand that until I am able to test that the blueprint is correct, and that I can indeed use the knowledge to manipulate DNA—I will not be issuing any release document to the president of New Rome?"

"I know that when you will be true to your word, and let my People go, when you have completed your tests, and that they will be unharmed until this happens. I know this, because I also know that you will still need my help. I have foreseen this. Until such times I respectively request that you allow my People to send hunting parties back across the Red River to hunt Buffalo—we will need to eat the Buffalo to regain our strength for the long journey to the lands of our ancestors."

"I will grant one hunting expedition a month—no more. And when you have completed your part of the bargain, you will be allowed to return to your people to await my granting the release—if everything goes as you say it will."

The Emperors' personal physicians and scientists had been on the brink of mapping the genome—indeed they had arrived at a theoretical "blueprint" already. The knowledge that they required involved being able to manipulate the DNA—to move beyond theory to the actual creation of life. No matter how they had pursued it, the elusive Spirit evaded their microscopes. Without understanding how, the brain of the Emperor had been changed—to be in sync as he put it, in order to "hack," and to reverse engineer amazing electronic equipment, using the Ark as a guide. Indeed, he boasted, that he could, if necessary build another Ark from scratch (but Soma doubted this—since the device was somewhat much more than just an electronic marvel). However, he was able to oversee the construction of powerful microscopes that magnified matter to the level where the illusion of solid reality ceased to exist. This turned out to be a dead end. The meaning of life was not to be found by logical means. When Soma explained what he had learned from the Symbols, however, this dangerous knowledge, (as Soma had named it) would become the inspiration for the Emperor to take the next step.

*   *   *

Upon returning to his People, Soma was utterly distressed. To save his people, he had (perhaps) betrayed the rest of humanity. His new found ability to "see across the void" had enabled him a glimpse of the outcome of his actions. He was well aware, that his vision was, as any prophetic dream, a view of a future if the wheel turned without changes being made. As with any powerful vision, however, any change would depend on the interaction of the main participants of the dream. His part in the change would protect his people (however temporarily) from the result of the knowledge, and the use of such, by the man whose thirst had brought it to light. He could only pray that the enlightenment would bring about a change in that man, that would halt, or alter, the latter's plans to "rescue humanity" from the reality of death. With the small possibility of this happening, Soma waited, and prepared for the worst.

Soma's first act was to gather together the tribal chiefs, and tell them about his time spent across the great waters. Next, he shared with them the plan that he envisioned to protect the Red People from what was to come, and to help them prepare for the journey back to the lands of their ancestors. This he had seen as actually happening (in his vision), but it would need to be a quick departure. He had seen (through the terrible result of Wounded Knee), that even though the Emperor would eventually send the decree to let his people go—the president of New Rome could not be trusted to follow anything but his own path of greed (as evident in the building of the Golden Gate Bridge). The newly constructed bridge over the raging Red River would be the way for the hunting parties to journey to the great plains of the land that the People were now naming "Kansa," in honour of the red people on whose land the "prison camps," or temporary reservations presently occupied. The people who had previously occupied "Kansas," (now named by the white settlers) were known (per the ancient translation) as the People of the Wind. Thus the name Kansa was thought to be a fit name for the Promised Land—the land given to the red race by the Great Spirit.

The first hunting parties were turned back, as Soma expected, but following a strong message being sent to the President of New Rome, the agreement was allowed to go forward. When the President learned that the reason for the Red Men to cross the bridge to Kansa (he laughed aloud at this naming), he told his captains: "let them go—it will save us having to feed them in the long run." So, one party of four men, from each reservation, was allowed to cross the Red River to hunt the Buffalo—once a month. Also the men were only allowed to carry bows and arrows (no guns), and they were counted, and granted a temporary "passport," that would be signed at the time of their crossing—with the provision that "should any man fail to return, his family would be killed." This was justified as a halt to any thoughts about this being part of a planned uprising.

The reason for the hunting parties was known by Soma and now the other Chiefs, as being not due to any planned future escape. No—the escape from these prison camps would not be forced, but in the passing of time until that was granted, the People would need protection of another type—as explained by Soma. The other chiefs could only trust the words of this man, who had come to be known as a great Shaman by the entire Red race. A Shaman, one Elder explained, is not a name that a man or woman calls themselves—this title must be given by the People who respect their deeds. This is a name that follows a person's heart-driven actions. Soma had become such a man—known also in vision and prophesies as the one who would lead the Red People to the freedom in the "promised land" land of their ancestors.

The meat that the hunters brought back would be scarcely enough to feed a complete reservation. Time would be tough in the days and months, and possibly years (?) that follow, and at first many would question the reason behind giving up the meagre food offerings from their white captors—but eventually, "you will see," was the promise of Soma. The men brought back everything of the Buffalo that was given—including the blood. "The blood will be needed—it is of vital importance," Soma insisted. Upon receiving the blood, Soma instructed each tribal Shaman in the way of creating a "powerful medicine," that would be needed in the time to come. Soma told the tribal Shaman to start giving a bit of this medicine to all of their tribe—from the smallest baby to the most elder. Then, with bated breath, he waited for what he prayed would not be the inevitable.

A year past quietly, and the men continued to hunt the Buffalo in the land across the great Red River, and bring back the meat and blood to their People. At first the soldiers jeered in derision at the hunting parties, and teased them by pointing loaded rifles, and saying things like: "bang—another dead injun." But eventually, even that became a boring action, when the warriors' only response, was to sit straight and with pride, upon their painted ponies and offer their pass books to be signed. These men had regained something not known to the white race that now enslaved them. There is a pride that is about following ones purpose in the eyes of the Creator and that man or woman's tribe—this is not an ego's pride. Sometimes this will involve going into battle, and only touching the enemy—called counting coupe. When the passports were signed at each crossing of the Golden Gate Bridge, each man smiled sincerely, in knowing that he was counting coupe for his People.

When a year had passed, the first sign that Soma dreaded appeared. In the world outside the reservations, farmers were given seeds to plant that were genetically altered. These seeds, it was explained, would grow faster, and be resistant to disease. "It has begun." He explained to his People by word of mouth: "do not eat the crops that grow from these seeds—and do not accept these seeds, even if it is a gift from those white people who truly care about the Red race. If you feel it in your heart—it is not wrong to warn these people about the dangers of changing things that are natural to Mother Earth. But also be warned that it is not safe to say anything beyond that, as there will soon come a time that they will begin to believe that their God has turned on them—and they will be looking to blame."

Chapter 13

The Blood of my Children
(continues . . .)

In the year following the introduction of genetically altered crops, there followed a number of serums—injections that would do much the same for the white farmer's livestock. In Soma's eyes, he first saw this as a sign that the Emperor was indeed attempting, in his way, to pass on the result of his new-found knowledge to the people under his rule. Or was he? Having experienced the vision of a future in which mankind—particularly this one man, attempted to replace their Creator, Soma had serious misgivings. Soma mused that even if they still possessed a belief in a God (that had chosen one People as his own)—they were violating this God's rules and should expect to pay a terrible price for his wrath. As far as Soma and his People were concerned, their faith involved the One Creator—who was Father (and Mother?) to every living creature. They did, however, know about a balance—between a Spirit Father and a Mother Earth, and when that balance is tampered with—there will be (as their white relatives would say): "hell to pay!"

Times became extremely lean on the reservation, while the world outside this "protected" environment, prospered, and grew (literally) fat. It became more difficult to persuade the parents of hungry children that their children (that returned from white schools) should not accept food—especially meat, from their well meaning white "friends." Then four years passed (one turning of the Wheel), and Soma received the news that he had dreaded. There was a rumour—of a new disease on the other side of the Great Waters (the original Rome). This disease, as the rumour went, had started in a far-off land called Africa. This disease involved the weakening of a person's natural immune system, to the point that the person was open to any passing disease. Then upon contracting an illness, this person's body would be without the ability to fight back, and the result (in most cases) might be a slow and painful death. Soma immediately saw the causes of this (rumoured) disease to be two-fold. The first cause lay in the birth of the disease, which was inevitably tied to the second. They both had their roots in the tampering with the Spiral of Life! When the disease and the altering of the food chain of the people came together, there was little that could be done When the people who ate the meat of the changed animals—consumed flesh without the spiritual energy that could have helped them (despite their lack of immunity)—there was little hope. This was the beginning of Soma's terrible vision.

In less than a year, the rumour became a fact—in New Rome, Soma and his People cried (in their hunger) for their relatives, but kept a firm lip, and told no one—unless the hunting parties to Kansa be halted. And Soma, and the other Shaman, increased the dose of the medicine made from the blood of the Buffalo for the babies and young children (particularly those children that were still taken away to the white man's schools). In the beginning, when the reservations were first established, the children, like Soma, had been taken away and most never seen again. The reasoning had been, if our church tells us that we are not allowed to completely exterminate these people (who stood in the way of our progress and greed), then the next step would be to "save" them. The best way to "Christianize" these people was to re-teach their children. That meant taking the children away, so that their parents could not teach them their "pagan" ways, and teaching them the "righteous Christian way." Eventually things changed, and it was decided that the next generation of children could still live on the reservations, but were obligated to attend schools in New Rome. One way or the other, Soma knew that the children represented the future survival of the Red People, and so, in another way now (not by war) they protected these children, through silence, and the blood of the Buffalo.

Nothing can go unnoticed forever, especially when there are people who care—people who have learned to walk the true "Christian Path." One such woman by the last name of Crowe. She coincidentally was a descendant of Pocahontas (who had fallen in Love and married a white man). This woman was a teacher in one of the schools of New Rome that the children from the reservations attended. She noticed that the children appeared undernourished, and having a history of being an activist for human rights (many times at her own peril) she lobbied for an investigation about why the food had been cut off to the reservations. She was subsequently given a curt reply via a letter from the Department of Indian Affairs that it had been at the request of the Natives themselves. Not being one to give up easily, and having a belief that whoever was responsible, the children should not suffer. She argued that enough mistreatment had gone on in the past, and it was time for children, no matter what colour, to be treated like human beings, and not animals.

When the woman called Crowe was granted an audience, the local representative told her: "but they ARE animals. In their own words, they are related to the animals they worship in their pagan ceremonies. Perhaps you should know this, better than anyone?"

Diane Crowe bit her lip. It would not be helpful to her cause, she reasoned, to try to refute the obvious stupidity in the remark—by a person who should have the Natives' best interest at heart. This man had not even made the effort to understand the culture of the people he was supposed to represent. "Even a dog has the right to be fed." She replied. "There is something else afoot here, and I intend to get to the bottom of it." With that, she curtly turned and exited the man's office, leaving him red-faced as the people of the reservations.

He called in his secretary. "That Crowe woman is about to stir up trouble." He stated. "We need to cut her off at the pass." He smirked at the joke he believed he had just made. "Get a hold of one of the local chiefs, and arrange a meeting for myself and her. We need to be one step ahead of her. She has a reputation. She will not give up easily."

"We could arrange for Homeland security to pay her a visit?" the secretary suggested. "She might be considered a threat—maybe guilty of treason?"

"Sounds like a thing to consider, but this time we have told her the truth (not that we don't always do this)." He shared a knowing smile with his secretary. If the truth was really known, he did not want his cushy job to be put at risk, nor have someone questioning the disposition of the money that Christian charities gave to help feed the Native people.

So, the teacher called Crowe got a meeting with a chief of a nearby reservation, and was told, face to face, that the Natives had decided to fend for themselves. He explained about the monthly hunting parties.

"But that cannot be enough to feed all of your people." She pressed the matter. "I do not like seeing hungry children in my classroom. The Lord knows what else must be happening—I have not even heard about what kind of medical problems there must be as a result of undernourishment? Much less this epidemic that is sweeping New Rome."

At this pronouncement the chief broke eye contact rather abruptly. "We look after our own." As restated to the man from the Department of Indian affairs. The latter reached to shake the chiefs' hand, and promptly urged the teacher on her way, with: "I think this has gone as far as it needs. Perhaps you are overstepping your position? Perhaps you might want to teach somewhere else?"

His meaning was more than clear, so Diane Crowe went home, with more questions than answers filling her head.

The next day, one of the teacher's assistants joined Diane at lunch in the open cafeteria. "About your questions?" the young woman looked straight ahead, and spoke in a hushed voice. "You need to wait. Let it seem that you have given up—for the moment. The best I can tell you is: this is a decision that was really made by the Red People, and everyone is healthy, though a bit hungry. One more thing," the young woman finished eating, and rose her feet. "They are more than healthy—there is not one case of the dreaded disease that we know of on any of the reservations."

In the days to come, Diane noted that the teacher assistant that she had spoken to, made the rounds, joining different Indian children for lunch. A couple of weeks went by then she met the young woman leaving said lunch room with a rather self-satisfied smile on her face. The assistant was bubbling over with her apparent success, telling Diane, "they have a medicine. The little girl I sat with today told me that they are given a medicine every morning and before bed at night. We suspected there was something."

Diane wondered exactly who the "we" that the young woman spoke about might be, but instead of pursuing that, she asked: "so what happens next?"

"Hard to say—the Emperor had issued a strong decree that the Indian reservations are off limits" . . . then she realized who she was talking to. "I am Christian, and so are you. It is a terrible crime how that disease is killing so many people. We need to do whatever is necessary to get a cure. Don't you think?"

Diane simply nodded in numb silence. She had witnessed the effects first hand of "whatever it takes," before the closing of most residential schools.

As luck (good or bad) would have it, before anything otherwise drastic could be brought into play, a sequence of events occurred that played directly into the hands of the "well wishers" that were desperate for the cure. In one of the schools, a little Indian girl went ill, and was rushed to the nearest hospital. She had a ruptured appendix. In the recent past—this child might have been sent home for the local Shaman to care for despite the almost inevitable results, but this child was given the best treatment that money can buy—in a white man's hospital—including a private room. After the surgery, it was decided that the young girl would be kept for a lengthy stay—to heal and to treat "the worst case of malnutrition" that the hospital had seen. Diane Crowe, upon hearing about the situation, highly doubted this diagnosis—she was more than aware of the true reason.

The mother of the child, who was encouraged to visit, did so, knowing that she would be closely watched. Time progressed, without incident and the child was moved to a ward for other children that were dying of the disease that was sweeping New Rome. It was blackmail—of the worst kind, and the families on the reservation petitioned their Indian Affairs agent (on the quiet). Their appeals fell on deaf ears. Soma also attempted to send a message to the Emperor, but his mail was either lost, or otherwise went unanswered. The mother of the girl, just 10 years old, asked for a council with the tribal chief—who would meet with other chiefs on the reservations. She cried—not only for her child, but the plight of the other (dying) children that she could not help but see during her daily visits.

Then one day, the mother of Molly, showed up at the hospital with a bottle of the much needed medicine. It was confiscated the moment she began to give it to Molly. Nothing more occurred, until, presumably the medicine was synthesized and the result was given to the other children on Molly's' ward. Only when most of the other children began to get appreciably better, Molly was granted a bill of health, and allowed to return with her mother to the reservation. Shortly thereafter, a major pharmaceutical declared a major breakthrough, and began to sell a "cure," at an astronomical price. The price, they explained was needed to recoup the millions of dollars in research.

"They created a synthetic version of the medicine," the teachers' assistant exclaimed in apparent disgust to Diane Crowe, upon a "chance" meeting at a coffee shop. Diane guessed that the young woman had a need to justify being used to spy on the Indian children. "From the early test results, it appears to be working—at least it halts the progression of the disease. But so far, it is not a cure. The sample that Molly's mother provided had to be from natural substances. I have a feeling that it would have worked with the body's' immune system better? Don't you?"

Diane nodded in agreement. "Whatever the Native medicine is made from would be natural—that's for sure."

"Well, I still don't see why the Natives held back the cure so long. You would think that they wouldn't want to see so many children dying needlessly? It makes me think that they really are mostly animals—like the government keeps telling us."

"Or they do not trust us?" Diane suggested.

"But they must know that Christians really care about what is good for all people?" The other woman was not to be convinced.

"Just consider what you said about the Natives being animals." Diane shrugged, and walked away. Under her breath, she continued: "It will be a hot time in hell before the Natives trust any white people again—especially Christians."

Chapter 14

At What Cost Freedom

It was discovered that the synthesized version of the medicine did not affect a cure—but halted most of the debilitating effects of the disease, while leaving the person dependent on an expensive pill. So taking the next logical step, another "cure" was created, duplicating most of the natural ingredients used by the Natives. In all but the most progressed form of the disease, the patient was found to be completely free of the effects of the disease—but their immune system remained weakened, and nearly non-existent. Based on this so called "side effect," the National Coalition of Drugs for Rome (NCDF) declared the new medicine created by the Natural Herbal community to be unsafe and untested, and would therefore be banned for use until the National Coalition had time to conduct tests. This despite the urgings of the natural minded people, that all that was needed was for the patient to be put on a proper diet to help their immunity. The actual truth, which most people of Rome (and New Rome) were aware, was that there would not be any testing (at least in the near future), because the major pharmaceuticals who supported the "research" done by the National Coalition, had found themselves a "cash cow" in the form of their new pill. None of this surprised the Native People, especially Soma, because he was more than sure that he knew of the source of the dreaded disease.

Another year passed, in which the citizens of New Rome were too busy coping, to be bothered with the Native population on the reservations, to the extent that the monthly hunting parties crossed and re-crossed the bridge to and from KANSA, with little more than a brief inspection. The hunters, on the other hand were very aware that should they bring back anything that would cause suspicion, they would be putting the lives of all of the Peoples in danger. The health of the People on the reservations depended on the monthly trips across the river, and so, the only thing that changed, was the travois that the horses pulled, which carried Buffalo meat, were re-enforced with birch bark. The People believed that Soma would somehow bring about their freedom, but through past dealings with the president of New Rome, they had serious doubts that they would be allowed use of the white man's bridge when that time came to cross the sometimes turbulent Red River. So, piece by piece, during the long winter nights, make-shift canoes were being built, and secreted away in the rafters of the shacks that the Indian People were forced to call home. It appeared that some kind of fate was on their side, as the white people were busy fighting their disease, and had been instructed to "keep away" from the reservations by the Emperor of Rome. The People hoped that the canoes might ensure a safe passage for the Elders and children—everyone else would be prepared to swim for their lives.

On the seventh year since his return to his People, Soma received the summons, he expected, but had come to dread. He had hoped the Emperor would, having realized his thirst for knowledge, send a letter to the President of New Rome, to declare the Indians free. But he also had troubled visions of a re-occurrence of Wounded Knee, so this—being called back to Rome, might be considered a somewhat more positive outcome. He therefore considered himself ready for whatever the Emperor had in store for him (remembering that much of his previous vision had manifested itself in the form of the disease). He was nonetheless surprised when he stood face to face with his former "employer."

"I called you here to help my son." The Emperor was downcast.

"Your son?" Soma caught himself; he nearly exclaimed that he didn't know that the Emperor had become married—no one in the world that was ruled by Rome knew of this, or that a son existed. But a shudder of realization shook him, and rendered Soma temporarily speechless.

"Yes, my son has contracted that deadly disease that is sweeping our world." The Emperor continued. "If I had thought this might have happened, I might have taken better precautions. I might not have tried to help mankind before protecting my "family,"—the way you and your People have done," He stared wide eyed and accusingly at Soma.

Soma paused, to collect his thoughts, and to consider the best way to approach the situation. He took a deep breath, before speaking in a measured tone (meant to calm the other man). "We were always ready to share our medicine, but my People were afraid of what the President of New Rome might do when the time came to do so. We feared that he might blame us for the disease. If you recall, I was very reluctant to give you the information that would result in your ability to manipulate—and even create life?" Soma was aware that he was treading on dangerous ground, but he needed to let the other man know that he knew what had transpired.

"Yes—I created life." The Emperor rose from his throne. "With the knowledge that I have now, I am like God. In fact I may be a better God than these people have known before. At least I listen to their cries for help. I created a medicine that I hope will someday be a cure for the greatest diseases—including death. And before you start judging me, I had the people of Africa's best interest at heart, when I picked them to try it out. What was I to do—they are a struggling, hungry lot. I injected my new serum into the cattle that were shipped to ease their hunger. It was my desire to feed them, and make them eternally free of disease at the same time. How could I know that there would be a slight side-effect—that my serum still needs work?"

Soma sighed in resignation. He felt partially responsible for what had occurred. "I am sure that you will be wise enough to make whatever changes that need be done. If it is not overstepping my purpose—after all you did ask for my help, I have a suggestion. You must know that my People's medicine works to combat and prevent the disease? You would not have requested that I come before you now, if that was not the case?"

"Agreed. I am open to suggestions. I need your help—I especially need you to heal my son."

"I will do what I can." Soma promised. "The main thing I can suggest, however, is that Life is Sacred . . ."

" . . . I've heard all this before—we can talk about this after you have healed my son." The Emperor said rather abruptly.

Soma was led to a bedroom in the palace that was much like the room that he recalled spending endless nights, dreaming and meditating during the translation of the "alien" language. The room was sparsely furnished—not the kind of room you might expect of a child's bedroom. Soma had a feeling that this was not the boy's actual bedroom, but a place the child was brought to be cured—or die. He bent over the sleeping form, and exclaimed in amazement: "he looks to be about thirteen—at least a teenager! How can this be? You did not have a son when I was here only . . . was it seven years ago?"

"It was." The Emperor agreed. "Do not trouble yourself with these matters. You are only here to make him well. He has this disease that has been ravishing my kingdom—this disease that started in Africa. That is all you need to know. Can you help him or not?"

Soma bent closer. "Can I wake him?"

The boy stirred, and opened his eyes. "Who are you?" He asked. His voice was strained and it appeared an effort to even talk.

"This is the man I told you about." The Emperor sounded genuinely concerned—an emotion that Soma could hardly recall the man as expressing, except when talking about himself.

"Could it be that the Emperor is really being changed by becoming a father?" Soma wondered . . . and then it struck him, as the boy began to speak again. It was like hearing the father echoed through the son.

"Have you come to make me well?" The boy asked. His voice and his mannerisms were unnerving.

As the boy continued to speak, Soma recalled endless conversations with this very boy—he almost knew what the youth was about to say—before he spoke. The truth struck Soma like a fist to his stomach. The conversations had been with an older version of the child. Soma had to draw a deep breath, in order to not say: "What have you done! Do you have any idea of the consequences of tampering with the Sacredness of Life?" Instead, he choked back the words. Yes—the Emperor did know. He did now, at any rate. That was the reason the healer had been summoned to this boy's bedside. Instead, he spoke in a quiet, reassuring, caring voice. "Can you sit up? Let me help you. I have some medicine that I want you to drink."

After the boy had taken a few sips of the medicine, and lay back down, to return to what appeared the peaceful sleep of the innocent, Soma sighed. "I brought enough medicine to start him on the way to recovery. I will need to have more sent from the reservation back in New Rome? There is a reason that the synthetic medicine created by your doctors will not cure this boy. He is too far along with the disease. You are aware that your medicine will only help in cases that are new—and then it does not cure. The synthetic drugs can be used to help boost a patients' natural immunity—until the bodies' immune system takes over. But the way this disease works, is that it attacks, and destroys a person's natural immunity. It is not the disease that kills. But I guess you know that?"

His answer was a silent nod. Soma continued. (Both men knew all too well the why and the wherefore—it was simply down to—what is next?) "There is something else that needs to begin, if this boy is to regain his health. What are you feeding him?" He did not wait for the answer to this as well. "Whatever it is—you need to stop. And you need to find somewhere to get organically grown food for the boy to eat. No meat or vegetables that come from a farm that uses drugs. And if you can find such a farm—they will have free range chickens (or cattle). This is the most important thing to remember. Spirit is only present in a creature (or plant) that has freedom, and has willingly given the Gift of Life."

The Emperor sighed. "Enough with the lecture. I disagree with you on the Spirit thing. Remember our conversations about Jesus. Jesus said that the Holy Spirit is within all of us."

This almost literally floored Soma. Here was the whole past Christian and Native relationship in a nutshell. The Emperor was quoting the Holy Man, and acting in a manner that was contrary to everything Jesus was about! The Native People did not have a problem with what the Black Robes had preached—it was what happened next that (almost) killed the Red man. Soma did not have an answer except: "We do have Spirit—all of us. Except this disease takes away our strength and will to live. It slowly weakens our connection to Spirit."

The two men exited the room, closing the door quietly behind them.

"I have taken the liberty to having your room prepared for you. You will remain here until my son is well again."

Soma simply nodded, and turned to do as he was bided.

"Wait. I have a question." The Emperor watched until the other man faced him again. "You should know this. Before I called you back, I tried everything you have already suggested—including a natural form of your 'medicine.'" Did you think I would not be able to analyze it? I know what the true active ingredient is. But it did not work—the way it seems to work for you and your people—none of the process worked. If it did, my son would be well now. I do not understand..?"

A long moment of silence passed before Soma spoke.

"It is a matter of Balance. In all things there are two sides. There is the medicine and there is the intent. Each must be seen as part of the Gift, or the outcome will be less than the desire."

"Tell me more?" For some reason, perhaps some genuine caring on the part of the man for his son, the Emperor was receptive—he was willing to listen instead of talk.

"My People would have been willing to share the medicine, if not for our fear—of what had come of the sharing in times past. But we also knew that Spirit would provide a Way if it was the right thing to do. And that happened. I am open to share the simple secret

131

to our Medicine Path—and you will do with it as you will. Begin with knowing that everything is the Sacred. We do not smoke the Tobacco—The Tobacco becomes the Breath of the Spirit. I do not "use" the flesh and blood of the animals that are our Relatives—I Honour the Gift of Life."

Another bit of silence followed and the Emperors' attitude reverted back to the way Soma had come to know him. "Go. Get your rest." His tone was once more a command, rather than a wish of well being. "You will need it. I expect you to be my son's personal healer—for as long as it takes." He turned abruptly and left Soma to find his way, under the watchful eyes of the palace guards.

In the days that followed, Soma was granted use of the kitchen to prepare the meals for the Emperor's son. He was assured that the food came from organic farms (under decree of the Emperor) and the animals were treated kindly and killed in a humane manner. He started the boy on chicken soup, and graduated to small bits of lamb, then beef (and vegetables). In a manner similar to the energy gained by eating the flesh of the Buffalo, he attempted to explain to the Emperor that an animal that possessed this powerful life force would be needed to provide the Gift of healing. The Emperor was not in any listening mode (which was probably just as well—Soma realized afterward, considering the reference to the Buffalo). The Emperor had given over the task of Healing, to the other man, and Soma was once more aware of the consequences, of failure on his part. Curing the boy would mean the long promised freedom for his People. Failure to do so would mean another broken promise. There was no doubt about that. If, however that healing was successful (and Soma sincerely cared about any child's life) there might be other dire things to cope with. Soma had begun to understand just part of the Emperor's plan, and it caused him to tremble with the knowledge.

As the boy began to regain his health, the "Father" became noticeably more talkative. Soma, for his part, would have preferred not knowing the things that were being revealed.

"My son IS getting strong again. Soon he will be ready to fulfill his destiny."

Soma winced inwardly. "I don't want to know this." He thought. Except he was far too intuitively inclined to not have guessed.

"I have come to the realization, that I have been granted the Ark, and the knowledge, for a reason. It has been my fate to be the living God of these people. They do not know this, yet, and may not ever suspect who it is that will answer their prayers. I have become the "Mystery," that you speak about so much." He beamed with the knowledge of his own glory (and Soma bit his lip in order to remain silent). "And like the prophesies in the Bible," the Emperor continued: "it is clear to me, that my son, is a sign of a new beginning—the "second coming," of the Son of God."

The man was too caught up in himself to notice that Soma had averted his eyes. He needed to hide his true thoughts—that the Bible and it's prophesies that the other man referred to in his ranting, was the same book that this very man had re-translated and edited to his own ends.

"I have heard it said," Soma spoke silently to himself, and to the True Mystery: "that Truth cannot be hidden or changed. I can only Pray that this will prove to be so!" He wondered, and trembled with the knowledge of his part in all this—to gain the freedom of his People. He wondered, if this "second son of God" would be required to sacrifice in some way—as the original had done? Soma bowed in (mock) respect, and slowly backed out of the throne room, to return to the sanity of his sleeping quarters.

Chapter 15

The Promised Land?

"Do you think we can trust the Emperor to keep his promise?"

Soma was asked this question at the emergency Council meeting that he called with all (that could attend) of the Chiefs of the many tribes that occupied the reservations on the banks of the Red River. They were able to be there, because the Department of Indian Affairs, and the government of New Rome, had issued a document. This document stated that only one member of a family could be allowed outside the boundaries of his or her reservation at a time. It didn't say, as the People saw it, that as long as your family was kept hostage, you could go anywhere you wished. This took into account the children that were taken by government buses to the white schools, where they were educated to follow the "good Christian ways" of the conquering race

This meeting was "closed doors"—being not open in the Way of the People to the rest of the residents of the reservations. "Are we becoming like them?" One old Chief asked: "that we keep the Truth from our People—with the excuse that it is for your own good?" A murmer of agreement passed around the Council Circle.

"I agree also—that this is not a good thing to do." Soma spoke gravely. "But we have always been able to adjust to what is right at the time."

The old chief spoke again. "There have been changes in the lives of those who live outside these reservation fences—in the lives of our white relatives. Their so-called Father that lives across the great water has been creating strict laws that his children must obey—for their own good."

"What kind of laws?" Soma asked. He did have a few ideas based on what transpired during his time spent with the Emperor.

"Two laws in particular." Was the reply. "I am beginning to wonder that these reservation walls are being extended? One law deals with Tobacco. The Emperor and his government have decided that since tobacco is not good for your health, anyone who is caught smoking outside their own home, will face a strong fine—will need to pay a great deal of money." Soma recalled a certain conversation, in which the Emperor stated: "now you will not be able to say that I don't listen to your advice." And he thought "yes—you do—but only when it has some potential benefit for you."

"And if this tobacco is such a bad thing—why was it not banned?" Another Chief asked. This was followed by a hearty laugh by everyone present—at the expense of their white "relatives."

"Think about the tax money that these white people pay to support their addiction." Another chief suggested. "And the penalty for being caught? Still it saddens me—these people are our captors, but they are being treated with less respect and trust than we give our children. Every day a new law is passed that restricts their personal freedom. It is now a crime to be homosexual throughout the whole of Rome. What is the reason for this?"

"The reason is that the doctors and scientists have found that the terrible disease is spread mostly through sexual practice. So they need to point a finger—they have found someone to blame, and have conveniently forgotten how this disease came into being." Soma's voice became hushed. "What we are sharing today, is a potential further danger to our survival. It is nothing that many of you have not guessed. But it tells me that the Emperor will act quickly on his promise to set our People free of this prison encampment that they call a reservation—and ensure that we do not have contact with the white People of New Rome. He must turn us into the enemy

135

once again—so that any mention of his responsibility will fall on unbelieving ears."

"We will make sure that our canoes are ready." Another chief suggested. "I believe our first sign will be the closing of the Bridge over the Mighty Red River."

*   *   *

One early morning, two days after the Council meeting, a scout reported to Soma that the bridge had been closed for repairs. "There is group of soldiers standing guard at the mouth of the bridge." he reported, "it is time," Soma agreed. "Spread word to the People to expect . . . ." He did not finish the sentence, for at that moment the door was kicked open. Two heavily armed soldiers stood in the doorway.

"Move!" One of the soldiers barked the command. "The orders just came down. Rome has sent the papers that you are to be sent back across the river."

"What . . . ?" The scout that had awoken Soma pretended surprise. To some extent he was. "Can I get my belongings together?" Soma asked.

"No. You will take only the clothes that you are wearing. Our orders state that we must make sure that you will not be spreading the disease."

Soma's heart jumped in his chest. "The disease cannot be spread through clothes and food." He began: "it requires more than . . . ."

"I am just following orders," the man motioned with his rifle. "You can take it up with the Department of Indian Affairs at a later date." He winked to his partner. It was quite apparent that there would not be a later date for the People on the reservations, if this plan went as planned. It was meant to be a quick operation—executed before anyone sympathetic to the Native cause had time to act. "Outside!" The soldier commanded, and followed Soma and the young scout into the crisp spring morning.

The rusty wire fences that stood between the People and the "freedom" that was the Red River, were being torn down. "That way!"

Another soldier herded Soma toward a growing group of Natives on the banks of the river. As the People were chased from their dilapidated homes, with only the clothes on their backs, the shacks were being systematically set on fire. The dry wood framed houses caught fire quickly, and soon became a raging inferno—stretching as far as the eye could see—along the near banks of the Red River. For the moment, the fire separated the soldiers, who had retreated to stand at the ready with their comrades, between the fire and the distant, waking city of New Rome. The land that the Red People had called the Reservations was barren, so the plan was quite deviously conceived. This Fire would not spread. It would not harm the City, and for the moment, it did not threaten the mass of People gathered at the water's edge.

"We need do something before the fire burns down!" One of the younger chiefs stated the obvious, frantically appealing to Soma for guidance. "There goes our plan involving the canoes."

Soma was about to turn his back on the fire that was now reaching skyward, consuming what had belonged to his People—taking all that they had owned for the past ten or more years. He halted. "Did you hear that?"

"What?" The younger chief tilted his head.

"The Fire—and the Wind." Soma explained. "They are telling us that we are free. We do not have a past—except in our memories and Dreams. We do not have anything to lose. We are once more a proud People of Spirit. We are the People of the Wind. Come,"—he urged to the younger man, and the people standing near. "Today we will survive—if it is the will of the Great Spirit . . . and our Mother Earth!" The People parted, and Soma walked with the pride that he spoke of, to the edge of the Red River.

"Great Spirit!" Soma raised his arms to the sky in a greeting. Then he bent to scoop a bit of the fast moving water in his hands. "Spirit of this Mighty River—you are the blood of our Mother. This same Spirit blood runs through the bodies of your children, we ask only that you recognize your Relatives. Please help us in our time of need. Your Relatives—the Red two legged ones, wish to cross to our promised land—the land of our ancestors. Great Spirit—if this is to be, we will cross safely—if not, it is a Good Day to Die!" With these words, the great Shaman, and leader, stepped into the swirling water. Within seconds the rushing water of the Red River slowed, and became quiet, and then slowed again to a trickle. Then as Soma completed his second step forward, the water flowed no more, and a river of stones remained. Soma turned and motioned to the great mass of People, some of who had followed him into uncertain waters and the others that still remained on the bank. He motioned to them, and the People surged forward over the steep river bank. Behind the People, the fire raged, holding back the Army of Rome and having consumed the wooden shacks of the reservation, burned on—from a Source unnamed, and unknown, until all of the People had found safety on the other side of the River.

Soma was the last of the People to set his foot on the river bank, on the other side. He raised his hands to give thanks, and the water began to flow again. The Red River surged with a power that ripped loose the supports and smashed the bridge that the engineers of Rome had deemed immoveable. The River seemed to be sending a message—to the soldiers, and a group of citizens of New Rome, who now stood gazing in wide eyed amazement behind a smouldering, strip of purged, blackened Earth.

*   *   *

Happy to be free at last, and to be once more in the lands of their ancestors, the People set up camp in a valley at the foot of the Black Hills. One significant result of the time spent in the reservations on the other side of the Red River, was that all previous tribal differences had been set aside—with the common goal of returning to the land that they had collectively named Kansa.

"What happens now?" This was a common theme that arose at the council meetings. "Can we return to the life we once knew? So much has changed. We are now a united tribe, and this feels right. But we have waited for the time to come that the People can reclaim their lands, and the ways of our ancestors. Some of these ways involve tribal differences. It is right to give up this new large tribe, and go our separate ways?"

"Let us live in the Mystery of what has been called "Native Time," and the answers will come." Soma suggested. There is no reason to hurry. This is a good place to call home. It is after all our home. Let us hunt, and live as the Spirit moves us."

When it appeared that the People were settled in the valley, the Spirit moved Soma to seek a Vision, high up in the Black hills. He found a flat plateau and began to construct a Medicine Wheel from rocks—in the teaching way of his Grandfather, and his Grandfathers' Grandfather before him. He built a wheel using stones—with four main stones at the Sacred directions. In the middle of this large, living wheel Soma dug a pit, and lit a fire. "This is the Life of the Wheel." He observed (and acknowledged to the Great Spirit). Then, beginning at the East, he sat and meditated on the Fire at the centre. The moment he quieted his mind, he heard a Voice that spoke from the Fire. He could not really be sure, however, if the Voice originated from the Fire, or within his mind—sometimes there were pictures, and other times, it was like talking to himself. It was similar to the effect of translating the symbols in the Emperors' palace, but had a purity, that was like no other feeling he had known. The Great Mystery was teaching him. He was being re-taught the Way of the Medicine Wheel—the Simple Way of the Relationships of Life on Mother Earth. The days came and went, as Soma lost track of time, in his clockwise journey around the Wheel.

One morning, Soma awoke. He found himself, by no co-incidence, perched on the stone of the North (the direction of Winter—in which the Earth will sleep . . . and Dream). The Fire was now smouldering embers. It did not occur for him to question what had fed the fire for . . . he guessed it must have been four days and nights? You do not attempt to explain the Mystery. If you try—you will lose your Way—you will forget that you are a part of the Dream. You will begin to believe that the Mystery is out there—somewhere. He had reclaimed the teachings of the Medicine Wheel for his People. The teachings of the four directions and the fire (at the centre) had not been lost. This knowledge of these four simple truths that had been all his ancestors needed to show them the Way—to walk the Path of Beauty. Now it was re-kindled within his heart (and his mind).

It was now his duty to take this teaching back to his People. "I have learned so much!" Soma surveyed the stone circle that had been the instrument that helped to inspire him. "How can I take this back with me?" His mind recalled the knapsack that he had brought with him on this quest. It had not occurred to him before this moment that he had not eaten in days—he had only taken sips from the canteen that was in the back-pack. Somehow he had been nourished? How could a man that has not eaten in four days feel so alive? He was not even hungry . . . and . . . and? His hair had grown down past his shoulders to the middle of his back! What magic is this? While pondering on the Mystery, he searched in his pack to find—birch bark, and feathers! "Of course! That must be why I brought these with me. I will make a Medicine wheel that I can take with me. It will be a sacred teaching, and a remembering tool."

Soma approached the one tree that grew on this plateau, and after asking with great respect, drew his knife, and cut one long, willowy branch. Back beside the circle of stones, he bent, and tied the branch into a circle. Then with the remaining strips of sinew, he fastened a flattened piece of the bark into the middle of the circle he had created. "It is like a Dream catcher." He mused. "Only this will capture and hold my memories of this teaching." So saying, he used ashes from the Fire, to draw animal symbols at the four corners of the birch bark, at the four directions of his "Medicine Wheel." Next, he hung four feathers at the bottom (the South). He surveyed his completed work (not without a sense of pride). "There is the Eagle at the East. There is the Hawk in the South, There is the Bear that is in the West . . . and the White Buffalo in the North." He dug deep into the dying ashes, and found one last glowing coal. This he placed in the center, and blew on it, until, there was a hole burned in the middle of the Wheel.

"This is Good! Now I can return to my People."

Chapter 16

Tarnished Gold
(Vega is also a Star)

Soma felt more alive than he could recall in the recent past years. He picked his way carefully down a path on the side of the Sacred Black Hills. The path was overgrown with grass, and it looked like it had not been used for years! "Maybe I came up a different way?" He wondered. He imagined that the People must be wondering about him by now. "It is a good thing that I instructed the council that I was not to be disturbed. The People have become like children. They have lost their traditional ways—no! The Ways have been stolen from my People. The White man has stolen their souls." His mouth was firm, as he recalled the hardships of the life on the reservations and the residential schools. "But this will all change now. We are free to live in the ways of our ancestors—in balance with the creatures that are our relatives on this Mother Earth." His heart was happy again with the knowledge that had been given him during his quest—this knowledge that he carried back in the form of the newly constructed Medicine wheel.

As Soma neared the foot of the mountain, he saw a boy stand and wave to him. He waved in return, and as he drew closer to the boy, he shouted enthusiastically: "Is all well with our People?"

"Yes. We are happy and healthy." The boy shouted back, as he ran to meet the Elder.

When the boy stood breathlessly beside the older man, he looked up with wonder. "You are the one that was called Soma?" He affirmed.

"Yes! Of course—but I am still Soma—not was. Why do you speak as though I am returned from Spirit?"

"I respectively apologize." The boy replied. "It has been a long time since our People have seen you. But I have not given up hope that we would see you again—even after everyone else . . . . I mean—in the beginning, as my father told me about you . . . In the beginning there was a watch for your return. A group of children would wait where you found me. My father was one of those children.., and he talked to me about the waiting."

Soma halted. "Wait. Wait—what are you saying boy? Did they give up so easily? And what is this about your father? I have only been gone for four days and nights."

At the boys puzzled face, Soma burst into laughter. "You are teasing me—for sure." He put his arm around the boys shoulder. "Here—I have something to show you." The two had reached the valley, and the sloping path became a flat, sandy area (where the boy had been sitting on a nearby rock). Soma motioned the boy to join him, and squatted beside the rock. "Let me show you what I have learned. Let me show you what I did on the mountain top." He was so eager to share the knowledge, he momentarily forgot the Medicine Wheel packed safely away in his back-pack, and proceeded to construct a replica (out of small stones) like the one he had built on top of the Black Hills. In the moments that followed, Soma poured out his teachings to the boy, who hung on his every word, and drank it up with an unquenchable thirst. "And this is how our People have passed on this Way of living in balance. Just as you and I—like a Grandfather and his grandson. This is the Way of our ancestors. This is the way of Respect." And Soma halted, and smiled. And I have neglected one other gesture of respect. I have not learned my Grandsons' name?"

"My name is Seattle, sir." I was born when my mother journeyed to look for work in the city of Seattle—across the Red River in New Rome. That was eight years ago. My Grandfather told me that someday I will be a chief . . . and I believed him. And I promised my Grandfather, and my father, that I would not give up the job that was given to our family. I promised that I would wait for the Great Shaman called Soma. I would have waited until it was my time to join my Father in the Spirit place of our ancestors."

At this point Soma came to an incredible awareness of how long he must have been absent from his People, how much time had passed so quickly for him on the mountain.

"So your Father is gone as well? I am sorry." Soma patted the boy on the back. "Who looks after you now—when you are not here waiting?"

"My mother." The boy replied. "She works all day in the city."

"Not in Seattle?" Soma spoke the obvious. What other city can she be at work in? Is there a way to cross the river that we did not know about?"

"'Course not in Seattle." The boys face got that puzzled look one more. "But we could use the bridge if we needed to."

"What bridge is that?"

"The only bridge there is—the Golden Gate." The boy answered.

"Oh?" Soma grew thoughtful. This boy had seemed so sincere? He did not seem to be the kind that would talk in a disrespectable way to an elder. So why?

"We should be going now." Soma suggested. "Like you said—I have been away a long time, and I need to talk with the council of our People. Is your home near here? Perhaps you should go on home now?"

"Yes." The boy agreed. "I live down the road that way. I am not allowed to go with you anyway. My mother says that Vega is not a city for children—I am not allowed to go any further that way." And he pointed in a westerly direction.

"You are not allowed to go to what city?" Soma was perplexed.

The boy pointed again. They had walked on as they spoke, and came to a well traveled road covered with fine gravel. There on the road side, was a large sign. Soma was able to read the white man's

English quite well. On the sign were the words: "WELCOME TO THE CITY OF VEGA—A STAR IN THE DESERT."

*   *   *

Wind-In-His-Ears became silent. In fact, the moon-lit park became silent, and the silence jolted Joseph back to the present—back awake.

"That's it?" Joseph was surprised by the sound of his own voice.

"There is more. There is always more. It is happening this very moment."

"No—I mean, is that the end of the story about Soma and his People?"

"What do you think?" The Older man stretched, as if he was preparing to get up from the bench.

"Well . . ." Joseph was pensive. "I was hoping to find out more about how these 'Sons of Soma?' As for the rest of this story . . . . I think I can guess what happened next."

"How could you?" Wind-In-His-Ears smiled slyly, and slipped back on the bench, spreading his arms, making himself comfortable once more.

"I guess you don't read much? Sorry—I don't mean to sound disrespectable. What I mean is . . . there is an old story—part of the white man's—I mean Christian Bible. You must have read it?"

"You were right the first time. In fact, I do not read a word of the white man's language. My story was told to me by my Grandfather. If, as you say, you can guess what comes next, then, how would the story continue?"

"Well . . ." Joseph took a deep breath. "After Mo . . . . I mean Soma came down from the mountain, and found that his people had degenerated to worshiping gold, he became very angry. Soma was so angry, that he broke his Medicine Wheel, and threw it away. Then, he returned to the mountain, and wrote a book of rules for his people to live by. He gave these new rules to his people, and then, taking as many as would follow him, went into the desert—where he wandered for forty years—looking for the Promised Land."

Joseph hesitated "How did I do?"

"Some of it is close." The Elder smiled, as though relishing a personal joke. "But this would be a white man's story—you are right about that too. And perhaps, your story did happen—in another Dream. But this Dream we are Dreaming belongs to you and I—and it is about the Second World. This is a Red Peoples' Dream. In this Circle—in this story, Soma was not angry. He left the child called Seattle at the edge of this city called Vega, telling him to return home until he could find out the truth of what had happened during his time on the peak of the Sacred Black Hills. And when Soma learned about the kind of city his People had built, he became very sad. "You have learned to live like those who had imprisoned you! Your Spirit has been stolen—it was taken from our children in the residential schools, and now our children have created a city without a soul."

After a few days in Vega, Soma left the city to seek out the home where the child he had met lived with his mother and Grandfather. Seattle's father had passed on to Spirit two turns of the wheel—when Seattle was six years old.

"My father believed that you would return—right to the end of his days on our Mother Earth." Seattle confided to Soma, as they shared the family meal.

"That is true." Seattle's mother agreed. "When he returned from work in the city, each morning, he would eat his breakfast, and spend his sleep-time keeping watch in the place that you found our son."

"I let my People down." Soma was sad indeed.

"No—our People made the choices to live as they do." Seattle's mother replied. "Vega is not a bad city. It is just not the kind of city our People would have built in another time. There are still those who follow the Traditional Ways, as best as they can."

Soma brightened. "This is what I must do." He said with resolve. "I have been given the teaching of the Medicine Wheel; so that I can help our People regain their connection with the Mother Earth.

I will gather together as many as are willing to follow the old ways, and find a new home for us beyond the desert."

"It sounds like a good thing." Seattle's mother agreed. "I would like to be part of this, but although the Spirit is right—Since my husband died, I have moved on as well. The old way is good, but I think it would also be a good thing to live in a new way—keeping the Traditional Values. My Father is too old to travel, and my son deserves the chance at a better life. He can go to a school in Kansa, and learn to live the way my Grandmother taught me. That is the balance that I believe in."

"I have found that there are more directions than one—to find your heart." Soma sighed. "I have shared part of my teachings with your son, and I believe now that this was the right thing to do. I have something for you." He spoke to the boy called Seattle. "I believe, as you told me on our way down the mountain, that you will be a great leader one day—a chief. Keep this Medicine Wheel that I have constructed, so that you will remember me—and not forget about the true ways of our People. When I shared this knowledge with you—I realized that it is alive in my heart, and that is the way I should teach it."

Joseph sat abrupt. "So that is how the Sons of Soma came to be?" He exclaimed.

"The answer is yes, but this is a two part answer. This is the way of my people. The simple answer is correct, but there is more to meet the eyes and the ears in the simple answer." When Joseph looked puzzled, Wind-in-His-Ears explained, "the Sons (and the daughters) of Soma were wandering People, that roamed the Desert and the land beyond, for almost forty years—until the passing of their Spiritual leader. Following Soma's unwritten teaching, they lived in peace, and harmony with the land, like our ancestors had before them. After Soma left this Earth, however, a young man was "elected" Chief, who had a different way of looking at life. He began to write down Soma's teaching, in a book of laws. He was called Iron Fist, and that was the way he ruled. His heart was full of blame for the life of his people—his mind was full of thoughts of revenge on the white man. This caused a split in the People who had been followers of Soma. Over half of the People left the desert, and rejoined their relatives and tribes in the cities and small villages. These People, who still live quietly in Kansa, still follow Soma's teaching, and they are respected for this. These Sons of Soma have intermarried and together they chose as a leader the boy who grew into the great chief called Seattle."

"So there are two groups of People that call themselves Sons of Soma?" Joseph was beginning to understand. He had not heard much about these people, but the little he heard was negative—to the point that he was warned not to talk about them. They were (he learned on the quiet) named terrorists, and subsequently blamed for any violent acts against the people of Rome (or New Rome).

"In a way of speaking—yes. But in Truth, there is only One—the one people who still follow the Peaceful Path, and there is another group that is angry and violent. These other People, who still live in the desert often, recruit our young—especially the boys who have become disillusioned and lost, to join them in their on-going war against the world outside Kansa."

"I originally found out about the Sons of Soma from the Internet. I guess I have lived a sheltered life?" Joseph shrugged. That is past. I want to know more about life—especially the ways of your People." He explained to the Elder, as he followed him toward the bus shelter at the far end of the plaza. Simon had left (hours ago?). The moon had now almost disappeared behind a cloud.

"I think you have other reasons for wanting to know about my People?" Wind-in-His-Ears smiled broadly. "If you are seeking my consent to court my daughter, you have it. For whatever that is worth." He chuckled. "My daughter has a mind and a heart of her own. But I am glad to call you friend and part of my family. The other thing you are asking about? The world wide web is a useful tool to find a seed of Truth—if you know where to start."

"Where would I start?" Joseph let the part about his interest in Mary, to slip for the moment. "How can I tell which Sons of Soma I am receiving information about—whatever method I use?"

"First, be forewarned that your government does not see a difference. All Sons of Soma are potential terrorists to them—so be careful in your seeking for knowledge. Second—the way you tell is simple. Listen with your Heart. If the information is peaceful and good for the whole of the two-legged People—then the source will be the same." They stood at the bus shelter, watching an approaching bus. "My daughter did not leave because of you. She was asked to leave by a representative of your government—the reason that he gave was that she had been photographed doing a forbidden Dance. There was more—but he did not need to tell us that."

"So—why did you and your sons stay on?" Joseph wondered.

"We had given our word. There was a contract of work that required completing by my sons. That is our Way. And for me—there was a story to complete—if the Great Spirit was willing. If not—I would leave with my sons tomorrow morning—knowing that I had done all that I could."

The bus came to a stop and the door opened. "About Mary . . ." Joseph began.

"I have done all that I can for you in that matter also." The Elder had one foot on the step of the bus. "Oh?" He seemed to recall something, and smiled his disarming smile. "My daughter is very traditional in the ways of the heart as well. It might be a good thing if you learned to play a flute."

Chapter 17

The Mirror of Dreams

"It might be a good thing if you learned to play a flute." This was the second time he had been given this bit of advice. There was a lot of Native flute music available in the record stores of New Rome. Joseph owned a couple of CDs himself. He put one on his stereo while he booted up his computer and connected to the internet. The music was both soothing and inspirational—more so now that he had acquired the first-hand experience of interacting with the People who created it. On searching the net he found, that one of the original uses for the Native flute was part of the courtship by a Native man and the woman of his choice. "Hmmmm? Do you need to be hit with a two-by-four to know what she was telling you?" he mused. He was buoyant at first with this new knowledge, as he searched for a place to purchase one of these flutes. "It has to be a traditional flute," he told himself, "to woo a traditional maiden." This meant that his search led him to an on-line source that was based in Kansa. He was able to order a traditional bird flute—to be delivered in the standard week to 10 days.

Having completed his purchase, he could not resist searching the Net for the words "Sons of Soma." A lot of "hits" appeared, and upon connecting to the sites in question, he was overwhelmed by a barrage of what could only be called propaganda—for and against. The information on one particular site jumped out at him. "'The

Sons of Soma' is a known terrorist organization based somewhere in the heart of Kansa. Any communication with this group will be considered an act of treason against the democracy of Rome and the United States of New Rome."

Joseph hastily disconnected from the internet. "What am I getting myself into? First, I have been living in a vacuum, and now it seems that I am about to consort with people who could be enemies of my country!" His mind churned out visions of someone from Homeland Security breaking down his door, and hauling him away. He turned off the computer and sat back in his chair, letting the images play out in his mind. The soothing flute music was still playing in the background. Eventually, he came back to the reality of the moment. "Consider this:" he began a dialogue with himself, "if the very thought of questioning the morals and ideas of the country I live in bring up the fears that I have just experienced, then there is something wrong! I am not a potential terrorist in any sense of the word. And I am not nor will I become a traitor to the fundamental rights and truths on which my country was formed. His friend Jenenes' words echoed in his memory: "Stand up and act like a Wolf (not a love struck pup)." Something to that effect. "Ok—this is more about being a man who is brave enough to think for himself, but I can't deny the love part either. There is more than a bit of feeling for Mary that has inspired me to come this far, and her family does appear to be all that they say." He squared his shoulders, and decided to conduct a personal search for the Truth, no matter where it led him. He would be as objective and pragmatic as possible. "Now that I have been granted the knowledge of the 'other side of the story,' I will see how it plays out in the history books that I read while I was growing up. I did not pay too much attention in school because my heart was on learning my trade. I will see if I can hit the books, and surf the net, to catch up on the world that I live in—with open eyes."

The history books he borrowed from the local library told a story—the story as written by a people who won a lop-sided war. The "Indian Wars," was a short and bloody conflict involving a civilized white race that attempted to "save" a savage pagan red-skinned people (the updated history books actually called them "people"). Joseph recalled something similar—something from his early schooling called the Crusades. This was one of the reasons he quit being interested in history—or school for that matter. It all came back to him now. He was a gentle-minded child—raised by peaceful parents. His father passed away at an early age, and his mother (in Portugal) taught him, by example, to be a true Christian. She was, and still is (he was reminded that he needed to phone her) a forgiving loving parent, that understood the importance of free will. When her son decided to quit high school (and the church), and enrol in a local trade school, she told him that although she did not understand, she would support his decision to make a life doing work he enjoyed.

Later, he had some regrets, and went back to night school to complete his education. In the long run, his time spent as an apprentice carpenter proved invaluable when he started a small business of his own after moving to New Rome. He was able to build up a solid clientele—mostly by word of mouth—as a man who cared about the little things and if there were problems down the road he would stand by his work. This drive to please, coupled with a desire for perfection, kept him busy to the extent that there was never room in his life for love—until now. He smiled to himself, and wondered about telling his mother. It would certainly go a long way to resolving a constant topic in their lengthy phone conversations. Almost certainly, the conversation would turn to: "am I getting any closer to having grandchildren?" She meant well, and it was more than about her status as a potential Grandmother. "God created us to share love," she would say, whenever he told her about the newest friend that Jake and Jenene had introduced. His friends eventually backed off (Jake at any rate), but Jenene still put in little digs. She was the first to notice how well Mary and he danced at the wedding reception. "She was impressed with you." Jenene winked. But when the real love-bug bit, he was shy and overwhelmed by her natural beauty and grace. And now? "When a woman that you respect, shows an interest—well I guess that Wolf nature kicks in? A gentleman is after all—a wolf with patience."

"And what about Mary MorningStar—now?" he resumed his Internet and History research, and realized that this interest was what started him on this path. He had been browsing the net one evening after work, about three years ago (was it that long—maybe more?), when he was interrupted by "the Truth cannot be Hidden or changed." Maybe your destiny is something that is not easily denied? "I have free choice, at least that's what my mother taught me. But how far does that go? Do I have the choice to make a bungling fool of myself by saying things that ended relationships before they began—or worse yet, could I have taken a wrong turn, and become a cold blooded killer?" Yes to the first, but a definite no to the second. "I am a middle of the road kind of man—strike that. I lean to the side of Peace, and live and let live." With that resolved, he opened his mind to whatever truth there was to be discovered.

He learned some eye-opening truths (with the benefit of the story as told to him by Mary's Father). The disease had been real. It was still a factor to be reckoned with. He now had a name and there was no cure, if not caught in its' early stages, despite the medicine that was formulated by the big drug cartels. There was a mention (very small) about the natural origin of the treatment. The article he read on the net said that good results had been obtained by some home grown clinics that based their medicine on a Native recipe. Those clinics and their treatments were tested, and closed down. Some moved South, and still flourished in the lesser stringent laws of Kansa. So much for that. And true to the "old man's" story—the USNR, the country Joseph now called home had laws against the practice of homosexuality. To be truthful, the laws were considered archaic in most states, but they were still in the books, to be resurrected when needed (like the law against Native dancing). And there was that (almost) common related misconception that AIDS was either linked to, or the result of homosexuality. There were also the publicized articles that said it originated in Africa, "food for the conspiracy theorists?" he mused, "or is this another bit of "the truth that cannot be hidden?"

Strangely enough, there was very little knowledge to be found (by regular means) about the Emperor of Rome. He was a shadowy figure that made an occasional appearance—or at least his successor did, at various times in the history records. It appeared that his family was like the former Kings and Queens of ancient Europe. They had kept to themselves (it was said) and intermarried, to keep the blood lines pure. More for the conspiracy group. Some pages that were allowed to flourish on the net said that each and every Emperor looked like his successor. They hinted that, being the World Religious Leader that he was, maybe he was the same man and that he had somehow conquered death? Joseph did not wonder why these sites were allowed to exist—it was good publicity for the church. "Hooo Boy! Wind-in-His-Ears—you have really given me something to think about."

Cigarette smoking was banned through the whole of the Roman Empire, but the sale of the substance that everyone called cancer sticks was not illegal. "Come to think of it, "Joseph noted that almost everything you ate or drank or took part in, was considered a cause of cancer these days. And this followed the knowledge that nearly all of the food available to the citizens of Rome and the United States of New Rome was force-grown using steroids and whatever else worked these days—livestock and grain included. "What a strange bit of irony—our athletes are tested for drug use, but they grew up eating drug enhanced animals, and vegetables—and like the general population, continue doing so for most of their allergy ridden lives." After returning from the camping trip, Joseph contacted a real-estate representative about purchasing a small cabin or home up North, where the air was cleaner, and organic grown foods were more readily available.

Back on the internet, another night, he came across a notice that as the Friendship tower was nearing completion, a change was made in the plans regarding its' purpose. It would not be capped off with a transmission tower to broadcast the Christian message world-wide, as previously planned. Its' purpose was to be scaled down to receiving the message from the Empire State Building in Rome, and re-transmitting that signal to the collective states surrounding the city of New Rome and to the city of Vega in Kansa. The implications were plain as day. The Emperor did not want a tower in the "New World" that was higher or more important than the one in Rome. Joseph could see this as being a slap in the face for the President of USNR. The Friendship Tower would instead be a place of commerce for all trade and a meeting place for business this side of the Great Ocean. Joseph could now understand the way the offices that he had helped install were in the planning from the start.

In a somewhat related topic, Joseph had read that the new supersonic plane, called the Concorde, was to be scrapped. The reason being that it was way over budget, and not safe. Things began to add up. The Concorde was built from the ground up with the help from local government grants. It would have been the pride of USNR. It would have made Rome more accessible, and it was rumoured to be faster than any current aircraft that Rome currently (and publically) had in the air. The plant where the Concorde was built was closed down, but another rumour had it, that the last working aircraft was flown out and dumped in the ocean beyond Kansa. At the end of this article, a small link was inserted "SOS." Does this mean what I think it means?" For just a second, Joseph paused, wondering if he should take the chance, and then decided that it was harmless enough, even if his activity was monitored ("Boy am I getting paranoid?) The link opened to a site with a warning: "If you are interested in the Truth, download this text file. This cannot be traced—the link that brought you here will not last long—SOS." He downloaded the text file, disconnected from the Internet, and saved the file to a floppy drive, before running a washer program that Jake had given him, and directed: "I use this anytime I download music. It will make your Internet experience harder to track—you pirate you!" Well Joseph was not a pirate, and although he would have used it to try out some music that he intended buying—he did not appreciate Jakes' gift until now.

Joseph had a laptop that he only used for his business. He made it a rule to never connect it to the Internet, because he had an irrational fear about identity theft, and losing his personal information. This had never made sense, but he declined using a wireless connection, and online banking. Now, he needed to buy a floppy drive add-on for his laptop, so that he could access the information in the file that he had downloaded. He went out to the nearest computer store, and smiled in response from the young clerk that kidded him about his purchase. "Didn't think anyone had floppies anymore? You should get this memory stick. It will store more than a gig. It is cheaper than the floppy drive, and it is more portable."

"What about the old files on the floppies that I have now?" Joseph asked. He didn't want to give them up—especially the file he had just copied.

"How did you create them in the first place?" The clerk inquired. Maybe you still have an old floppy drive? Do you have a desktop pc, or just the laptop you told me about?"

"Oh? Good grief." Joseph clued in. "I have never been much of a techie. So, I can use the old desktop to transfer my information from my floppy to the memory stick—thanks. I'll give it a go. And thanks again for the help."

Back home, Joseph pulled the plug from the Internet connection before booting up his pc. He was honest about not being a computer geek, and did not want to take any chances—but he was learning fast. Soon, he had the information copied to the memory stick. Before shutting down the PC and reconnecting it to the net, he ran Jake's cleaning program one more time, and made a copy of the install program to load on his laptop. "Just call me pirate Joe," he chuckled. Later, he would learn that most of his actions to hide his non-paper trail were redundant, but at the time it gave him peace of mind.

The file was named SOS3346.txt. "What the heck was version 3345 about? This must be a long story? Well I am not about to try to find out what went on before, or if there was a before—that is beyond my capabilities. If I am lucky (?) they will resend it for us late-comers?" This was to be proven true.

The file had come from an attachment to the story about the scrapping of the supersonic plane called the Concorde. When he opened the file, the title read: "Do you believe in UFOs—your government does." Joseph scratched his head. He continued to read:

Your government—the real one in Rome, has faster planes than the Concorde, but they don't want you to know about them. Just think Roswell—and I will get back to that in another update. This instalment of SOS is about another kind of UFO—and Red men from outer space. The Emperor of Rome recently received visitors, in the form of four horsemen—who claim to be part of the fulfilment of the prophesy. Your Biblical scholars might know them as the four horsemen of the Apocalypse? As the story goes—and this is from a reputable eye witness—four Red skinned people on spotted ponies rode up to the Palace in Rome and asked to talk to the Emperor. No one knows where they came from, and they were literally untouchable. They were like ghosts or holograms, but also real and tangible (when they wanted to be). The palace guards exhausted numerous rounds of amunitinion, but they might as well have been firing into empty space. And then, when the Emperor did make an appearance (surrounded by an armed regiment of troops) these horsemen were able to hand him—by proxy—a birch-bark scroll. We do not know what was written on the scroll, but it most likely had something to do with the speech by the one who appeared to be the chief:

"This is your second chance. This is the second world known to my People. You may not be aware of this, for the same reason that you have denied the words and all but erased the memory of the One who came before. He has become a Dream to you—a memory that you only give lip service. The time has come for the end of words. Let us tell you first, that he has not been the only one, but he came to you, because this was your prophesy. It is this prophesy that brings us here today. We are here to tell you that all prophesies are self-fulfilling. They are a Truth for the ones that have the inspiration, but they are not unchangeable—if this was not so—what would be the purpose of a Vision—a Gift from the Creator of All Things?"

All of the conversation—the speech by the four horsemen, who were untouchable was recorded. After a moment of silence—after letting his words sink in, the Chief continued:

"We are here to tell you that another One will come to Earth. Another Son of the Creator. This is part of your story as well—but you have it confused. This is not a second coming! I can say no more—it will be part of the Mystery for you to try to understand. But another One will be come. I will not tell you the exact date or time, because one of you might wish him harm. I will tell you, that his birth will be signalled like the first. This child will be born in your country, but not of your race. He will have red skin, but he will be white. He will arrive on the next occurring cycle of seven, and then when the cycle has completed four times more plus nine, we will return. When we are close, at that time there will be a reckoning—not a judgement. If you have not changed your ways, when we return, this reckoning will take effect. This will be an end to your Dream. This will be an end to the second world."

Then the four horsemen turned and quite literally, rode off into the sunset. They rode away into the west, and disappeared as mysteriously as they had appeared.

You should be aware that this happened (so we have been told) one moon less than six of your years ago. That is enough for you to think about at this time. . . . SOS

"Cryptic or what?" Joseph pondered the words on the screen of his laptop. "I guess they needed to be extra cautious—in case the Emperor should discover when and where the child will be born? Holy Bat-Riddles Batman!" he smiled—he needed to make some light of a possible prophesy of doom! "Not just doom—but the second coming (or not?) of Jesus? I am shaking in my former Christian boots (and beliefs)."

"Let's do the math. This happened one month less than six years ago. So, add a cycle of seven (years?) and the child is fated to be born . . . . NEXT YEAR . . . give or take a month! I am guessing that whoever his parents are, they better get busy pretty soon to make this all happen? This kind of eliminates most people I know—unless Jake and Jenene (A Red and White parent) have plans that I am not aware of? Or am I going bonkers? I am starting to believe this! If it were to happen—it doesn't need to be someone that I know—does it?" He began to wonder about the telling of the Native story to him by Mary's Father. "Good grief! You don't suppose they think . . . . Mary and Joseph! Sorry people, there is not time for that to happen. I still have to learn how to play that flute—besides that, I love her, and respect her too much to rush into anything." Then he slapped himself on the side the head, and had a good, much needed laugh at himself and this crazy conspiracy theory he was getting involved in.

*   *   *

A day or two went by, and then it was a week, and a card appeared in his mailbox to say that he had a parcel being held for pickup at a near-by UPS office. His hands shook when he brought the parcel home; and he carefully opened it with his pocket knife. "Beautiful!" Was all he could say, when he held the exquisitely hand-crafted flute in his hands. The "fetish" as he learned what the bird figure was called, was a golden Eagle. He had read a bit about it on the net. The placement of the bird (hence the name—bird flute) was moveable, but positioned so that it would modulate the sound in some way. He raised it to his lips, and blew into it. The raspy squeak that he produced was . . . ." Maybe I am suited to a Crow flute?" he chuckled, "this will take a bit of practice, if I am going to woo anyone but a flock of Black Birds."

He practiced for about an hour, using the small instruction book that came with the flute. Eventually he gave it a rest—but not until he was able to do the scales. He still didn't sound much like he recalled the flute on his Native music CD. The pamphlet suggested that to really learn to play this Native instrument, one should not compare it to anything you have heard. "Amen to that! Or what does Jenene say—Miigwetch? She thanks every little thing that works out right—and even some things that don't"

With the flute safely stored in the box it had been shipped in from Kansa, Joseph decided to resume his search for the illusive truth. He recalled something from the file he had downloaded. He typed "Roswell" into the internet browser. A significant number of hits appeared. He clicked on one that drew his interest. Part of the information that stood out was: Project Red-Book. Project Red-Book is an ongoing operation by your local government—headed up and initiated by Rome. It consists of a study about the possibility of life on other planets—life that might have contacted, and may still be contacting, the people of Earth. In our recent history there have been numerous sightings—many that have remained a mystery. The most glaring unsolved mystery remains at Roswell New Mexico. Until the late nineteen—forties, the lazy town of Roswell was unknown—that is, until it became the site of one of the most famous UFO incidents in recent history. The rumour has it, that an unidentified craft—a UFO, crash landed in Roswell. Until this incident Roswell was simply an area (surrounding a village of the same name) of unclaimed land in the southern part of Kansa. A point of interest twigged Joseph's brain. This land had been unclaimed, because the Native People do not claim land—they share all of Kansa—though it has been divided amongst various tribes living south of the Red River.

The Natives had "copied" the way the States of USNR were portioned, with the exception being the borders were more loosely defined, and each had a Chief, who reported to the Grand Chief of all First Nations (that they had named themselves). So—like the not so distant past being revisited, when the crash occurred in Roswell, a contingent of the Army of Rome moved in, and a base was set up called Area 51, to investigate and help protect the citizens of Kansa. And similar to what happened in the past, the "Big Brother," did not ask, nor pay much attention to the complaints of the Natives about treaties and land claims. Until this incident, there seemed to have been a degree of "respect" for the Native rights south of the river. Joseph could not find a history book printed in Rome or USNR that explained the re-settling of the land that was named Kansa. Something of a Spiritual nature occurred—that led to a mutual agreement between USNR (and Rome) and the Natives that had been living in reservations along the banks of the Red River. Now, with the set up of the base in New Mexico, the "honeymoon," appeared to be over. The Airport and the secretive Area 51 that was set up to study and monitor UFO activity under the code name Project Red-Book, had become a full time presence, in the heart of the Red man's land. The other thing that amused Joseph about this was how the white man moved in, claimed the land, and renamed it to "New-this-or-that," as if their being there still had the effect of "saving" these savages (and their land). He wondered who was fooling who?

Over the next few months, Joseph practiced diligently with the flute, and intermittently checked out sites of "interest" on the net. He found a few more links attached to similar information sites. He quickly learned to tell the difference between the "SOS" that he could trust, and the sites connected to the terrorist group, from which he kept his distance. The difference was, as Mary's father had suggested. Some files that were "posted" for download under the guise of SOS reeked of revenge and psychological manipulation. These he deleted after just a cursory scan. The files that Joseph did read before deleting contained open ended statements—they were about conspiracy to be sure, but they did not have an underlying motive. The information that Joseph chose to read, (sometimes skeptically) was mostly about something he could test in the "real world"—outside the internet. Other kinds of information, he would compare to the story as shared with him by the Elder known as Wind-in-His-Ears. When the stories matched with events in his history books, and his controlled intake of the evening news on TV, he would let it be—until proven otherwise. The file he read about Roswell and UFOs led to further disclosures that gave him reason to wonder in great depth whether he was really awake or not

He found a follow-up file titled: "Who are the real Aliens that abduct us?" And the article read, as follows:

"You have read about how your government suggested that, to help protect our children from harm—particularly the danger of being kidnapped. There was a bill put forth to make it a law that all children be "tagged" at birth, so that they could be traced, should they be lost or abducted. This bill failed to pass on numerous occasions until it disappeared into obscurity—or that would be what you are led to think. If a bill is required that Home-land Security believes is in the best interest of those that need protection, this bill can be given priority by the higher powers. We do not need to suggest who those "higher powers" might be. There is one person on this side of the Ocean and One other that lives in Rome. You might not like this, but for some time, the Emperor has been testing the inserting of computer chips—first in animals and then in humans (babies at birth). His staff has been ordered to conduct this testing since the invention of the computer—and since it appeared necessary to know the whereabouts of Native children. This practice was quietly altered to include all children—for their own well being. This was when (after the fact) that the bill to make it law made its first appearance. If you have children that were born in the last ten years, it is a possibility that they are "tagged."

Another possibility is that you may be the proud owner of a tracking device—either through the latest bank cards, or through a recent trip to the hospital, or . . . have you had dreams about being abducted by aliens? It has been rumoured that during these abductions that result in an implant, the abductees are also subjected to brainwashing. Afterward, they have re-occurring dreams of little green (or grey) men who do nasty anal testing on them. We might suggest that, it is not some aliens from another world that are "screwing with you" (pardon the pun). We are not saying that there is no life on other planets—and that they have not visited Earth. We ARE saying that the visitors, at least the ones that we know of look just like you and I. These are the so-called aliens that your government would have you be frightened of—as they are. The possible disclosure of truth should not cause Fear. Remember the words, in the Book that you have come to believe: "Truth Will Set you Free!" . . . . SOS

A week later, Joseph downloaded, and read another "update" that went on to suggest that the craft that crashed in Roswell was actually a prototype—a supersonic stealth plane that Rome was using to spy on the People of Kansa. According to rumours (again?), the stealth fighter from Rome was in pursuit of a disk-shaped object when the unidentified craft changed course, and took off at a right angle—straight up. It left the ship from Rome literally standing still, and the pilots in a state of shock. The press release from Rome reported a dangerous encounter with an alien ship and that the "saucer" shaped craft crashed in the hills near Roswell. Following that incident a contingent from Rome took over the small airport nearby to conduct tests, and make sure that the citizens of Kansa would be safe. Within a week of renaming the airport as area 51, and claiming it as a security sensitive site, they released a follow up report that nothing had crashed except an experimental weather balloon. Area 51 however, to none of the local Chief's surprise, remains to this day in the hands of Rome.

"Too much truth for me!" Joseph's head was spinning. He was on overload. He put in his time at the completion of the Friendship tower, and followed up with the purchase of the cabin north of New Rome. He decided that "flute or no flute," he needed a vacation. He felt the urge to seek out his personal truth—to follow his heart. He picked up the phone, and dialled Portugal—to talk to his mother, and fill her in on his plans. He felt a lot better after a lengthy telephone conversation, and then, just before he said good-bye, he asked:

"Mom? Tell me where I was born again?"

"You were born in a nursing home. There was no time to call the doctor, so a mid-wife delivered you. Why do you ask? You have never been concerned about this before?"

"Not to worry Mom?" And after a moment. "Did I need to go to the hospital when I was little?"

"No. Haven't I told you before that the Angels must be watching over you? You have not been ill a moment while you were growing up." Then she laughed. "Except two times you got a stomach ache, and stayed home from school. You never did like school any way. I guess you didn't like needles any more than school."

"Why is that mom?"

"Because those two times you were ill, were the days that they were giving needles at school. The authorities phoned me and asked if I wanted you to get your shots at another time, and I told them no. I told them it was against our religion. I thought—why mess with a good thing. You have always enjoyed good health, so I thought that the Angels were looking after you, and you didn't need their medicine."

"You are so right," he thanked his Mother. "I am sure that the Angels have been looking after me—and you too Mom. Bye for now."

162

The very next day, on what he called an overdue whim, he jumped in his Jeep, and drove to a Pow-Wow that he had seen advertised in Kansa on the net. It was near the reservation where Mary and her family lived.

He watched the Grand entrance, and soon after that, they declared an Intertribal Dance. An Intertribal Dance—as the announcer explained, was open to anyone who wanted to join in. Joseph watched from the bleachers, deciding that he was not ready for this yet. He was not really surprised, however when a familiar figure appeared, in full Native Regalia—clutching the same shawl she had that night when he had watched her dance in the forest. Mary danced by below on the grass—and then she looked up. She stopped momentarily and smiled. The next thing Joseph knew, he was following her beckoning hand to join her in the dancing circle.

Chapter 18

Starlight
(How it looks in the Mirror)

Joseph spent most weekends during the year that followed, in Kansa with Mary and her family. He put a lot of millage on his Jeep. His new home in the rural setting near the small town of Bethany, was a little over an hour drive North-West of the city of New Rome, but his part in the construction of the Friendship Tower was now finished. He resumed his carpentry business—finding more than enough work on both sides of the Red River.

He was now a familiar face on the Pow-wow trail, and became involved in every aspect of the traditional Native ceremonies and beliefs—except the Sundance which admittedly frightened him, for reason he could not define. One early winter evening, after sharing a particularly hot sweat lodge ceremony with Mary, they both walked off into the nearby forest. His knees were still a bit rubbery from the sweat, so he just enjoyed not talking—listening to nature. They came to a small stream that was partly frozen. The water that still flowed created a musical sound in the stillness of the approaching night. Joseph leaned back against a nearby tree. In a purely inspired moment, he took out his flute from the arrow holster on his back and began to play. It was a song he had practiced just for this occasion.

When he had finished playing, Mary asked: "Is that cupid's arrow?"

"Yes." He answered. Will you marry me?"

She leaned back against another tree, facing him. "I have wondered when you would ask. In fact, I have been waiting for this moment . . . . but . . ."

His heart leaped in his chest. "But? I hope I haven't misjudged . . . ?"

"No—I do feel the same about you." She reassured him. "But I need to tell you something. And then you can ask me again. There have been things happening, that seem part of a dream—and at the same time too co-incidental to be anything but the plan of the Creator of All things."

He nodded in agreement and waited for her to continue.

"I have told you, that when I was born, a White Buffalo was also born. Do you know of this prophesy?"

"Yes—I read about it. If you are the White Buffalo Calf Maiden in the story, then I am happy to be the one who will let you show me how to open my heart—you have already done that. I accept my place in your prophesy."

She smiled. "I know that. But there is more. This is about your People too, and their Dreams, and their prophesies. Remember when you told me about your Bible (after I said that I had not read it)? Remember the part about Mary and Joseph? We had a good laugh about that. Something happened to me in the Sweat this evening. That is how I knew this would be the time you would propose."

"Something good—I hope?"

"I believe so, but you will be the one to know how you feel about this. In the Sweat, I went somewhere. There was a woman—a Spirit of glowing white. She did not have wings, like your bible stories, but I know that she was a messenger from the Creator. She told me that I will have a son—and he will be a Son of the Creator come to Earth. She did not say anything about a second coming, as your people talk about. She said that he will be like all other Sons and Daughters that are born, but unlike other children, he will remember who he is."

Joseph took a deep breath. "Oh my God! This is a bit scary and wonderful at the same time. I feel . . . I don't know what to feel. I do not feel worthy of this, and I would doubt all of it, if you were not the one to tell me. I do not doubt anything that you would say to me. After all we have been through so many of those co-incidences that you mentioned. But . . . but? I have to ask how—I mean, in the bible story of Joseph and Mary, she was Spiritually . . . . impregnated as a virgin. I don't mean to . . . . I mean are you . . . ?"

She blushed. "I am not pregnant. If that is what you are asking." She lowered her head momentarily, and then looked into his eyes again. "But I am a virgin. I have waited for my husband, for you, if that is the wish of Spirit?"

"Then how? I can't say that I have not been intimate with other women before, but since the very moment I saw you—I knew that you were the one I wanted spend the rest of my life with. All of my interest in other women disappeared at that moment. I have not dated anyone since—even though Jenene tried her best to set me up. She gave up, when she realized what I am telling you."

"I believe you." Mary reached out, and he took her hands in his. "I think there is a different way to see the workings of Spirit than the one written in your Bible. Both ways could be right—like a white man and a red-skinned woman. In my way of seeing, you are a son of our Creator. His Spirit is in you, and when you share love with the woman that you chose—the two of you will be Creators of new life."

"And if there is not a baby created?"

"The Sharing of Love is the purpose of Life." She answered.

"Does this mean that you will marry me—if I agree to my part of this Mystery?"

"Yes."

*   *   *

"Doesn't this change the prophesy that was told by the four horsemen to the Emperor in Rome?" Joseph wondered out loud. He lay on a secluded beach in Portugal, looking up at the stars. Mary's head snuggled into his shoulder. The only thing that covered their naked bodies, was the large "marriage blanket" that they were wrapped in. The native marriage had been simple. They stood together (clothed at the time) in front of a group of their closest friends—and tribal relations. The Shaman of Mary's tribe asked both: "do you chose to be with this man (woman) the rest of your life—in Love?" They both answered simultaneously "I do!" The Elder then put a large blanket that was made by Mary's Grandmother, around their shoulders. "HO! This is done—this is so!" The Shaman said, and in the eyes of all present, and the Creator, they were man and wife. The Christian marriage (for Josephs' mother and family) in Portugal was a bit more formal, but when all was said and done, their vows were not to be consummated, until this moon-lit night on the beach.

"What does it change?" Mary's voice came muffled and sleepily to his ears.

"The prophesy . . . . ? The one about the four years and nine months that would be the date of the child's birth. The one that was told to the Emperor."

"I only listen to prophesies that speak to my heart." Her voice was clearer. She joined his view of the star-filled sky.

"Which means? . . . I mean that if our child is to be the One, then he would be born tonight—this morning and not . . . maybe nine months from now? Doesn't that make sense?"

"This is part of why we are now joined in marriage, my husband. Our People will need to learn a new way of thinking—that will include both the logical, and the Spirit. In the way of my People—if our joining, and our sharing of Love this morning creates a child—in the way of my People, today will be thought of as the time of his birth. This will be the time that his Spirit came into our world."

"Woman that I love," he planted a kiss on her lips, "you are messing with my mind. I am not saying that I disagree with that, but I don't understand a thing you are talking about."

"This is the morning of March thirteenth on the calendar that you follow?"

"Correct." He answered. "We have been making Love all night." He sighed. "And yesterday—when we were married for the second time, was March the twelfth, by my calculations."

167

"And by the calculations of some of my People, this is the morning of the seventh day of the ninth moon—in a year that has thirteen moons. It seems that the man, who came from the stars, spoke in a riddle that might be known by a person who can think like white and a red person combined?"

Joseph thought for a long time, and then he hugged his new wife. "Neat! Joseph and Mary may have just brought into this world a baby, whose astrological birth date will be Pisces—the two fishes, which strangely enough is considered the sign of Jesus. Did I cover it all?"

"That will be enough for now, except . . ."

"What?" He wondered? "Do we even have a choice of a name for our son?"

Mary laughed. "Of course we do. But I like the name that Spirit suggested." She waited, but when he did not reply. She said: "what do you think of Shiloh Joseph Renauldi?"

"You mean that Spirit even knew who you were going to marry?"

"No silly. Spirit suggested the name Shiloh. It is a peaceful name. I had the choice of who would be his father—and so did you."

"OK. OK. You've got me—literally and for life. It was all my choice as well. And I would do it all again—and again. Now how about giving our son a better than average chance of being born today? I am more than willing to give Spirit and Love, a chance—how about you?"

*   *   *

Mary and Joseph Renauldi found themselves in unfamiliar surroundings. They had been driving since early the previous morning, searching for a place to spend the night. Every motel that they stopped at, or passed on the freeway, only confirmed the blatant, flashing signs outside: "NO VACANCY!" The old jeep was overheating again, had been doing so, most of the afternoon that had become twilight. It was at this moment, that it hit Joseph. "What are we doing here?" Better yet, what had possessed him to bring a pregnant Mary on this trip? If he had to take it back, he would have done things different. But here they were still on the road. They would have to make it home—their other home in Bethany—the one he had bought nearly two years ago, and forgotten to give his lawyer the final check for the tax account. The papers had been in his brief case for a year—until the lawyer tracked him down—in a manner of speaking. Lawyers, it appeared do not have time for trivial things, until they get a call, a reminder from the State of New Rome. Pay up or face foreclosure.

Joseph had given Jakes' name as a reference—a person to contact in New Rome if he was unreachable. When Jake made the call, Joseph came down from the cloud he had called home. His mind and heart had been on Mary—and now the baby on the way, since he had came to Kansa with the one single focus—to make her his wife. Mary had been to their doctor in Kansa only a week ago, and she and the baby was given a clean bill of health. "The baby is on time." The doctor pronounced. There is nearly a month to go. Nothing to worry about." Joseph had phoned his lawyer back, to tell the man that he would take a quick drive to deliver the cheques to clear up the tax account. There and back, with a quick stop at the neglected home to rest. He could do the whole trip in a day, if not for the stop at the house in Bethany. "I want to come along for the ride. I have not seen your (I mean our) other home in New Rome." It was late fall, and very little snow on the ground. Mary would not need a passport to cross that bridge, since she was his wife, and all of his papers were up to date. "Ok." He agreed. Any thoughts about prophesies and such had long been swept to the back reaches of his mind. Mary and the baby were foremost.

Now, on the road the prophesies came back. They passed a sign that read: the City of Bethany, Population (the numbers escaped him). Half an hour and they would be . . . . a cloud of steam erupted from under the hood of the Jeep, and the motor coughed twice, and quit. They coasted to a stop outside a small motel tucked back off the road in a wooded picturesque setting. He could see the quiet sprawling ranch-like homes back in the trees, but what really caught his eye was the neon sign that blinked: "Pine Ridge Motel—Vacancy."

Mary and Joseph exchanged looks. She smiled. That smile said: "see—I knew that Spirit would look after us."

"Would you mind waiting her for a moment?" He suggested. "I'll walk to the main house, and see if someone can give us a lift." He didn't think it would be good for Mary to walk that far.

"I feel fine." She pronounced. "It would be good to stretch my legs. Shiloh and I have been sitting too long. We need some exercise and fresh air."

"Ok." Joseph reluctantly agreed. "But only if you promise to go slow."

The walk was farther than it looked, but with Josephs' insistence, they rested half way to the main house that displayed a small sign on the side of the building (only now visible) that said "Pine Ridge—motel office." Mary was a bit out of breath when they stood and knocked at the door. "We need a room for the night—our car broke down at your front gate."

"You must have someone looking after you." The woman who answered the door had the kind, weathered face of a farmer (or rancher). Let me get Mike—my hired hand, to take you to get your luggage, while I show your wife to the bunk house. She looks like she could do with a bit of rest. How soon is the baby do—honey?" She asked Mary.

"Not for a couple of weeks—maybe a month." Mary answered.

"If I were to guess." The Woman replied, taking Mary's hand. "Whoever told you that is a bit off. I was a Veterinarian before the ranch went under, and my husband (bless his soul) passed away. We salvaged what we could, by selling off most of the land, and turning this into a Motel. But what I am saying, is that I have always been a good judge of when a birth was near—for horse or woman." She smiled motherly. "And Honey—that child of yours is about to make an unexpected appearance."

Mary managed a warm smile in return. "He has his way of picking his own time—that is for sure."

The owner of the motel assisted in getting Mary comfortable, while Joseph and the man called Mike went to retrieve their luggage from the Jeep. When Joseph returned, the woman, who asked to be called Marg, cautioned him. "I am a light sleeper. If you need help at any time during the night—just knock on my door. I advised your wife that she should let us take her to the nearest hospital, but she declined. She said that she was OK, and that everything was being looked after by Spirit. Do you know what that means? I hope you are not part of some religious group that would put your babies' well being second to your beliefs?"

Joseph was alarmed by the woman's words, but he quickly assured her that Mary and the baby meant more to him than anything—including his own life. When he opened the door to the room, however, he found Mary in distress. "My water broke." She grimaced in pain. "Our baby is about to be born."

*   *   *

With Marg's assistance, the baby boy that Mary and Joseph had decided to name Shiloh was born. "Young lady." Marg announced. "I have not been a midwife to a simpler birth—If you will pardon me saying, for animal or human mother. It might interest you to know, that before the renovation, this was originally horse stables. I think it is an amazing co-incidence that your baby was born in a manger."

It was a co-incidence that blew Josephs' mind. When the bed linen was replaced, and mother and baby were settled to rest. It really started to dawn on Joseph, the series of events that led up to the birth of his son. It was as though everything was planned—orchestrated, in a way that he could not have believed if it had happened to someone else. Some greater force had to be at work. Everything had come together—right down to the minute—and the day, and the month and the year. "The year?" It came back to him now. This was supposed to be the year that everything came apart—the millennium. This was the much feared nineteen-ninety-nine that the computer world waited with breathless anticipation to come to an end. How could they know, that this special birth would take place. Maybe God planned it this way, so that the birth of his son would go unnoticed. "Good Grief! I am going crazy. What am I saying?" He glanced at a calendar that hung askew on the wall—and reached to put it right. Instead, it came loose, and fell to the floor—upside down, and the year . . . ? He had to sit on the end of the bed. Upside down 1999 looked like 6661! The mark of the Beast!

For a long moment, his mind went crazy. All of his Christian beliefs came crashing down—like that calendar. His mind was in turmoil! "What is happening here? God?" He silently cried out. "What are you doing to us?" And then, calmness came over him—as though this God—or Great Spirit, whatever the name—had answered. A shining light (the moon?) came through the half closed window blind, and filled the room and illuminated Mary and the baby until they glowed. There was a knock—a light tap at the door.

The door opened, and Marg appeared. "You need to come out here. There is something you need to see." She said in a hushed voice.

Joseph joined her at the open door, and the moonlight streamed through.

"It's not the moon." Marg explained. "The moon is over there." She pointed to the western part of the sky. "It is some kind of planet, or Star that was not there an hour ago. I would have noticed it. It just appeared. Oh my God! I am not a Bible thumper—but I can see that this is some kind of miracle! It is like the Story—happening for real—right before my eyes. The only thing missing . . . . ?"

A sound caught their attention, and they saw riders approaching. Four riders—on spotted ponies thundered up the path from the road where Josephs' jeep had broken down. They came to a stop in front of the motel door, where Marg and Joseph stood waiting, in open mouthed awe.

"We have followed the light from the Star." The leader was a Native man dressed in the complete regalia and headdress of a Chief. He dismounted and the other three riders followed suit. "We have come with gifts to welcome the Son of the Creator of All Things."

Joseph looked from the Chief to Marg, then back again. "I have to be dreaming?" Was all he could say?

The Native man extended his hand. "Perhaps you are right about that." He conceded. "Perhaps we are all dreaming? But it is a good Dream—don't you think?" Joseph grasped his hand and arm in the traditional hand shake. "Depending on your ability to believe the Dream—I am (or was) known as Seattle." The Chief introduced himself.

"Then . . . who are you now?" Joseph shook a hand that was not ghost-like by any stretch of the imagination. The man had a firm, solid grip. "And where do you come from?"

The Native man laughed aloud. "I am still the man called Seattle—a Chief of my People—and we have come a long way to see your son. Our Home is that Star." He pointed to the sky. "I cannot explain this—you would not understand—at this time. I am as real as you. I am as real as the baby—your son. And I am Spirit at the same time, as HE is, and his Mother, and you as well. The best I can say is that you are more than you believe you are."

"OK." Joseph's head was swimming. "You seem real. So . . . why are you here?"

"We come with Gifts for your son. Gifts that will help him to remember his purpose."

"His purpose?" Joseph experienced a chill.

"Yes! Do not be afraid—it is not part of his destiny, to meet an end like the One that came before. That was true for that One as well—but that is another story—for another time.

"Joseph?" Mary's voice came from the inside of the motel room—the room that once was a manger. "Who are you talking to?"

"Someone that wants to meet you—and our son. Someone who has come a long way." Joseph stepped back inside, and motioned the riders to follow him. Soon they stood in a semi-circle around the bed. "This man . . . ." Joseph began, and then simply motioned that he wished the chief to introduce himself.

"I am Chief Seattle." The chief stepped closer, and Mary returned his smile. "I bring this gift for your son. This is the Medicine Wheel that was given to me so that I would know the Sacred Teachings of our People. As it was passed to me, now I give it to the Son of this man who is the Creator as surely as the woman he loves is the Mother of all things. This Medicine Wheel was gifted to me by a man who stepped beyond time, and saw that this Life is a Circle. It has no words, but it is a story that has been told—and will be re—told by this child."

Another one of the visitors stepped forward. He wore decorations of all kinds, but did not have as many feathers as the Chief. He wore a vest, and had a twinkle in his eye. Joseph guessed that he was a Shaman. "I am called Crazy Horse." The man announced. "And I do not have a problem with the need to explain this Mystery. I am open to new ways of seeing life. My gift to your son is this Spirit shaker—a rattle." He demonstrated. "At Wounded Knee we danced a Sacred Dance called the Ghost dance, and I wore a Ghost shirt, like the one that I am wearing today. Sometimes Spirit is Coyote Medicine, and although it does not lie, we need to see the truth in a different way. We wore the Ghost Shirt, and danced the Sacred Dance, believing that the white man would be taken away. The white man did not go anywhere, but my People did—to a safe place where we could not be harmed by the white man's guns. This was not an easy truth to experience. There is a new prophesy that the white man will remove himself from this Earth, and our People and those that follow the Path of Peace will return—but I for one, do not believe that this is necessary. We have moved on. This Spirit shaker will help your son to remember that his true form is Spirit, and Spirit is not imprisoned in any form, or Dream."

The next person to step forward with a gift was a tall muscular man with one feather. Just by seeing his confident way of being present, Joseph guessed that he was a warrior. "I am Geronimo. I give your son this Arrow. This is the Arrow of Truth that was removed from the body of the man called Custer at the Little Big Horn. With this arrow a Spiritual Warrior will be aware of the difference between Right and Wrong action, and why we will say: Today is a good day to Die."

"This has always caused me to fear. And now more than ever—I fear for my son, and the destiny that might be his." Joseph said. "Is there no way to have Peace without this Sacrifice?"

"I will answer this question." The fourth rider spoke. "I am called Pocahontas." She was indeed the most beautiful native woman Joseph had ever seen (except for Mary). She wore a dress of doeskin and had three feathers in her long braided hair. She stood with the pride of Geronimo, and with a gentle strength that (again) Joseph had not seen in any person—except for Mary. "When I chose to marry a white man, many looked on me with scorn—including some of my own People. I was thought to be a traitor by my People and a whore by many of the white skinned race. That is my part as the Fourth Horseman. I am the reason why the ones who wrote the story have feared our coming. I am the one who will give your son a Drum. This Drum will be his Heart. In our Heart we will know that there is another step beyond the Arrow of Truth. This step on the Path of the Heart takes us beyond Judgement. There is a time to act, and there is a time to do nothing—this is called Compassion. The destiny of your son is to awaken Compassion in the Hearts of all People on this Mother Earth. This message cannot be denied. This time you cannot kill the messenger to delay your fate. The people of the Earth have been told that they have a choice in this Destiny."

"How are we to use these gifts?" Joseph asked. They had moved outside, and Chief Seattle stood beside his pony. The other riders were already astride their mounts, awaiting their Chief. "Especially this Arrow of Truth—isn't this like some Christians' explanation of Sin?"

"My People do not have a word for Sin." The Elder spoke with measured words. "Until the European people came with their black robes, we did not need this word. We have always known right from wrong—it is in your Heart. But we needed to be open to Change. This is our way of honouring this truth. We do not think or teach with written words—or with words that are unchangeable. We tell stories. The gifts that we have given your son are to be used in this manner, by two loving parents. You will teach your son by example—the Creator has chosen two parents that are the living examples of Love. When you feel he is ready for one of these teaching gifts, you will give it to him. Perhaps the Drum might be a good start for a red skinned boy? It was how I began. And if this is right for your way—the Arrow might be a gift when he turns into a man? Every child begins innocent, and it is our teaching way that changes or helps this grow. He already knows—it will be a mother and father that will help him remember."

Chief Seattle mounted his spotted pony, and the four riders followed him out of sight, into the bushes beyond the path that led to the motel. He had explained previously to Joseph that they could not stay—since they did not wish to draw unneeded attention to the child. He also said that the "Star" he called Sirius, would remain in this part of the sky for seven hours, before returning to their home constellation. "We will return four more times." He explained further. "But the next three instances in the folding of the Blanket of Space and Time will not bring our home world this close. The fourth time, however—when your son is twenty-eight years on this Earth, we will be very close. This will be the time of Reckoning. I will say no more. This is a simple story that has an ending that is not written—and therefore may be changed. We must go now to add to the confusion that your people call UFOs. This will give your wife time to heal so that you can move her and your child to another place of safety."

When the riders had gone, Joseph collected his thoughts. He checked to see that Mary and the baby were resting peacefully, and took a walk out to check on the Jeep. When he returned, he asked Marg for some water to fill up the radiator of the Jeep. He went out, and then returned with the Jeep, parking it on the beaten path rather than the pavement by the motel "There is a water leak. It doesn't seem bad, so if I fill the rad before we leave, we will be able to drive to the cottage. Once there, I can find a service centre to check out the problem. What a co-incidence." He joked to Mary, who was awake, bright eyed and admiring their new son. "The Jeep lost its' water about the same time as you. We will be OK. I will never doubt now, that someone is looking out for our family."

*   *   *

The next morning, Mary announced that she was ready to travel. "Not too far, but we need to get away from this place. The Star is gone, but so will the ships that Rome will be tracking. Sooner or later they will come looking."

They bid good-bye to Marg, promising to call her when everything was calmed down. "I will not tell you where we are going, so that you will not need to lie to the people who will most likely come nosing around. Remember the Christmas story—well this is happening again—in real-time, as you so rightly noticed. Someone who is afraid of what a child might do to their comfortable way of living, will be looking for us. We will probably head back in the direction of Kansa. "He said a bit louder, noticing that Mike, the handy man was within earshot.

As luck would have it (or was it luck—at this point?), Joseph had not gotten around to signing in at the motel, what with the baby arriving so suddenly. When he visited Marg at the Motel office, following the arrival and leaving of the visitors, she accepted payment in cash, "under the table." "The book will remain blank for the night you spent with us." She told him. "When you leave first thing in the morning—use the garden hose to fill up the radiator, and if anyone does show up to ask—I will tell them that you skipped out without paying. I have trusted Mike in the past, but the least he knows the better. He knows that I would help anyone if asked, and I don't think he heard your last names—and neither did I, for that matter."

Early the next morning, Joseph and Mary and Shiloh were on the road, without a hitch. It was about half an hour drive across town to the cottage. He listened to the radio on the way, and the news reported an above average build up of traffic on the Golden Gate Bridge—due to some unknown problem at customs. He breathed a sigh of relief that he had decided to stay over at the cottage. What choice did he have with the car problem? He realized that maybe Mike would have to be trusted—since he did know about the car. But just in case, they would lie low, and talk to Jake and Jenene before venturing back to Kansa. He called Jake on his cell, and inquired about getting his car fixed on the sly.

"Joseph you old Pirate. What kind of trouble have you gotten into?" Jake ribbed him.

"No trouble—nothing illegal at any rate—unless it is against the law to become a father in this state now?"

"No kidding!" Jake was floored. He listened to part of the story. "I have a friend who is a mechanic—sounds like a water pump to me. Jenene and I will be up to see the baby after I contact my friend. He works out of his house about half way between here and Bethany. We Portuguese boys look after our own you know."

"This is a fairy tale!" Jenene gushed. I am about to be God Mother to a baby that will change the world!" She rocked the child in her arms, cooing and fussing. It took less than two hours for Jake and Jenene to appear on the Joseph's doorstep. "Jenene can stay with Mary while we take the Jeep to get repaired." Jake had everything arranged. He reached out. "My turn. Let me hold him for a minute. Mary—did you notice—this boy is glowing—and so are you! Jenene is right. This is some kind of fairy tale—or miracle. This does NOT happen now-a—days." Jake and Jenene could not have children of their own, due to a birth defect in Jake. They had learned about this only after years of trying, and numerous trips to the doctor. Jake and Jenene had become the perennial baby setters and God Mother and Father to any and all children of friends and family (on Jenene's side).

Later that evening, Joseph and Jake returned with the Jeep repaired. "Water pump." Joseph confirmed to Mary. "The Jeep is good as new. I think we should hang around here until you are better able to travel, and just to make sure." Mary agreed, and so did Jenene. Mary was learning to feed the baby the natural way, and Jenene was playing at second mother. "Sorry I can't help you with that she quipped, but when you get to the bottle stage—I am eager and willing."

A couple of weeks went by, and Joseph met with the lawyer to finish off the bit of legal work that had brought him back to New Rome. "Luckily this cottage is winterized." He said one blustery day. I think it would be good to spend Christmas, and return home in the New Year?" Mary agreed again. "Wow!" He noticed. "What an agreeable wife I have. Will you ever not agree with something I say?"

"When you suggest something that does not seem right—you will be the first to know." She kissed him gently. The glow that Jake had seen was harder to see now—for both Mother and child, but it was still there—if you looked just right. And Joseph knew just the way to look—something she had taught him early in their courtship. Mary did not lie—ever, but if she were to be holding back "some of the truth," so to speak, he learned to sense what he could only call a "closed off" feeling in his own Heart. Now, since giving birth, she was open one hundred percent of the time, and the glow spread out from her Heart to his. He learned later, that the Natives called what he was experiencing, "seeing with the eyes of the Heart."

Christmas came and went. It was a special event to be sure—to share this time with his new family—and friends. It would take something pretty amazing, however—another miracle of the proportion that he had just experienced before Joseph would come down from his high (or so he believed). For now, everything was so good, that it couldn't possibly get any better. He did come down to Earth rather abruptly, the day they decide to pack up and return to Kansa. It was fear—that grew inside him as they approached the Golden Gate Bridge. What if—what if Mike at the Motel had taken down their license plate number and given it to the authorities? What if . . . ? Before leaving, he gave Marg a call, and she told him that one man in a dark suit had come asking questions—looking for a friend and his wife. Marg had told the man nothing—because that was all she knew. That was Mike's day off—she informed Joseph. Besides, she still trusted that Mike would say nothing—he was a good man, and had no reason to tell about something that most people might be witness to once in a life time."

Waiting in line to cross the bridge to Kansa, Joseph turned on the radio—almost by instinct—to catch the latest news from Kansa. He tuned in instead, to a talk radio broadcast from New Rome. The host was inviting people to phone in and share their memories from the Christmas holidays just past. A man phoned in, to say that he had been witness to a "Christmas miracle."

"We have Joe on the line." The Talk show host announced. "Ok Joe, what did you see this Christmas that we could call a real honest to goodness miracle?"

"I saw a baby being born."

"Ok—that is a miracle anytime." The host agreed. "But it would be a special Christmas miracle, if your name was really Joseph, and your wife was Mary, wouldn't it?"

There was a slight pause, while the man on the line collected his thoughts. "Yes." He agreed. "That would be a special Christmas miracle." And he hung up.

"Ok people." The music in the background was signalling a commercial. "You heard it first here—Joseph and Mary—and a Christmas miracle. See you after the break."

Joseph reached over and turned off the radio. He smiled, and Mary smiled back. They were next in line to talk to the customs and security person.

Josephs' fears had disappeared.

Epilogue 1

This is a Circle

The West is a Spirit Circle
The End is also the Beginning
This Spirit Dance
Is the Mystery Dance.
Spirit is the part Of the Mystery that Remembers.
This Circle Is a Journey of Remembering.
. . . Steven WinterHawk (1992)

The End…

The warrior who held the Arrow that would end the life of the "man with the yellow hair" at the battle of the Little Big Horn can sleep peacefully now. It was a good Dream. Mary and Joseph, and their baby are safe. Although he is content with his memories this man, who is also called Shane, is aware that this Circle is not complete.

When the baby is of the age to fulfil his destiny, there will be those that recall the story in a different way. Some will be prepared to forget that this man of peace ever lived—or deny his message that is "the Arrow of Truth." Others will continue the mistreatment of their brothers and sisters, including the animals and all creatures, and the Mother Earth. The trees are cut down and the waters (the life blood of the Mother) and the air is polluted. In the world that Shane calls home, many of these people, those that claim to remember, will be prepared to accept the death of the man who was born of Joseph and Mary. They will say that the blood of this man will save them, and they will no longer be responsible for the so-called mistakes that they continue until the end of this world. But as the ancestors of the red skinned People were aware, "This is a Circle."

Shane is left wondering if there is a better Way.

And what of Sarah? In his obsession with his dreams, their relationship has changed to the support of friendship, which is also good, but the fire of passion has become a smouldering ember. The gift of the buffalo calf maiden is one of his distant memories. And he sleeps alone.

And so, the Vision Quest continues . . . and so he turns over in his sleep, and the Dreams begin again.

. . . the beginning

They were running, the woman and the child. He was too young to know why. She had tried to tell him, as best she could:

"We need to go someplace safe."

That was all. That was enough. He was too young to understand more. There was no time. She was out of breath. Sometimes she carried him. Sometimes she pulled him along . . . tugging gently, urgently at his hand.

"We need to go in the direction that the sun comes up in the morning . . ."

The sun was lower in the sky with every ragged breath. They hurried on.

"Safety is in the East."

How did she know? There was not enough time to explain. Her mind raced back to the cabin, their home (her home) for as long as she could remember. Everything had changed—abruptly, with the arrival of the strangers. The strangers that came by horseback. Horseback? She marveled (no more). She had not heard about a horse since she was a small girl . . . almost as tiny as the boy at her side. It didn't matter. Nothing mattered any more. Everything was gone. Everything was in ruin. Her life was lost. Her family (except for the boy) now dead. Murdered by the strangers. Their cabin burned to the ground far behind them now. Like a distant, smouldering memory.

"They will think we were in the house." She mumbled incoherently, to herself. The boy was too young to understand. "I pray to God! Oh God why?" Partially she knew why, or tried to force her mind to believe . . . that a fellow human would kill a family for . . . a bit of food? What else was there? They had nothing else worth . . . ? Her mind raced, out of control again, recalling the looks of the strangers.

Three men had come . . . asking for food. They were grizzled, bearded, mountain men? No . . . yes? But where had they gotten the horses?

"I thought all of the horses had gone . . . disappeared . . . been . . . eaten . . . after the, the . . . there was no word. " . . . the end of the world?" She was not old enough to remember the "end." She was not old enough to remember a real horse. But she had seen pictures, and her grandmother had told her about the time before, when there were animals. When there were horses, cows, deer, dogs, wolves. "What has happened?" she asked again and again, but even her Grandmother's memory was vague. There were stories that her Grandmother recalled about something called Armageddon. This final battle between the forces of good and evil that was prophesied to occur at the end of the world. Her Grandmother was told that Armageddon had occurred, and they were among those "left behind." But in the Bible, it seemed so clear as to who was the evil and who was on the side of good. When the end came, the people of the "beast"—those that were blamed for what happened, were the People who had red skin. Her Grandmother was fleeing the extermination of her kind, and had taken refuge, only to stay and marry the white man whose cabin had become their home. Not everyone believed the story as told by those who were looking for someone to blame. There had been other settlers nearby, and the boy's mother had found love in a boy who grew to manhood only to give his life that she and their son might live on—to continue her Grandmother's search for a myth—a place of Peace and Safety that was called by her People "the Eastern Door."

They had fled, the boy and the woman, slipping out the back door of the burning cabin. Her husband remained, firing out the window at the front of their home, sacrificing his life for the safety of his family. The smoke from the cabin was far behind now, days, and nights behind. The mother and boy hid during the day at first and traveled eastward, by her memory of the direction, during the night. On the fourth day, she decided that it was safe to travel in the daylight, one of the reasons being, she discovered that they had gone in circles, recognizing the places they had hid the day before. She had lost her bearings, her ability to follow the stars, as had generations of her family before her. She only knew that the place of safety lay in the direction of the rising sun.

She did not build a fire until the night of the seventh sun had passed overhead. Until she believed that anyone following was left far behind—for seven nights, not counting the first three spent wandering in circles, the woman and boy huddled together in the bushes for warmth. Their food, packed hastily before the escape from the burning cabin ran out—the last of the berries that she had picked in the woods around their former home. Perhaps her Grandmother would have known what was safe to eat, and what was not, but this mother had long forgotten the teachings of her ancestors. When berries were not available, she pulled up roots from bushes, and the two chewed on these to ease the hunger pains.

Luckily, or not (?) the brush was dry, so her fire making skills were, at least rewarded. A small, meandering stream crossed their path more than once, seeming to be coming from the direction that they were traveling (thankfully), so they were able to quench their thirst. A warning surfaced the first time she tasted the water—a memory of her Grandmother? "I remember when the water was polluted . . . not safe to drink. Many of our people died in the early days . . . following the Time of the Earth Changes. The only safe water we had was from a small stream that came from the East." These last words, of the warning, alleviated the fear, a bit, for the mother and boy badly needed to drink, when she found the stream.

And now, she had a fire burning, to keep them warm. Her motherly instincts were comforted, for the moment. A sense of, almost contentment, settled in as the night wore on, and as she watched the boy sleep, with his head on her lap, it brought a drowsy feeling, until her head began to snap back. "Can't sleep . . . need to keep awake . . . unless?" Finally she gave in, and stretched out on the ground beside the boy. In a few moments, the warmth of the fire, and the happenings of the past dozen days, brought about a deep sleep.

"A sound! Was it in her mind? Was it part of her dream? No—there it was again, closer—sound of footsteps on the parched earth."

The first sound had been a distant twig breaking. Beneath the blanket, where she slept, the mother tightened her finger on the trigger finger of the pistol. She recalled, like a dream, her husbands' voice, when he had thrust it into her hand, as she was gathering their meager belongings, quickly taking only that which might not slow down their flight to safety. "There are two bullets in this gun . . . . just in case." Did he mean . . . ?. She didn't have the time to argue. There had not been any wildlife to be fearful about for some time. No larger animals—all of the few remaining bears, and wolves had thought to be killed off long before, in her Grandmothers' time, for food. It appeared now, that the only animals they had reason to be weary of, were not the four-legged kind!

She had arranged their bed-rolls in the centre of the clearing, with their legs facing east. The heaviest bushes grew in the east—it always seemed to be so, so, in her mind, before retiring for the night, anyone who was able to catch them unaware would most likely seek the cover. She had been right . . . partially. Her half closed eyes caught the movement at the edge of the denser bushes near the circumference of the clearing. "They had followed her and the boy!" Her heart thudded in her chest. She gripped the pistol tighter. She still had the element of surprise—they (?) did not know she was aware of their presence, and did not know that she was armed. "How many were they?" She could not guess. There had been three men at the cabin that night. She prayed that her son would not hear, and that the strangers would become confident enough to walk into the flickering light before her lidded eyes. She doubted her ability to use the pistol effectively, otherwise . . . . but then the boy stirred. He had sensed something, and he sat up.

A faceless form—and then another rushed from the bushes. She threw aside, the blanket, and fired the gun, while urging the startled boy: "Run—and don't look back!"

The small boy ran—for his life. As he lunged into the undergrowth at the edge of the clearing, his ears echoed with the sound of a second shot. His small legs faltered, but he ran on, until the sounds (of fighting?) grew faint, and a scream rent the air. "His mother!" He fell to his knees. Being as small, and young as he was,

186

some part in him still grasped what was happening—what must have happened in the clearing not far behind. His small hands searched in the sandy earth beneath him. Finding a rock that he could use as a weapon (in his small mind and hands); he turned and ran back the way he came.

Without any other thoughts, except to go to the aid of his mother, he would have burst into the clearing, and . . . and? It took him a few moments longer to get back to the clearing, than his hastened escape. Some part of him took over, cautioning him, causing him to halt at the edge of bushes, and peer out. His use of language was not fully formed, at his young age, or he might have "voice-talked" in his mind, taking in the scene, and planning the best way to help his mother, but his eyes told him all his small mind needed to know. One man lay unmoving directly in front of him. But another, very much alive, straddled the boy's mother, raining down endless blows upon her weakly protesting form. The discharged pistol lay near one of her bloodied hands, barely discernable beneath one of the man's knees. Her other hand was in use attempting to fend off his blows.

The small boy screamed, and charged out of the bushes, holding the rock high. The man, momentarily startled, halted his attack on the boys' mother, and swung around to meet the challenge. His eyes went from being large to slitted . . . menacing.

"All right—you little pup. Cum'ere . . . !" the man snarled, diabolically, as both hands reached for the boy, easily fending off the rock. These were to be his last words. The empty pistol cracked against his temple, with all the strength the mother could manage.

She waited, with the hand gun/club, poised over the mans' inert body. When she was sure that he was out (for the moment at least), the mother dropped the empty weapon, and reached out for the rock that had been knocked from the boys hands. It was bigger than both his small hands together—larger, and heavier than the useless pistol. She grasped the rock. And smashed it down with a vengeance on the back of the intruders' skull. "There! He will not be able to hurt you now!" She mentally added: "When I am gone." With the last of her strength fading, she collapsed on her back. Then she surveyed the reality of the knife that protruded from her chest. Blood was oozing from the wound, but if she were to remove the imbedded blade, her end would be quicker.

"Come . . ." She motioned weakly with her free hand. "How much would her son understand?" She wondered, hoping that it would be enough. He was not yet talking. Her husband had suggested lovingly, that he was a bit slow? Still she had to make the boy understand: "I will be staying here . . ." She began. She talked through the night, until she could talk no more . . . stressing: "When the morning comes, and the sun comes up—go to the sun. Go in the direction that the sun came up. Remember this—it is important. The sun will come up over the mountains—when the sun is high overhead keep walking in the direction of the mountains where the sun comes up . . . and when it starts to get dark, find somewhere to hide, until morning, then, start out walking again in the direction of the morning sun." Before her strength was completely gone, she instructed her son: "In the morning, go to the sun . . . I cannot come with you . . . do you understand?" She saw the tears beginning to well up in his eyes. Yes—he was beginning to understand. "I will be OK." She lied? "I will be going to another place. I will be leaving my body here. I will be going to be with your Gran. Like I told you when she had to leave us?" The tears streamed down her cheeks, to match those of her son. "Promise me that you will go in the morning . . . because I will no longer be here . . . promise me?"

The small boy nodded his head, and buried it in her protecting arm. In the morning the sun shone in his eyes, awaking him to his purpose, and she was cold . . . somehow . . . he knew that she was gone.

*   *   *

My memories of my birth mother are dim. It is as though my childhood did not exist. I am an unknown quantity—part of the Mystery—Grandmother smiles when she speaks about this unusual truth. When I wandered into this valley, Grandmother told me, I could not yet speak—although I was ten years old. I learned the language fast, because I sensed what a person was about to say, before they spoke. This ability lessened somewhat, as I began to communicate using words. Grandmother has looked after me since that first day. She took me into her tepee like I was her blood . . . she told me that we were all the Creator's children—every living creature . . . she taught me that even the rocks, and the trees are part of our family. She also taught me about a, time when there were tribes—when there were many animal tribes that roamed the Mother Earth.

The people living in this valley, my new family, are a red-skinned race. The reason I mention this, is Grandmother once told me a story about four different colored races that inhabited our Mother Earth. She told me a story passed down by our people, about a Bright, Living Star that fell to Earth, and shattered into many rainbow colors, to become all of the living brothers and sisters in the four directions, including all of the Relatives that we once called animals . . . winged and four legged, and the plants. Now, to my limited knowledge, only the plant people and our red-skinned race remain. However, Grandmother has hinted of a knowing that some of the other colored races might still be alive somewhere, and perhaps even animals.

The people of our tribe are quiet, loving, and caring. They help each other, and talk very little. Their communication is mostly through smiles, and gestures, since, like me, they can feel what each other are feeling, very little spoken word is needed. Still, they have Mysteries, due to the Respect. One of these Mysteries (that Grandmother will only smile about, when I ask her), is related to the paring of Women and Men. Although, as I have mentioned, we keep no secrets, this is not entirely true. The men and the women do have secrets that they Share, only with their mates. In fact there are times that they go off in groups of twos, to Share a private time that I can only guess about. "What are they doing together that must be kept secret?" I asked. Grandmother laughed aloud, the last time my inquiring mind would not be still. "You will know, some day," she replied, her eyes twinkling. "And considering your inquisitive nature lately, I would guess that you will be finding out soon . . . or you will burst!" And she laughed, again, before turning back to tend the Fire that she attended, beside her teepee.

"How will I know?" I wondered aloud. "There is no one my age to share this secret with." This much was true. All of the tribe was older than me, and everyone seemed to be paired, that desired to be. Another truth was there were no children, nor young adults. Everyone has been the same age as long as I can remember. No one, since I came to this valley, has aged except me! They all remain at an age that seems right for them . . . this much I can see. Another strange thing, whenever anyone does leave the valley, which does not happen very often, they do not return! And no one seems very sad about this. "Your time will come soon enough." Grandmother assured me.

"My time? For what? For leaving or finding a mate?" I cannot see either happening right now. "Why would I ever want to leave my tribe who has been my family, my brothers and sisters . . . mothers and fathers?" And finding a mate? Well, besides this being impossible (as I explained before), the only reason I would want to, would be to satisfy this curiosity that has been growing inside me. "What do they do? What is the secret (or secrets) that they Share?" Another thing? Grandmother says that since I am becoming a man, soon, I will need to go on a Vision Quest. I will need to go on a voyage to another place to seek my Totem, and my Path in this Life! I have no desire to leave this camp, and definitely no desire to leave this valley. When I said this to Grandmother, she smiled again: "You will not need to leave this valley. You will not be asked to do anything that your Heart does not cry out to do."

Our People had everything they needed, as far as I can see. The plants and the trees provided us with our food and our clothing. The tribe planted gardens that everyone looked after. Everyone had a job to do, and everyone enjoyed sharing the duties and equally shared in the harvest. We all took turns. One day it was my turn to dig in the ground, to prepare for the planting, and then it might be my turn to plant the seeds that were saved from the harvest before. These were two things that I enjoyed most, because what I like most is to be close to the Earth—to feel the earth with my hands, and the energy, and the steady Heart-beat of our Mothers Life. When I put my hands on my chest, it was much the same, only stronger. The Heart-beat of Mother Earth is stronger, and steadier than even one of my Mother-friends. The Heart-beat of the Earth is comforting and re-assuring as the whisper of the winds through the trees. This entire valley spoke to me, and listened to my thoughts and fears—yes, I do have fears. In the beginning, especially, when I first came to this Sacred place, I had many fears that I have yet to understand. My greatest fear was about being alone, and Mother Earth knew this, and gave me comfort with the ever present beat of her Heart.

The Earth, and the trees, and the wind, and the Sun overhead told us when to plant, and when to gather the fruits of our harvest. We gave back to the Earth, by taking no more than we needed, and by Dancing and Singing our thankfulness, and prayers. I have no idea how much time went by. "Time is suspended in this Valley." Grandmother told me, one night by the Fire. "Time is waiting for change—for the right moment for it all to begin again." She was speaking in response to a question that I asked about children.

"Why are there no young people like me?" I asked.

"Do you know where the children come from?" She asked in return.

I responded that I had wondered, but: "no—do they grow from the Earth?" I was completely innocent of this knowledge. I had, however seen how everything else seemed to originate from a seed, that was planted, nourished, cared for . . . . that grew, and ripened, and in its time brought forth fruit, and seeds, and, in its' time, died, and returned to the Earth, only to grow again at the next planting. "Do children grow from a seed?"

"Yes—we are like the Earth. We are part of Creation. But the children of our People do not grow from the soil, directly. They grow from the seed of a man, that is united with an egg that is in a woman. This egg is like the eggs of the winged ones." Sometimes, we have found eggs that have fallen from the nest of the Great Eagles far up on the side of the mountain . . . . so I did have an idea of the process of eggs that would hatch into the Great winged ones.

And then it began to dawn . . . . as though some memory awakened within me . . . almost. "So this is the one of the secrets that the men and women share . . . but then, why???" I stopped speaking, lost in thought and wonderment.

"Yes this is one of the secrets . . . the miracle of birth, but this is part of the secret. The rest is something you can only know through personal knowledge, through the Sharing of this Sacred Relationship." Just for a moment, Grandmothers' eyes went far-away, and I knew she was remembering . . . . "But in this Valley the time has been suspended, for our People—the two legged. There are no children being born . . . we all grow to maturity, to a point of time in our lives that awaits the Change that is to come."

"And what is this Change about? What are we waiting for" I asked.

"For some, it means the leaving of this valley to start a life in the outside world, where time has not stopped. But for me, and most of our People, it is about waiting . . . for it to Begin again."

"For what to begin again?"

"The Circle that never ends. This Gift of Life is a Circle, and for me, it is marking time." She took my hand then held it to her heart. Her Heart was like the strong, steady beat of the Mother Earth., like the heartbeat of another Mother-friend who had held me and comforted me to her breast, while I was a small child. "Now hold your hand to your own chest, and tell me what you feel?"

I did so, and when I started to take the hand away, Grandmother gently placed it back on my chest. "Wait a moment." She instructed gently. And I found a difference! Why had I not noticed this before?

"My heart beat changes! It speeds up, and slows down. And it began to beat faster when I noticed the change!"

"Yes." She smiled. "You are growing, and changing. One day, you will reach a point where your Heart will slow to a steady, strong beat that could last for eternity. This Heartbeat is the Pulse of the Earth in this Valley. This is the Mystery of this Valley. All other life changes. The plants and trees grow and age, and die. All other life continues as part of the Circle, except our People. This is our

Sacred agreement with the Mystery. The Circle completes, and we are given a chance to begin again. For all other life—all of the Creator's children this is not necessary. All of the rest of Creation has a heartbeat of its own, which we would Share, but at some time, for some reason, we have lost touch with that beat. The people before us, in the outside world have denied this connection to the Mystery, and we are the result."

"I do not understand?"

"Nor did I, at first." She touched my shoulder, re-assuring. "It is a Mystery. This is the true Mystery. Humankind have been given a Gift to know the Mystery—or at least to think that we do, and that can be our downfall—quite literally. Some wise people have called this the Fall from Grace . . . . even though they may not have truly understood what they were saying. It seems that, sometimes, only the minds of poets, can communicate with their Heart."

My young mind sought to understand.

"Do not try to understand." Grandmother sighed. "This is not to be understood with your mind. You are young, and growing. You are still part of the Mystery, since you have not been taught otherwise . . . . and that it is part of the Knowing . . . the Other Wise. There is another Knowing that cannot be taught with words."

"The Gift," she continued. "As you will learn . . . . Is about Choice. In this Valley, you enter through the Eastern Gate. This is the Beginning. It is about the Gift of Life. It is about living. It is to be lived Now. I would be happy to tend this Fire for Eternity, but another part of me is always ready to begin again."

"What about the men and women. What about the men and women of our tribe? . . . Oh Yes, the time is stopped . . . ."

Grandmother chuckled. "Yes, that is what you will need to find out . . . isn't it?" She gave me a serious and wise look, before breaking out into another wide smile. "Let me give you a hint—it is another Mystery. It is about another Sacred Gift. I can say no more. Please make your Grandmother a tea? There is no more that needs to be talked about. Perhaps it is just as well that there is no Grandfather here to try to explain. One day, you will know, without knowing."

*   *   *

The time for my Vision Quest came at last. Grandmother prepared the paint for my face from Grandfather Stones. There were four Sacred colors, and each member of our tribe applied paint to my face, beginning with a single dot in the centre of my forehead. "This is where you will begin," Grandmother instructed, "this is more than the center of your head it is the door to your Heart."

"But my heart is in my chest? I can feel it beating." I mildly protested.

"Of course it is." She chided me. "But . . . this is where you will find the Key to open the door to your Heart. The key to open your heart, to the Dream of Truth, is called Trust, and to find this key you must first open the eye of your Imagination to See the Mystery. This can be very frightening for some people, since opening this eye will show you what is in your Heart. This is part of what the Mystery is about. It is why the Creator has taught us about the Circle. This is the Circle of Truth, and of Life. Your Heart and the Eye of Truth are connected, as all of creation is." And then she finished her favorite phrase that drove my young mind crazy: "This is all that I can say about this Mystery." . . . . And seeing my eyes roll skyward, she added, with a smile: "Truth is not about words; it must be lived to be understood. Go to a place on the mountain, and find your Truth."

Epilogue 2
The Vision Quest

"Go to the Sun in the morning. Keep following the river, in the direction that the Sun comes up." My Mother's words echoed in my mind, in my memory, as I was that small boy again. I did not want to be following this path that took me away from my mother. One part of me fought against the part of me that knew that she was no longer back in that fateful clearing. Still another part of me, the small boy, did not fully understand, and only wanted to turn around, and run back into her arms.

I have heard, since then, since I have grown, since I have lived the lives that lead me to write this down, too many people use the word: "Knowing," as if it were a "one fits all" explanation for Spiritual Truth. But I will use it here, non-the-less. As sure as I am telling this story, some part of me, that is doing the telling, was there with that boy—urging him onward, to a destiny that neither of us knew, but sought out, because my mother had said it was the right thing to do—even more, because her words awoke a Truth in me, to follow a path, that I instinctively believed in. Ok—there is another all—too used phrase here: how "part of me" wanted to go back, while the other pushed onward. This is about the Mystery. I was there, as I am here now! This time I am the dreamer.

As day followed night, and brought another, and another day, the small boy stopped to drink from the stream, and when hunger took him off the path, seeking berries, he found himself, with the sun going down, at the entrance of a small cave. This seemed a safe place to stay for the night. He dropped to all fours, and crawled inside. The cave was warm, and filled with a particular smell. This smell that filled his nostrils was pleasantly familiar, to the extent that it increased his sense of safety. He curled up in one corner, snuggling into a warm, welcoming softness, and was fast asleep.

It all became unclear from this point until . . . . ? There was a sense of time passing . . . and then I awoke again, within that same dream. My mind was foggy, and it took awhile for my eyes to focus. I was in a small clearing. The day was dawning. Other people were present, around a dying campfire. I heard a man's voice:

"It is time for you to continue your journey. We will go with you as far as we can, but then you must go on alone." His voice was kind, and I felt a sense of confident strength. I knew he was the leader of this tribe, and I trusted that completely. "We are your people, your tribe. You can come back to us whenever you wish. You are one of us. Some day you will understand."

"Understand what?" I gazed about the clearing, with new eyes. These red skinned people looked at me with comforting eyes—eyes that changed, from dark brown, to shining yellow, then back again. My mother? I recognized a woman who had raised me as her own. I raised my hands before my face. They were no longer the hands of a small boy . . . . still youthful, but not the tiny hands that I remembered. And then my eyes saw a familiar face. A young woman\girl sat next to me. She had long black hair, and those same shimmering eyes.

"Come back to . . . ." Her words conveyed a double meaning. In my head, I heard her say "come back to us," and deeper: "*Come back to me,*" And then, I realized that the words—were not spoken! The words of the leader, and the girl who bent close to look in my eyes . . . the words were in my head. This did not seem wrong. In fact it seemed quite right, and normal (even in the mind of the dreamer).

The dreamer noticed something else. These people, this tribe did not wear clothes . . . or did they? My dreaming eyes adjusted

196

and they were all clothed, in buckskin loin-cloths, and tops, in respect for their bodies (as my Grandmother had taught me), like the people in the valley. When I made this observation, I heard the leader chuckle, and his gentle voice:

"It is time for you to resume your journey."

I opened my eyes, out of the dream, to see the eastern sun peeping over the far mountains. The first night of my vision quest was complete.

As I watched the sun climb higher and higher in the eastern sky, I drank from the gourd that my Grandmother had given me, and thought about my dream. I tried to recall more, but the events that had transpired after the small boy went to sleep in the cave, until he woke by the campfire, still eluded me. From that point on, I could now trace my steps to the entrance to the valley, where I parted company with my new family, (my Tribe). The deep connection between myself (the grown boy), and the girl, who in my fresh memories, was now the same age as I, was the only thing that became clearer:

"Come back to me." She called out in my mind anew.

There was nothing else I could do, except hope that more answers would come, so I sat quietly, and tried to surrender to my quest, as my Grandmother had instructed. But the day passed uneventfully, and I watched the sun cross overhead, and dip lower in the West.

The sun sent out a last arrow, in the direction of a certain cloud people. It seemed to be drawing my attention, rather than intending harm, but just the same, the oddly shaped cloud was left tinged blood-red, as though wounded. I focused on the shape of the cloud person in the western sky. It was some kind of animal. It had four clearly discernible legs, a long nose, and bushy tail. I have seen this animal—it was in my dreams! But my knowledge of the four-legged was not adequate to name it. I thought about how my Grandmother said to watch for my totem animal, which would give me my name, and therefore, tell me about my path in life. At this moment, I heard the cry of a bird, close overhead, and evening shadows encircled me, like the blanket about my shoulders.

I looked up—in the new dream, it was morning again, early morning. A large bird passed overhead, accompanied by a loud roaring sound. It was like no bird I had ever seen before. I am sure that it was not the bird that cried out to me a moment ago—the bird that called me into this dream. The sun flared from this huge bird's wings, and at first, I imagined it to be on fire, but then, as it came down into the trees to my far right, I saw that the sun was reflecting off its feathers. I decided that this bird, however fearful it seemed, must be a messenger from the Great Spirit, so I stood up and set off along a rocky beach.

The beach seemed to stretch on forever. I had never seen this beach before, even in a dream. Even more astounding, was the body of water that sent endless waves crashing upon this rocky shore. Peering out to my left, I could only see endless rolling water—to a far horizon. There was a clean, but distinct smell in the air. The smell filled my nostrils, and my lungs, refreshing me, however, when I stopped and brought a handful of the water to my lips, it was bitter—I had to spit it out—undrinkable.

I continued walking toward the trees where I had seen the great bird come to earth. My curiosity had gotten the better of my fear. I also hoped to find water that was drinkable—my mouth was parched, since I had tasted the water on the beach, and although I now knew that this was another dream, the thirst, and the curiosity would not go away.

Finally, I entered the forest that was on a piece of land reaching out into the water—I found this to be true, because, I came to a wide pathway that was cut into the trees, and beyond that, was a small standing of trees, and . . . .

. . . . and there it was . . . . the large shiny bird. It was on the strange pathway, further inland. I was considering going closer, when I heard voices—many voices. The voices came from beyond the next stretch of trees. There were so many strange things, that I now know for certain that I had to be dreaming. I followed the voices, and came out of the forest on to another beach, where a large group of people were gathered, all talking at once, staring out at the water. Out in the water, was a canoe (I recognized it from a story that Grandmother had told me)—a large canoe, with a tree in the middle, draped with cloth?

Almost immediately, a man left the group, and walked to meet me. As he walked toward me, his back was to the sun, rising out of the distant horizon. I thought it must be the water, or the sun at the back of this man, but there was a light surrounding his body. There was a peaceful power about him—even more powerful than the leader of the tribe in my last dream. He extended his hand.

"Miighan." He said (I heard mostly with my mind-sense).

I thought this might be some kind greeting in his language.

"Mighan?" I answered, and clasped his arm, in the manner of my people.

"Mayingun." He said, as though to clarify, as a broad smile crossed his face. "That is the name I know you by this time around. We have met" . . . . and then he sighed, and, still smiling broadly. "Perhaps it would be better to say that we will meet—in another place and time?"

"I came here to find answers. I came to find out who I am. My Grandmother said that I might see an animal in my dreams, and that four-legged would be my Totem. I did not think I would meet a Shaman." I was overcome with wonder at my good fortune.

"A Shaman?" He mused. "Yes, you could call me that. But then I would need an appropriate name as well—since this is your dream?" His smile touched my heart. You can call me . . . . but wait, you have questions? I am getting ahead of myself." And he laughed right out loud. "And considering that we will have met in a future place, I guess we both are . . . . ? But there are no coincidences. My Father would have us meet for a reason—perhaps I can help you on your Quest? Share your dream with me, and we will both learn about your name."

This man was a friend that I had not yet met! I could feel this. I would Trust this man . . . . with my deepest secrets. I would trust this Shaman, this Sacred man, with my life. So I sat down on a rock near him, and began to tell him about my previous dream, and how I came to be on the Vision Quest.

He listened quietly, and then said: "The Eagle whose cry began this dream—and opened the door, is not your personal Totem. Although Eagle will never send you somewhere you are not meant to go. Your Totem will be a four-legged that you have met—your ancestors were wise to look at their animal brothers and sisters to find their way on this Earth Walk. His eyes shone, and he gazed toward the sky. "What did you see, just before this Dream?"

"I saw a cloud person, in an animal shape!" I exclaimed.

"Now think back to your first dream." He instructed, "did you see this four-legged in that dream?"

My mind retraced—one dream to another, and then, at the point of the first dream, after I had bid my companions farewell, I stepped to the entrance to the valley, and turned back to see . . . . the tail of an animal disappearing into the trees. My heart thumped in my chest. I was about to awaken again. I had seen my Totem—my Spirit-naming animal, but my mind could not grasp the truth? This Shaman, who had helped me, was fading—only the touch of his hand remained.

"Wait—who are you—How will I know you again?" I called out.

"You can call me Two-Fishes—that is my Shaman name. And you will always know me." And then he was gone from my dream, and I wondered at something—My Grandmother (?) or someone had told me, that if a Shaman reveals his or her name, they have made themselves available to you. I do not know where this knowledge originated, but I was immediately aware that I had met someone that must be the embodiment of Trust (and perhaps Truth?).

* * *

As this Dream Vision ended, I was aware that the meeting with this Shaman had altered me. Even as the morning sun's rays touched my face, I felt that my heart had been opened, and I was still connected to that dream. Throughout the next day, I sat in meditative silence, unable to let go, with an acute anticipation of the next dream that was to come.

CPSIA information can be obtained at www.ICGtesting.com
Printed in the USA
LVOW080916080112

262772LV00001B/5/P